VAMPIRES AND VIDEO GAMES

A Spooky Games Club Mystery Book 5

AMY MCNULTY

Crimson Fox
PUBLISHING

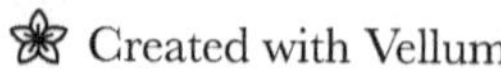 Created with Vellum

Chapter One

"All right, all right. It's not like we'll never see each other again." Ingrid wiped a single tear from her cheek, her white, pixie-short hair just a tad untidy, like she'd slept roughly. Her other arm was still wrapped up around the neck of her strapping son, who'd been practically poured into his pale lavender dress shirt bedecked with maroon tie.

Leave it to Cable Woodward to travel to the airport—and clear across the ocean to Scotland all those many miles away—in a dress shirt and tie.

"Never see each other again?" asked Milton warily from behind his sister, scratching at a particularly noticeable liver spot on his wrinkled forehead. His late wife's glasses hung around his neck on a chain, needlessly, the wiry few strands of hair on his head poking upward in every direction. He'd already hugged his nephew good-bye, but he hadn't really understood the man was leaving. He sometimes didn't quite recall that the little boy he pictured being his nephew was now the bulky, bespectacled, brunet thirty-two-year-old in front of him.

Ingrid stepped back and patted her brother's shoulder. "Just for a few months. We *think*."

She shot me a look that was halfway between stern and curious. As if waiting for me to correct her, explain the plan…

Only there was no plan. Not really. Not in the long term.

My companion broomstick, Broomhilde, or "Broomie" as I called her, let out what could only be described as a sorrowful moan as she lifted her brush head from where it had drooped over my shoulder. She'd miss having Cable around. And not because she liked to scare him.

Well, probably *a little bit* at least because he was the only one so easily scared by her pranks.

Even Roderick didn't so much as flinch whenever Broomie popped out at him—though that might have been because he was made of stone. So she'd given up teasing him. Cable was her one and only teasing target.

Just like he was the one and only true love for me. So said the magic that flowed deep through my very bones.

But Cable and I… We were both too awkward to really talk about that.

Cable bent down to pick up his briefcase that had been at his feet in the driveway, just inches from the snow-covered lawn. It helped that the Woodwards had a witch for a neighbor. My magic worked better to clear the driveways and roads of Luna Lane than any amount of snowplows and rock salt could do.

Cable swallowed, then tried to smile, but it looked more like a grimace. "I don't have to leave at all."

Broomie perked up at that, shooting off my shoulders and into the air, swirling in a circle above Cable's head.

"Broomie—no. No, we talked about this." This much, at least, we'd talked about.

Cable had only been in Luna Lane for the fall semester. He had a job teaching American literature in Scotland. The point of his sabbatical had been to produce a research paper associated with the university and then get back to his job. To his life. Far, far away from my sleepy little town in the Midwest United States.

For a moment, I'd wondered if I might come with him. For a time, anyway. But now…

I looked over my shoulder. Over the fence separating Milton's house from mine, the burnt-orange witch's hat of my cousin—first cousin once removed, to be precise—Lien Poplar, drew the eye. Above her head, her own broomstick companion, Broomhelen, was shooting up and down into the piles of snow, sending sheets of icy flurries into the air with her bristles, which looked more like tufts of fur than straw.

Roderick laughed, a throaty, grunting sound, as he flapped his stony wings up and down through the snow after her. With his pointed ears, his protruding fangs, and his harsh brow, he looked more like the kind of gargoyle you'd find perched on a European cathedral than the stone boy whom I'd summoned to my aid on the train, but that was the form he was most comfortable in these days. It'd taken him a week to even come out from his boulder form in the first place. It had been birthday cake earlier this month that had done it at last—along with the squeals and laughter of my best friend's children.

"I know you can't leave Luna Lane," said Cable, as if acknowledging why I was staring my cousin's way. I hadn't been able to leave Luna Lane practically my whole life—until just two months ago. Then I'd gone on a brief cross-country trip with Cable, and before I could blink, I'd been back to being stuck in Luna Lane again.

Lien insisted I was safe here. That she'd warded the entire town so that no witches besides her could enter, and now my grandmother, the wicked Queen of Witches Isadora Poplar, could not reach me—to kill me, to stamp out the "tainted" genes in her bloodline.

Because technically, I was a witch princess and heir to the witch "throne," whatever that might actually entail. I wasn't interested.

And not just because my biological father was a gargoyle, which Isadora considered to be an unforgiveable befouling of her bloodline.

Turning back around, I took Cable's hand in mine, squeezing it. "You have a life you can't just give up because of me."

"I don't see it as *giving up my life*—"

"You have to at least teach this semester," I reiterated. Broomie sighed, her bristles drooping as she flittered down and wrapped herself around Cable's shoulders like a shawl. "The university has a whole plan for you to travel the Continent when not teaching to present your paper's findings."

"Yes, but—"

I held out a finger to cut him off, my breath starting to grow a little steamier, my body growing a bit chillier, as my enchantment to keep us all warm was wearing off. "One more semester, and then you can decide what you should do." I forced myself to smile, this heaviness at the back of my throat threatening to choke my words. "And by then, I might not be stuck here anymore."

"The *reason* why you're stuck here is all the more cause for me to stay."

"It's cold out. Is it January?" Milton shivered and looked around him, as if taking in the snow for the first time.

I opened my mouth to perform an enchantment to warm us all up again, but Ingrid shook her head at me. "Yes, it's January. We just celebrated New Year's—and Dahlia's thirty-first birthday—a couple of weeks ago." She smiled at me. "Let's get inside, Milton. Give them a few moments." She looked at her son. "Don't forget to call your mother."

"I won't." Cable smiled at her. Ingrid was usually traveling the world herself but had opted to stay behind in Luna Lane for a few months to take care of her brother, a task that had sent Cable here in the first place during his sabbatical. She hadn't realized how much his dementia had progressed until she'd seen it firsthand, she'd said. But I thought, too, that maybe spending some time with her brother and son again, maybe she'd realized how comfortable it could be amongst your roots.

"I'll be fine, Cable. I have Lien," I said under my breath as Milton and Ingrid shuffled up the driveway arm in arm to reach Milton's front porch. "She knows what she's doing." I gestured around me. "And half of Luna Lane could put up a fight. That's why my grand-mother targeted me outside of town to begin with."

"Yes, but the fact that you're in danger…"

"All the more reason." I put a finger over his lips. They were warm, soft, and just a tiny bit full. "I'll feel better with you out of danger—away from me."

"*I* won't," he said, his voice growing quiet.

At the end of the driveway, Sheriff Roan Birch sat in the idling pickup truck he rarely had use for around town, which was loaded with the rest of Cable's things. He didn't honk or anything, giving Cable all the time he needed to say his good-byes. Even if each minute took them closer to the hour his plane was set to take off.

"Come on," I said, squeezing his hand again. "You're going home! Try to look a little more pleased about it."

"I don't *feel* like I'm going home." He looked beyond me, around us at the snow-covered houses lining the street, at Vogel's general store across the street, run by the Mahajans. They'd come and said their farewells to Cable at yesterday's final meeting of the Spooky Games Club that would have our visiting professor in attendance.

At least for now.

After this semester, who knew?

Who knew where Cable would be, where I'd be, where I'd want to be?

Luna Lane was home, but… A home was only really a home with the people you wanted with you in it.

"I have a phone now," I said, wiping a set of tears that had escaped first from one eye and then the other. "I mean, if even my vampire ex—er, if my vampire friend has a phone, I figured it was about time I got one, too." Cable didn't so much as flinch at the mention of Draven, my hundreds-of-years-old ex-boyfriend.

A gust of wind blew past as Broomhelen and Roderick let out their bristly and grunting laughs and sent snow up in the air. My long, wavy red hair flew across my face in the swirl of snow, and I had to let go of Cable's hand to brush it out of my face, tucking it back under my pointed black witch's hat with purple band above the rim. "And now I have the Internet, too, so I don't have to go to the library when I want to use it," I added, louder this time to be heard over the swirl of snow. "You bought me that notepad for my birthday."

"Tablet," said Cable, grinning, despite the light precipitation caused by the playful gargoyle and broomstick leaving drops on his wide, circular glasses. "And don't forget you can't write on it."

"With a pen," I added, having learned my lesson. "Only stylish pens—"

"*Stylus*," he corrected.

I rolled my eyes. "I cleaned it off with an enchantment, didn't I?"

He chuckled. "Convenient, that."

"What? Magic?"

"Yeah. But if you couldn't use magic to speak to me in another country, then, it was time for a bit of a welcome-to-the-world-of-normies upgrade, in my opinion."

"It definitely was." I wondered how my life growing up might have been different if I'd had such an open window to the rest of the world from Luna Lane. Though Faine, my best friend, assured me a lot of these normie human advances were from a time far more recent than my childhood.

"So where *is* your phone?" Cable looked at my outfit—long-sleeved black dress, shawl, a pouch at my belt for carrying potions and ingredients for potions, but it was empty now.

"At home." I thumbed over my shoulder at my cottage. It was past the twelve days of Christmas, but the icicle-style holiday lights I'd enchanted from real icicles were still hung up, glowing softly even in the early afternoon.

Cable chuckled and Broomie shuddered out a little laugh, as if she and Cable were in on a joke together.

"Well, don't forget to start carrying it around with you so people can actually reach you with it."

Oh. That was the joke. It was a big, old clunky thing to carry around. Besides, Cable was right here —for a little while longer. Everyone else, I'd see at some point during the day.

A light tap of Roan's horn reminded us that there was a time limit on our good-byes. And if Cable didn't go now, I wasn't sure the words would get any easier to say.

I turned my head to look at the idling truck wistfully, then slowly turned back—right as Cable pressed his lips to mine.

"I love you," he said, for the first time ever, as he

pulled away. His cheeks turned scarlet, and I could feel my own reddening.

"I love you, too," I whispered.

Broomie nudged her rough bristles against his jaw and he reached up to pet her.

"Be careful," Cable said. "I can come back in half a day if needed—"

"I'll be fine," I reiterated. Here in Luna Lane, I felt safe.

Just empty, a bit, if Cable was going away.

Letting out a sigh, Cable took a step back, clutching his briefcase and shivering, the cold invading past the warmth enchantment I'd cast for him. For a moment, I was tempted to cast it again— but he'd have the warmth of Roan's truck soon, and then he'd be out there, in the world, without me. Without magic to assist him.

To protect him.

I opened my mouth, extending my hand toward his retreating back as Broomie glided off his shoulder and into the air.

He'd gone his whole life without magic to protect him.

He'd be okay now.

This was a good-bye—but it wasn't for forever.

I lowered my hand as the wind whistled softly through Broomie's bristles, eliciting a melancholy sound. She swirled languidly in circles above my head as Cable got into the truck. Roan waved our way, a tight smile on his lips, his bald head covered with a hunting cap for the cold weather instead of his usual sheriff's hat. He was the only police officer we had, but nothing much was likely to happen in town as he drove Cable to O'Hare and back again without him.

This was Luna Lane. For the most part—barring a handful of abnormal murders that had occurred here—this place was safe.

I kept waving as the pickup truck headed down the street, not a single other vehicle on the road to join it. Cable stared at me until the truck took him out of view.

The front door to Milton's house opened and out stepped Ingrid, a brown wool coat and white knit hat tossed sloppily on, the coat hanging wide open. I jumped, wondering if Cable had forgotten something—my heart beating wildly at the thought of stalling him for just a few more moments—but she headed toward the fence separating my house from Milton's, her green, rubber boots crunching through the snow, which came up to the rather short woman's knees.

"Roderick!" she called. "Roderick Usher!"

I'd thought about giving him my last name, but it was my grandmother's too—and besides, he'd been christened with a full name as soon as Cable had suggested it. The protagonist from "The Fall of the House of Usher." Cable's forte was classic American literature, and so he'd looked for a way to combine something of mine and something of his when suggesting it. My contribution being the general spookiness of the tale, of course.

I followed Ingrid, my laced-up black boots crunching through the snow. As I was five-foot-nine, the snow only came halfway up my calves.

My gargoyle boy stopped flapping his stony wings and landed in the snow with a *thud*, sinking in almost as deeply as his head. In this form, he was only about two and a half feet tall.

Shaking his stony head, he took careful, slow, grating steps toward the fence, Broomhelen chuckling in that bristly, furry way she had as she flew behind him.

Ingrid stood up on her toes and pulled something out from her coat pocket, handing it down over the fence toward the stone gargoyle child.

The sunlight, already reflecting brightly off the crystalline snow in the yard, shone off the screen of the long, rectangular object, too. "I found this in one of my storage units and brought it here, thinking Cable would like it back—but he said he hasn't played a game in years, and it's 'out of date' besides." She let out a derisive snort.

It was a handheld game system. I remembered the Mahajan brothers had had the same one. Faine's had been another brand—I'd liked hers more, I remembered. Mom had never understood the things, but Roan had bought me my own a year after Faine had gotten hers.

I'd only had two games, but I'd played them religiously for months after. I wondered where my own system was now…

Roderick cocked his stony head, the movement causing a grinding noise, but held out his gray hand and took the gift.

"What do we say?" I said to him—trying to encourage him to speak. Lien assured me that, though gargoyle guardians rarely liked to speak—they *could* speak if the witch they were supposed to guard asked it of them. If their bond was deep enough.

Roderick had yet to say a word.

Roderick looked at the handheld game system in his hand, then up at Ingrid over the fence, then back at the system. Broomie flew over the fence and swirled around his head excitedly, Broomhelen wagging the tip of her shaft like a puppy tail as she looked down at him.

"Push the button," said Ingrid, pointing.

Roderick carefully tapped a rigid fingertip to the button on top of the device. The screen lit up in bright colors, and Roderick's jaw dropped open with a flinty noise.

He nodded at Ingrid, a slight smile breaking out across his lips.

"You're welcome," she said. She leaned back onto her heels. "Just don't ask me how to work it beyond that. All I know is Cable pushed all those buttons, and I had to constantly ask him to turn down the volume." She winked at me.

"You might want to get him a pair of headphones."

"Thank you," I said as she plodded through the snow back toward Milton's house, shivering all the way.

"MRAW." I motioned with my hands at my body. I didn't like wearing coats and winter hats and mittens and scarves—too much hassle. It was easier to refresh my warmth enchantment whenever it wore off, especially since there was a huge gap of bare, peachy pale skin between my skirt and my boots. The snow was melting just slightly at my ankles, the warmth affecting my whole body.

I walked down the driveway to the sidewalk and back into my own yard. The two broomsticks flew in enthusiastic circles over Roderick's head as he took slow, rocky steps toward the front porch of my brick cottage.

Lien ambled down the driveway to meet me, as unaffected by the cold as I now was, despite her orange dress being lengthy but not very warm, her long, shiny black hair contrasting against the color. Her sharp, brown eyes narrowed as she met me halfway up the driveway.

"I didn't want to sully your and lover boy's good-byes," she said. She hadn't been particularly rude when I'd first met her—but she'd been under-cover as a double agent of sorts working against my grandmother and great-aunts—including her own mother—in order to keep me safe. But she'd been practically all-business since arriving in Luna Lane. The most socializing she'd done had been to sit in the corner during my birthday party at First Taste, the local pub, a frown on her face and a cocktail in hand and no interest in participating in any of the Spooky Games Club's games.

"His name is Cable," I reiterated.

Her lips pursed, but she didn't comment on that. "I have to do some recon over in Creekdale again. I'm sensing… Well, something off."

My breath caught in my throat. "'Off' like witches?"

"Off like *something* paranormal anyway."

"You want me to come with?"

Lien snorted. "And have you set foot outside of Luna Lane? No, I'm not having you blow all of my efforts to keep you safe for something I can handle just fine on my own." She turned over her shoulder and whistled, and Broomhelen snapped to attention, gliding over and into Lien's extended hand. Broomie watched, her brush head tilted in curiosity. Roderick didn't look up from his handheld console screen, standing on the front porch under a string of free-floating, enchanted icicle Christmas lights.

"Are you still sore about the para-paranormal?" I asked, my voice gone quiet. We'd had this argument several times, including just the night before, so it was likely fresh in her mind. "I told you, I don't agree with how that stuff's created. There might be some of Eithne's left somewhere in town—"

"It won't help us if we lose our connection to magic around it, too. We need a sample of para-paranormal one of *us* created. Or better yet, we can both create some and use each sample in turn, or at a proper distance from one another. That way, we can still cast enchantments and any witch we bring the substance around won't be able to—"

"*No*! You *know* how it's created."

Lien huffed. "A witch and another paranormal have to… sacrifice a life." She mumbled that last bit.

"Whom do you propose we kill?!" It wasn't the first time I'd asked.

"Not any of your *friends*, don't worry." She sighed when it was clear the vein on my forehead was not going away at her little *reassurance*. "Someone who deserves it."

"And you get to decide who 'deserves' it? My aunt and mother messed around with that stuff and look what happened. My mom *died*! And it's caused me and the whole town nothing but trouble since."

"Never mind." Lien fluffed a hand at me. "It's clear to me you won't consider a reasonable solution."

"And it's clear to me *you* were raised by witches. And maybe swap that 'w' for a 'b.'"

Broomhelen's furry bristles shook so hard then, it was almost like the broomstick was growling.

Lien clenched her jaw for a moment. "Witches may be cruel, but at least they get things done. The royal witches may avoid relying on para-paranormal as a rule because it's considered rude to deprive a fellow witch of her connection to magic, but they're getting desperate. Desperate witches do desperate things."

"Considering they're already aiming to *kill me*, I think I'm plenty aware of what they just might do."

Lien's nose rose in the air. "You stay here and keep living your little carefree small-town life," she said, sliding on Broomhelen's shaft. She often rode side-saddle, I'd noticed, at least when not dealing with a train moving at runaway speeds.

"Well, excuse me for having a *little* life here," I said. "You're the one who told me to stay here—"

But she was already high above me, heading off toward the direction of the nearest town.

Creekdale. A town I'd heard about my whole life —they had a few thousand residents, whereas Luna Lane was home to only about three hundred. But I hadn't set foot in Creekdale until last month, and that had just been on my way through off to greater adventures.

But now, being on the border protecting Luna Lane from the witches who wanted me dead… the humdrum town of Creekdale was in danger of becoming a paranormal hotspot of sorts itself.

And I could do nothing to help. Which Lien seemed to resent me for, despite the fact that it was on *her* orders that I was unable to set foot there.

Broomie let out a little coo and nudged my

shoulder. "Let's go inside," I said, taking a deep breath of fresh air. "I can make hot cocoa—and hot cornhusk soup," I added, the latter for my beloved broomstick.

Broomie shook her bristles wildly in the air in excitement.

Chapter Two

A day had passed, and though Cable had checked in with me from halfway across the globe, Lien had not returned from Creekdale, just a few miles away.

"We'd hear if something bad had happened." Faine, my best friend, sipped from her cup of hot cappuccino. She had on a red, vintage woolen jacket with four big, black buttons across the front. Her long, brown hair spilled out from beneath fuzzy red-and-black earmuffs. The only thing brighter red about her was her lipstick against her pale-white complexion. She was like a pin-up model from days of old, if pin-up models covered themselves almost entirely in winter gear.

"Yeah, I suppose." Sitting on the bench beside her, I took a sip of my mocha, made by Faine's husband, Grady, before we'd left their café, Hungry Like a Pup. It was after school on a snowy Monday, and Faine's three kids were frolicking in the park beside the library, along with Roderick and Broomie. "She's the only one who sensed anything wrong in Creekdale to begin with. Mayor Abdel didn't say anything, right? Wasn't he just in Creekdale over the weekend?"

She nodded. "He took his whole staff there"—the "whole staff" consisting of Abdel's "granddaughter," Chione, as well as Ryan and Erik—"for a dinner with the mayor of Creekdale. They're trying to forge a more open relationship between the towns. Though not quite *that* open yet." She shrugged. "Chione came in for lunch today, and she said she had a nice time."

Chione wasn't paranormal herself, but she was descended from a living mummy. Surely, he would have at least sensed something if there was anything amiss.

"If you want, I can head into Creekdale tonight after we close the café to check for her."

"No, it's fine." I took another sip. "I don't imagine Lien is making herself easy to find if she's investigating a paranormal presence. She might even go so far as to say you blew her cover or distracted her if you showed up." She was good at the undercover stuff, as far as I could tell. Lien had been in disguise as a train employee the first time I'd met her and I hadn't really noticed anything strange about her.

Well, I thought as I stared down at my cup of

coffee, *except for her habit of sipping hot drinks when she's nervous.*

Was that what I was? Nervous? Cable was safely settled back in his flat in Scotland, meeting with other faculty today and diving right into teaching classes he'd been prepping for the past few weeks.

He was fine. Safe. Despite looking no older than thirty, Lien was decades older than I was, more experienced. She could handle herself.

"I think the protection over the town would fail if something had happened to her," Faine pointed out.

"Right. There's that." I wasn't *trapped*, per se, not like I had been with Eithne's barrier keeping me hidden inside Luna Lane, but I could sense where Lien's scope of protection ended. It was one-way for witches other than Lien. If I left, I wouldn't be able to get back in without her lowering the barrier for me.

Faine cupped a mitten-covered hand around her lips and shouted. "Falcon! No climbing trees without your claws! You don't have the same traction with human hands!"

Flora, Faine's eldest, who was almost eight, was also shouting up at her brother to come down. The three-year-old was almost halfway up the trunk of a spindly oak, grinning wildly as he stared down at her. They'd just turned into wolves a few days ago and it was harder for Falcon, at his very young age, to shake the feeling between werewolf cycles.

"Should I enchant him down?" I asked.

Faine frowned and stood to her feet. "*Falcon!*"

The boy's giggles carried across the trodden snow between us, and he slid down. His big sister, every bit a miniature of her mom in spirit, even with her stronger resemblance to her father, began wagging her finger at him, her other hand on her hip, but he ignored her, launching himself on all fours toward his other sister, Fauna, who was building a snowman with Broomie's expert assistance.

"One of his mittens is off," I pointed out. It dragged behind him on a string poking out from his black snowsuit sleeve.

Faine sighed and sat down, waving a hand in the kids' direction. "Oh, he'll remember it once he realizes one hand is cold."

He roared at Fauna, who screamed, then picked up some of the snow she'd been packing on her snowman and sent it flying in Falcon's direction. Fauna's puffy, brown pigtails poked up and down around the snowman, the light-brown complexion she shared with her siblings popping out against the snow as she hid from first Falcon's and then Flora's assault. Little Fauna had newly turned six just a week after my own birthday. We were birthday twinsies, as she liked to say, despite the seven days between the occasion.

"Have you given more thought to school for

him?" Faine asked, gesturing toward Roderick with her cup.

I was distracted for a moment by Broomie popping out from the top of the snowman—she'd burrowed herself in it from below like an earthworm in dirt— and all three of the kids shrieking while laughing and running away from her, the poor snowman now forgotten behind them with a hole in his head.

But unaffected by all the chaos and impossible to miss with his dark stone skin clashing against all of the snow was Roderick, holding the handheld video game system Ingrid had given him and not bothering to look at the other children at play.

"He doesn't speak," I said.

"That's no reason he can't have an education. Vesper is excellent with teaching both normie and paranormal children."

"I know that." She'd been our teacher, too, all those years ago. "And he does understand me, it's just… I want to give him a little more time to adjust. We're working on reading at home. Considering he was born just a month ago, I'd say he's making good progress."

"I can't deny that." She bit her lip and watched Roderick barely move as Falcon dove around him, gripping the gargoyle's bare shoulders. Gargoyles didn't feel the cold.

Falcon's attention turned from his sisters and Broomie to the game Roderick was playing. He pointed over Roderick's shoulder at the screen and then jumped excitedly in place. Roderick actually turned his head and seemed to smile.

Games. The boy liked video games, at least. Seemed like he could make connections through them, maybe.

"Do you still have your home console?" I asked, gesturing at Falcon settling down next to Roderick in the snow, who adjusted the way he was holding his screen so the little boy could see it better. "Maybe the kids can play video games together."

"He does seem to like them. Hmm… Yes, I think I do still have it somewhere. My closet, maybe?" She winced. "But shouldn't I get something newer? I mean, games these days are nothing like we remember."

"Let's see how they do with the old system first." Roderick was clearly loving the handheld system from twenty-plus years ago. Maybe simpler was better for a newborn gargoyle.

"We should head back. We're losing the light." Faine stood and disposed of her cup in the nearby trash can. I took one last sip of mine and handed it off to her when she offered to do the same for me. "Kids!"

It took a lot of wrangling, though Flora did her best to assist us, and I had to trudge out into the snow-covered grass to nudge Roderick into the present moment, but eventually, we headed down the sidewalks of downtown Luna Lane, a bevy of paranormal children in front of us, Broomie bringing up the rear as she jostled back and forth in the air above our heads.

It was only five o'clock and it was dark out already. We were nearing Hungry Like a Pup to meet up with Grady about an hour before they were set to close the café when a small group of people headed down an adjoining street met up with us at the curb.

"Doc Day!" shouted Fauna. Sure enough, there was the town's sole doctor, her trademark floral-pattern shirt poking through the slight dip in her navy-blue winter jacket that was so puffy, it looked about to swallow her up. Her silver hair was bundled under a cozy-looking white yarn winter hat, a pom-pom on top.

"Hello, dears," said Doc Day with a smile on her lined face. "Enjoying the snow, are we?"

But instead of excitedly telling her about their playtime in the park, as they might usually do, the three werewolf children stopped abruptly, lined up side by side, equally horrified expressions on their faces.

Broomie cocked her brush head at the kids, and Roderick, his footsteps slow and steady, bumped right into Flora's back, only then looking up from his handheld game.

The game's little beeps and musical notes was the only sounds outside of Roderick's stony jaw grinding as it dropped.

It wasn't the fellow human next to Doc Day who had caught their attention. Balding, with his salt-and-pepper hair worked into a combover, the doctor friend from the Creekdale hospital whom Doc Day relied on to, uh, *fudge* certain paranormal-related events going on in Luna Lane was standing beside her. He came every so often to enjoy a drink out with his friend—and he was well aware of the paranormal citizens living openly in this town.

Which was a good thing because there was a skeleton in a top hat standing next to him.

Lazarus did a little bow, tipping his black hat to us and leaning on the silver ball topping his long, black walking stick. Other than the shiny, black shoes over his bony feet, the man wore no other items of clothing.

He hardly needed to wear what little he did.

"This is a rare sight," I said as Broomie tilted her brush head toward Luna Lane's funeral parlor director—and the sole employee of said business— the reclusive skeleton before us who had last left his parlor probably seven years before.

He only ever wanted to "air out his old bones" every so often.

"Doctors Day and Corbin have invited me for a drink," said Lazarus, gesturing to his companions with one skeletal arm. His voice was almost hollow, ringing out with a rattling rasp. "And though I have no need of draughts, I have found I have begun to enjoy fascinating conversations."

"Kids," said Faine, putting her arm around Falcon and Fauna at the ends of her line of children. "This is Dr. Lazarus. He runs the funeral parlor."

"Charmed," said Lazarus, bowing again. The "doctor" title Faine had given him had no technical degree to back it up. It was quite difficult to bring the dead back to life. Vampires, being undead, didn't quite count since they died only during transformation through the use of vampire venom and were not resurrected from a corpse, whereas mummies relied on their enchanted bandages in order to continue life. But Lazarus was not comprised of the bones of a human long gone from this world. He, like the other reapers of his kind, had been born a skeleton. They often lived in dark places, like caves and abandoned homes—or the occasional messy closet. As one who ventured out of his home every seven years or so, Lazarus was downright sociable for his kind.

"I believe you had a brood of only one baby last I met you," said Lazarus, his skeletal jaw opening into what could best be described as a smile. "How your litter has grown."

All three of Faine's children leaned back against their mother, watching Lazarus warily. They'd been to the funeral parlor for the funeral of Leana Woodward, Milton's wife, almost a year ago, but Lazarus had kept to the shadows even then, allowing Mayor Abdel to take over as funeral celebrant.

Broomie had none of the hesitation the were-wolf children experienced. She soared over and around Lazarus's top hat. He turned his sunken, empty sockets upward slightly and his ribcage bounced up and down as his teeth clacked in an unsettling, clucking laugh. "And Broomhilde, how good you look! Though I have seen you quite recently. When was it, when you snuck into the back of my parlor nosing around for a cornhusk and a hello?" He tapped a bony finger against his bare teeth.

"That was almost a year ago," I pointed out. "The last time we needed to use your parlor."

Well, there'd been the murderer Fred, who'd died in an escape room *incident*, but no one had held a funeral for him in town. County had come and picked him up.

"Has it been so long?"

Doctors Day and Corbin chuckled, most likely at their friend's inability to grasp the passage of time.

"Yes, well, I am happy to be so little of use as of late. The mayor made me aware that our rather unfortunate spate of deaths was all the result of one ill-intentioned vampire." He clutched the top of his walking stick again, then his skull-head turned toward the beeping and electronic music coming from Roderick's video game. The gargoyle boy had stepped around the werewolf children to get a better look. "Well, what have we here? You are no werewolf child."

"He's... mine," I said. True enough. "Roderick Usher."

"What a fascinating name." Lazarus bowed slightly to him. "You know, there's a rather moving tale of a man with that name, and the fall of a house."

"Yes, we named him after that," I said.

"Oh? Have you gotten married then, little witch?" Staring into Lazarus's eyes was like looking into a black void. "You and that vampire boy—"

Down the block, the door to First Taste, Luna Lane's only pub, shot open next to the Hungry Like a Pup café.

"You cannot! You simply cannot!"

Speaking of the "vampire boy," hundreds of years old but perhaps still young compared to Lazarus, it was *his* heavily accented voice that carried down the street. The thicker his accent, the more upset he was. I knew that from the years we'd dated—which I supposed had still been a thing when Lazarus had last ventured out into town.

"Not married, no," I said quickly. I walked over to Roderick and put my hands on his shoulders. "Roderick is my guardian."

Roderick shifted his stony head to look up at me, his nose stuck up just slightly, as if proud to be called such a thing.

"I see," Lazarus said. But he, like everyone else, had his attention glued down the street.

It was nighttime now, so it was not a complete surprise to see a vampire walking the streets of Luna Lane. His shift at First Taste didn't start for another hour, but Draven and his coven sister and roommate, Qarinah, were wont to spend more time out and about during the winter, when the nights were longer.

What *was* surprising was seeing Draven storm out of the pub, Qarinah on his heels, holding her hand out as if to touch his shoulder, to soothe him. He flicked her gentle gesture away.

The two of them never fought. Qarinah was so sweet-natured, for one. She was never bothered by Draven's general moodiness.

"You cannot leave me alone!" Draven shouted toward her, his blond brow furrowing over his deathly-white complexion. He crossed his arms sourly over his chest, his black leather jacket revealing the top of his chiseled chest, his wavy, blond hair just brushing the top of his shoulders. He wasn't too cold. Vampires did better in the cold.

"I'm not *leaving* you, for pity's sake," said Qarinah, her own accent revealing her Middle Eastern origins. Her smooth skin a pallid brown, her red-rimmed eyes gleaming as brightly under the moonlight as Draven's own, she filled out a dress like a 1930s lounge singer, complete with wavy, black hair falling over one shoulder.

"You are! You are quite literally leaving me alone! Just like Ravana did, in her wickedness. Just like my mother. Just like Dahlia." His head snapped in my direction and his lips grew tight.

Too many heads turned my way.

Before I could speak, before Draven could say another word, he popped into bat form in the air, his little squeaks competing over the batting of his membrane wings as he flapped off into the night.

Chapter Three

Qarinah let out a sigh, putting a pallid brown hand against her heavy bosom as she stared after the zig-zag flight pattern of the retreating vampire bat.

"Is everything all right?" Doc Day asked, the first to break away from our group and head down the sidewalk to our worried friend. The rest of us followed suit, though Faine, the kids, and I stopped in front of Hungry Like a Pup's front door. Broomie floated nearer to Qarinah and the doctors, as if to eavesdrop, only she was hardly blending in with the way she flew back and forth overhead.

"Let me see what's happening," I told Faine as she held the door open for her kids, who bounded inside the café, their chatter re-engaged after the shock of the reaper skeleton and Draven's outburst outside.

"Roderick? Do you want to come inside with us until the café closes?" Faine asked.

He looked up from me to Faine and back, the handheld game system at his side in one hand still playing music, though a "Game Over" message was on the screen.

"It's all right," I told him. "I'll pick him up at your place after you close up?"

"Sounds good." Faine smiled and Roderick shifted warily inside on stony feet. He didn't need to eat like humans and many paranormals, but he had the option of doing so if he liked—and he was tempted by everything in Faine's dessert display case.

"Just be wary around Draven," Faine said softly.

"'Wary?'" I parroted. Draven was a lot of things —narcissistic, stubborn—but he never hurt anyone. He was often grumpy because he didn't drink enough blood from volunteers. Both because his cool attitude was off-putting to those who might have been interested in providing their blood and because he didn't really *want* to.

Something about how it only made him miss *my* blood. Despite the fact that I'd so rarely let him drink any.

"I just mean…" Faine started. "Well, you saw him at your birthday party. He barely left the corner."

"Yeah, him in one corner, Lien in another." I shook my head. No wonder she irritated me. Her temperament reminded me more than a little of my ex-boyfriend's.

"He hasn't been as friendly as he used to be lately."

"'Friendly'? Are we talking about the same vampire?" I laughed, but Faine didn't join me, so my smile fell. "I'm just going to see what happened," I told her, wrapping my shawl tighter over my chest. My warming spell was wearing off— or there was some other cause for the sudden chill I felt down into my bones.

The rest of the group was headed inside First Taste, so I followed suit, Broomie settling into my hand by the shaft, her brush head upward. The doctors headed for a table in the corner just as a crack of thunder echoed out overhead—sound effects, to give the pub more of a Transylvanian atmosphere. Paintings of spooky castles on darkened hills dotted the walls, and the lighting was dim. From another corner, Mayor Abdel—the mayor wrapped from head to toe in white bandages, though he wore a suit over most of it—let out a deep chuckle as he lifted a mug into the air and the other town hall employees clanked their mugs against his. They often all went to the pub together straight after work. Their shift had ended a tad early today, judging by how deep they were in their draughts.

Qarinah was behind the bar conferring with Jamie, a young normie who was one of Doc Day's boarders and who worked the day shift at the pub. The overly thin, tall man stretched out in every direction like a willowy beanpole. His bronzed complexion was more often dotted with sweat ever since his own close encounter with a murder a few months back.

I was sometimes surprised he'd stayed after that, but once you got some paranormal into your system, it was hard to get it out, or so I thought about the normies who flocked here.

I hoped the same applied to Cable—once he got through this semester anyway. Only I didn't know how he could work as a professor in a town with no college and I didn't want to be responsible for the man I loved giving up his career.

Worries for another day.

I slipped onto a stool at the bar.

Qarinah stopped whispering to Jamie, who scratched at his neck, at the two puncture wounds I knew indicated he was a volunteer "bloodbag" for the vampires in town. Or just Qarinah, if I remembered right. He'd expressed some dislike at the thought of Draven feeding from him in such an intimate way.

Jamie shuffled off to the table of doctors, including his landlord, and I didn't have time to gauge his reaction to Lazarus because Qarinah was in front of me, a rag in hand. "You haven't been here in a while, outside of your birthday party. What can I get you?"

"Just a soda, thanks," I said, remembering the last time I'd gotten drunk, really drunk. I needed a clear head for this, or I might find myself leaning all over Draven again.

Qarinah grabbed a glass and flipped it over, scooping some ice in and using the nozzle at the bar to fill it with sparkling soda. I settled Broomie against the bartop and watched the fuzzy, vague silhouette reflection of Qarinah in the mirror behind her. Vampires did, in fact, show up in reflective surfaces—just not clearly.

And you could take pictures of them or paint their portraits. Strange how that myth had gotten blurred a bit.

"I saw that, uh, argument out front," I said as Qarinah slipped the soda on a coaster in front of me. "Anything I can help with?"

Broomie sniffed at the soda, her bristles shaking, and Qarinah let out a sigh, her manicured hand resting lightly on Broomie's head. "Draven just isn't being supportive." She stopped petting Broomie, whipped the rag from where she'd stored it over her shoulder and started scrubbing at the already clean bartop.

"What he said… Does that mean you're leaving Luna Lane?" There were plenty of places a vampire could move to, and Qarinah had only lived here less than a couple of decades—nothing for a vampire. But I'd thought she and Roan had a thing going.

Frankly, *him* being upset at her leaving I could understand.

I picked up my glass and took a sip.

"I'm not." Qarinah paused in her wiping and smiled broadly, deepening dimples in her plump cheeks. "I'm just moving in with… my husband. After the wedding."

The glass slipped from my fingers and to the bartop with a loud thud. The raucous laughter from Mayor Abdel's direction stopped.

I leaped to my feet. "You're getting married?!" I shrieked.

"What? Who?" asked Abdel, standing up. "Qarinah? To Qarinah!" He held his mug up in the air again and Chione, Erik, and Ryan stood up too, no doubt eager for any excuse to clack their mugs against his.

The doctors all clapped, and Jamie froze halfway from their table to the bar again, his jaw slack.

"Oh, uh, did no one else know?" I asked, slipping back onto my seat. Broomie shook her bristles in a giggling sort of way. "Sorry."

"Well, I wanted to tell Draven first," she explained, pushing a lock of dark hair behind her ear. She went back to scrubbing, her heavily-lidded, red-rimmed eyes staring downward. If color could reach her face, she might have blushed.

"Who's the lucky guy?" I asked. "Roan?"

Qarinah looked up and laughed. "Of course

Roan! Did you think I found myself a different husband behind his back?"

"I don't know. I'm in shock."

Broomie flew across the bartop and did a little dance around Qarinah's shoulders, rubbing her bristles against her cheek. Qarinah giggled, a beautiful soprano sound, and pet the broomstick's back.

"Congrats. I'm happy for you both. But then, er..." I gripped my glass with both hands, the condensation moistening my fingers. Roan was like a father to me, in some ways. He'd had this unrequited thing for my mom, and he'd never pushed it, but he'd been a good friend to her. He'd always been there for me growing up—and in the days since her death.

I'd been happy when he'd finally started dating Qarinah. I was just surprised he hadn't told me they were *getting married*. Then again, I hadn't seen him today yet.

"We've talked about it," Qarinah said, her grip on the rag replaced by a steady petting of Broomie's head over her shoulder. Her eyes were unfocused. "Whether or not he should become a vampire."

A shot of ice ran down my back. I hadn't even considered that. But Roan was a normie in his fifties, and Qarinah could live for hundreds and hundreds of years. I wasn't sure if vampires could ever die, actually. Not of old age, anyway.

"Of course, we'd have to get approval from Mayor Abdel," she said. There was that. No vampire was supposed to drink more than was necessary to survive in Luna Lane. Though Ravana had skirted around that rule undetected for decades. But she'd also gone abroad to make a new vampire for her family because that sort of thing just wasn't done in Luna Lane. "And the Transylvanian Vampire High Council will need to approve both the transformation and the union itself if we're to have more than a simple human marriage that lasts a few decades. But I doubt we'll have trouble with that. He's just worried he's 'too old and ugly' to be a vampire." She *tsked*.

Roan was hardly what I'd consider either. Though age had added quite a few wrinkles, taken his hair, and added a gut, he was still as handsome. But I knew where he was coming from. Vampires were intimidatingly beautiful. They needed to be by nature to entice normies into giving up blood.

Qarinah stepped back and gestured at herself. "I told him, did he realize I was eighty when Ravana turned me? Vampirization works some magic—when done right."

My eyes widened. I hadn't known that about Qarinah. She'd been bitten in my lifetime—so I assumed she was actually about Roan's age, based on her appearance and adding the years since she'd turned. But I'd never pried.

"You look good for a hundred," I said.

She giggled. "Thank you. But even if he stays a human, I find my Roan *very* handsome." She looked down at the counter and started rubbing at it with the rag again. "And so sweet. I just want to spend more than a few decades with him, you know?"

I bit my lip. I'd had so much to think about, it had barely crossed my mind that Cable, as a normie, had seventy more years at best. And that was stretching it.

I was a witch, and I knew of witches who were easily in their second or third century.

Not that an accident or a gaggle of royal witches trying to kill me couldn't change my life expectancy.

I chugged back my soda, swallowing it all to cover the racing thoughts entangling my mind.

Then I shook my head as the brain freeze worked its way through my system. "Wait a minute, though. Why was Draven so *mad* if you're just moving to Roan's and will still be in town?"

"And I will still run First Taste with him," said Qarinah, whipping the rag over her shoulder again as Broomie floated over the bar and curled up on the stool next to me. "Draven has… anxieties," she said delicately. "Despite his gruffness, he does not like being alone."

I knew as much. That was partly why he was an active member of the Spooky Games Club despite looking as if he'd been dragged to each meeting kicking and screaming.

We all knew there wasn't anywhere else he'd rather be on Saturday nights.

"And there's, well, the fact that the wedding is

this Saturday." Qarinah grabbed both of her cheeks and fidgeted in place, as if she could hardly believe the words.

"*This* Saturday?" I said, loud enough to make the whole place go quiet again, aside from the gentle rumble of fake thunder.

"Oh, I know it would have been better if we'd thought to get married before Cable left. But we will invite him to… How do the normies say it? Zooma-ling in to the wedding with a computer?"

"Or on the phone." I nodded. I'd spoken with Cable on my new smartphone via video chat. "But why the rush?"

"Why not?" Qarinah said. "We're not getting any younger, you know. This isn't the first rodeo for either of us."

Well, I didn't know about Qarinah's human past —she didn't like to speak of it—but it *was* Roan's first time getting married, at least. But after dating no one for decades just because of his feelings for my mom…

"You will come, of course?" Qarinah asked.

"No question," I answered. Broomie cooed and nodded. Then I thought to add, "As long as you're getting married within Luna Lane."

"But of course," Qarinah said. "We shall tell everyone all of the details once we've arranged it with Abdel." She was about to walk away, perhaps to do just that, but she bit her lip with a jagged fang and stopped. "It is not my place to ask you to do this, not after your shared history, but would you consider checking on Draven? I am sure he just went home. He could use a friend. And there's no one he cherishes more than you."

Taking a deep breath, I picked up my empty glass, the ice clinking against the edge as I tapped it atop the coaster. Broomie watched me warily.

"Yes." I plastered on a smile, my stomach growing a bit tight. I loved Draven—as a friend—I really did. I just wasn't sure he wanted to see me.

My name had been listed among those women who had "left" him. And frankly, I was the only one in that list who had really willfully left him, unless there was something about his mother he hadn't told me.

"Maybe a drink before I go, though?" I asked. "Something stronger this time."

One small drink couldn't hurt things.

Chapter Four

Slightly tipsy wasn't how I'd hoped to knock on Draven's front door. Broomie held herself stiffly in my hand, brush head upward, granting me some balance as I stared straight ahead at the gothic three-story manor home. At eye level, there was a cat door—or, more accurately, a bat door—in the front door for easier comings and goings of the vampires in bat form.

When no one answered, I pushed open the flap and stuck my whole head in. "Draven…?" My voice sounded just the slightest bit shaky.

I'd only had one little drink. But my nerves were making my stomach do tumbles.

"Dra-vennnnn." I singsonged his name out into the empty, cobweb-filled darkened entryway.

There was a chance he'd fluttered off elsewhere to stew.

"Oh, for blood's sake," he barked. "The door is unlocked. Just come in."

Or not.

I pulled my head back out and turned the antique doorknob. Broomie chirruped into the large space, her trills echoing out and upward.

The house was deathly quiet, no sign of life. The vampires were frequent hosts of the Spooky Games Club, and it was shocking how just a few games and some laughter could transform this intentionally gloomy place.

"I'm in here," snapped Draven from the drawing room.

"I was just waiting to be invited in." I giggled. Because he was a vampire, you see? And he had to sense he was welcomed in residences to set foot in them.

"Dahlia, you have been drinking." It wasn't a question.

I definitely had been. His voice was turning shrill and tinny in my ears, squeak-punctuating every other word. For a second, I thought I saw him in bat form sitting on an uncomfortable-looking red upholstered chair beside the fireplace.

"ERIF," I said, waving my hands at the logs waiting for someone to start a fire. They burst to life, and Draven's vampire face flickered into view, his fingers steepled in front of his face as he sat stiffly in his chair.

"Brooding in the dark, I see?" I whispered, as if

speaking louder than the crackling of the fire would disturb him somehow more than just speaking at a normal volume.

"Why have you come?" Draven was all-business, his full lips in a too-tight frown.

This drawing room had been practically *designed* for one person brooding. We usually played games in the dining room—it wasn't like they used it for food.

I sat down across from him on the piano bench, a plume of dust shooting up as I did. Broomie slipped out of my hand and strewed herself across the top of the piano, hanging her brush head upside down off the side of it like some seductress about to burst into a low-register, woeful song of love gone wrong.

Snorting, I covered my mouth. I didn't want Draven to think I was laughing at him.

"You get silly when you—"

"Drink," I finished for him. "I know."

He, one of the town's *pub owners*, had always gotten on my back about how strange I acted when I had a drink. Never mind that I drank alcohol all of twice a year.

I clutched the skirt of my dress. Despite everything that I'd experienced over the past half year—the murders, the revelations, the once-and-for-all loss of a connection to my mom—it had been the thought of having this little one-on-one with Draven that had made me want to drink again.

I wish I knew why he was so hung up on me. It was clear we weren't compatible—not in a sense beyond friendship.

I took a deep breath. And a *friend* could do this.

"So," I started, after it was clear Draven had nothing in particular to say beyond lecturing me. Best to start this conversation casually. "Not sure you noticed, um, before, but I ran into Lazarus before coming here. His first time out of the funeral parlor in years."

That perked Draven up just a tad. "Really? No, I was…" He cleared his throat, then he sat straighter in his seat, leaning his elbows on the armrests of his chair. "Fascinating. The reaper doesn't usually countenance company."

"He was on the way to the pub. He saw you, but you left before he could say *hello*."

Draven looked away again and grumbled.

So we were at the heart of the matter. "Qarinah told me the good news."

Draven scoffed. The firelight flickered in his steel-gray eyes, rimmed in red.

"I'm *happy* for them," I said. I'd have to tell Roan as much soon—and alert Cable. Only I was sure it was too early in the morning in Scotland for a call.

Besides, I'd left my phone at home again, despite Cable's gentle reminder that I should bring it with me wherever I went.

Draven grumbled again.

"How can you not be happy for Qarinah? She's like a sister to you—"

"I know perfectly well how I feel about my last remaining coven member, thank you very much!" he barked. Broomie let out a little shuddering sound. Then the sharp edge of Draven's brow softened and he flicked his eyes toward me. "I apologize. You are right. She is a sister to me, and I am glad she will be happy." He spoke the words without malice but without genuine feeling, either.

"She'll still be living elsewhere in town," I pointed out. "Still run First Taste with you—"

"Yes, yes, I am aware." He waved a hand in my direction. "And *you*. You are trapped here, too, despite my worries you'd fly off across the ocean at the first opportunity. And yet, I am still alone."

I tapped my fingers against the piano fallboard. It was cold, the sensation pervading even my warmth enchantment, without which, I'd no doubt be shivering in this place.

"If I hadn't been forced to stay—"

"You would have run off with your new lover. I am aware."

I frowned. "I was going to say, I don't think I would have left. Not forever. I don't know." I shrugged and stared at the piano. "Luna Lane is my home."

"But now that you know love, it feels a bit empty, even with all of your friends *elsewhere in town*," he said softly.

He wasn't wrong. But I didn't like how his eyes gleamed red in the near-dark, staring straight into my soul.

"Still, I will agree. Better to have you in town than worry you are off somewhere, putting yourself in danger."

I scoffed. "I do not *put myself* in danger."

"Oh?" Draven's brows arched. "And who insisted she was in no danger on that speeding train, and yet when my very core said you were lying—"

"I was trying to keep you from worrying! I handled it!"

"With *my* help."

"Yes, and you put yourself in danger to do so. Draven, I…" I snapped my mouth shut and took a deep breath. "I thanked you for your help and I meant it. But I never asked you to put yourself in danger for me."

"And what would have become of you if I had not?" Draven pounded the armrest of his chair, and Broomie raised her head up, moaning sadly as she looked at me.

As if she agreed.

"Your taste in normie men will not keep you safe." He bit down on his lip.

"My 'taste in normie men'? What does that even mean? Cable's my first boyfriend since you—my second boyfriend *ever*—"

"And your true love," said Draven sadly. "When

were you going to tell me? Only a true love's kiss would break the curse upon you?"

"I… Uh…" I wrung the material of my skirt in both sweaty palms. He hadn't been present for that part, when Cable had kissed me and I'd no longer been cursed to grow a stone scale on my skin every day if I didn't complete a good deed before sundown. There'd been plenty of witnesses, and I knew the news would get back to him eventually, but I hadn't had the guts to tell him myself.

"And what was this talk of witch royalty?" Draven shifted in his seat, leaning forward, as if eagerly awaiting my response.

Now *that* no one else had been a witness to, though Lien knew, of course.

"Keep that to yourself, please," I said.

Draven cocked his head. "You mean, no one else knows? Not even Mr. Normie Professor?"

"*Cable* would just worry. It's not important."

"But you're the heir to the witch throne," he said. He'd gotten the gist of that on the train during Isadora's assault.

"Which is meaningless to me," I said. "And it's the sole reason there's a target on my back—from my own family, I might add. If you want to talk about being alone." I crossed my arms gruffly across my chest.

Draven had the sense to shirk a bit at the bad thoughts he'd brought up. "But your home is as full as it's ever been. At least you have that." Draven gestured around him. "Whereas mine is emptier."

Lien, Broomhelen, and Roderick had all moved in with Broomie and me. Though Lien and Broomhelen seemed to spend as much time casing the town's borders as they did at my little cottage.

"Draven, you're not alone, even if you live alone in this house." I looked around at the desolate place. A half-covered painted portrait I'd never seen uncovered before hung on the wall beside the mantelpiece, within Draven's line of sight.

The woman depicted in the portrait was beautiful. Dark-haired, with fair, peachy skin—though not as wan as a vampire's. Her cheekbones were sharp, her cheeks rosy, and her lips transfixed in a permanent pout. She wore an elaborate cream-and-white dress, her hair threaded through with jewels and affixed in an elegant updo style. I couldn't quite place the time period to which she belonged.

Draven must have caught me staring. "My mother," he said simply. "The first person to leave me. Willingly. Happily. She could have had eternal life—by my fang. Instead, she died too young. Not yet forty-five. I was told she fell from a cliff and I… I never even had a body to bury."

"I'm sorry to hear," I said softly. I knew what losing a mother too young felt like.

"And now my coven-sister leaves me just the same."

"Qarinah isn't *leaving you*. You're taking joyous news awfully *personally*."

"You are not wrong," he said softly. "And Ravana, too, did not leave willingly, I must say, though her desires always have and always will trump my own." Ravana and Draven had never been lovers, but as his sire, she was a mother of sorts to him—and had been for centuries.

"Your mother was never a vampire," I said, referring to the woman in the portrait. He'd told me that much even before today, though he'd been reticent when it came to his human life hundreds of years ago in Eastern Europe. "All normies die—"

"Something you and Qarinah might want to keep in mind," Draven said abruptly.

It wasn't that I hadn't thought about it. Though my life wouldn't be as long as a vampire's regardless. "Qarinah said she's going to ask the Vampire High Council. That she might turn Roan into a vampire, with their and Mayor Abdel's blessing."

Draven steepled his fingers together again. "So this is a forever thing, her leaving me? If her husband is to live as long as she does?"

"It's not *about* you."

"Yes, well, I can't deny that, however I feel." He looked up at the portrait. "My mother, though… She had the chance to change into a vampire. To stay with me."

"And she chose not to?"

Draven nodded, ever so slightly. "She was the

first and only normie I've offered to turn into a vampire."

I'd guessed as much. If he'd sired any vampires, they likely would have been here in Luna Lane with him—or at least they might have stopped by every so often to keep in touch.

"I would have offered it to you," he said, "but I was certain the Vampire High Council would disapprove of a witch vampire. Besides, your presence was clearly being kept a secret from the Continent. I just hadn't known why—until those witches came after you on that infernal train."

"Wait. Back up. You wanted to *make me a vampire?*"

Draven flinched and stared down into the fire. "I would have asked first, of course."

"Well, good because I don't think I would have taken you up on that."

Draven's lip trembled as he stared at me, his face falling like a crestfallen puppy's.

Broomie chirruped beside me and I patted her shaft as guilt seeped into my bones. Not guilt for my opinion—but for stating it so flatly and hurting him like that. "I don't know what becoming a vampire would do to me," I said. "I already have some vampire venom in my blood—"

"I most certainly do not leave venom in the blood *years* after I've bitten someone!"

"I don't mean from you." I cleared my throat and Draven's jaw dropped. As if learning I'd gone behind his back to let another vampire suck my blood. As if. "My father was a gargoyle, remember?"

Draven's expression softened. "And witches need vampire venom to treat the stones with which they bring gargoyles to life."

"Just as they do for many a witch's curse," I pointed out. "Witches have a long history of working with vampires, if I understand it right." Draven didn't answer in the affirmative, but he didn't deny what I'd said, either. "And in my father's case, it may very well have been Ravana's venom that gave birth to him."

"Supplied to Eithne." The wheels were turning in his head.

"In any case, doesn't that make us sort of like uncle and niece, in a fashion?"

Draven's nose wrinkled. "Of course not!"

"Ravana sired you *and* my father—"

"Giving her venom to a witch for a witch's own business is *not* the same. My goodness, is that why you've been pushing me away?"

"*No,*" I said. This wasn't even the point I was trying to make. I ruffled Broomie's bristles. "I just mean, well, I might already be part vampire, and I don't know what having more vampire venom in my veins could do to me. I could stop being a witch." Broomie cooed sorrowfully. "I won't risk that. You *know* I didn't like that time I let you bite me—"

"You said I could!"

I held a hand out. "I don't deny that. I just mean, once it was happening, I was… uncomfortable."

"And I stopped," Draven said hoarsely.

"I know you did. I'm just saying… There was never a chance, Draven. Never a chance I'd become a vampire who'd live an eternal life with you."

The room went quiet again, not even Broomie's soft noises to interrupt the crackle of the fire between us.

"I would have lived with you, Dahlia the witch. Just as you are. We could have had over a hundred years together." His voice was soft, cracking. "We still could have at least some time together after your normie lover…" He left the rest unsaid.

My eyes widened, and Broomie shot up.

Draven held up a hand, though his face was still listless. "Or I could make him a vampire for you. He could never become a witch, and werewolves don't live much longer than normies. A vampire might be his best option." Draven's eyes glistened as he looked at me. "Only for you would I do such a thing."

My voice caught in my throat. I didn't know how to respond to that.

I certainly wasn't about to agree to such a thing on Cable's behalf.

But for a second, the idea that Cable would outlive me, that I'd never have to live on and on and on without him…

No. I wouldn't do that to him. *I'd* be the one leaving him behind too early in that case. Even if we still had centuries together.

"Draven, you need to focus on yourself right now," I said—just a tad harsher than I'd meant to. Adrenaline coursing through my system at everything Draven had told me was clearing my mind, pushing away that bit of edge the drink had given me. "You need to learn to be happy alone so you can invite someone to join that happiness with you. Because you may have a lot of time left on this Earth, but that also means so much more time to find the right person for you."

"Oh, *do not* talk to me of setting me up with someone—"

"I wasn't! I just meant—"

A knock at the door cut us both short.

Draven sighed and got to his feet, dragging himself with slow, plodding steps toward the door. I took hold of Broomie by the shaft and followed, unable to look him in the eye.

The knock resounded again, though it wasn't too urgent.

"Yes, I am coming." Draven sounded sour and surly. He opened the door.

On the other side stood Grady, Faine's husband, a tall, thin, dark-skinned man whose warm demeanor made him smile even in the face of Draven's surly attitude. His thick, fur-rimmed winter coat covered up the mangled scars on his arm from my botched job healing his werewolf bites from his blood-mad son. He had a gloved hand on Roderick's stone head.

"Roderick?" I asked, coming forward beside Draven.

The gargoyle rushed forward and hugged my legs.

"Qarinah told us you might be here," Grady said. "Roderick was playing with the kids at our place, but he seemed unsettled." Grady looked down at the gargoyle boy, who held his videogame system in his hand at his side, but he wasn't playing it. "When I asked if he wanted to go look for you, he nodded, so we headed next door."

The lights in the Vadases' house were on beyond the fence separating the properties, the two-story house so much more warm and inviting than the cold vampire manor.

"Thank you," I said to Grady, patting Roderick's cold scalp. Broomie cooed and slipped out of my hand, wrapping around Roderick's oversized head and landing in a circle on top like some kind of flex- ible broomstick hat.

Roderick leaned back and let out something akin to a grumbly laugh, patting Broomie gently with his free hand.

"Well, everything looks all right here, then." Grady nodded at me and Draven in turn, his smile never fading even as Draven shot him an unsmiling look that could kill. "Take care, buddy.

The kids would love to play with you after school again."

We said our good-byes—well, really only Grady and I did, as both Broomie and Roderick were largely silent and Draven was as grumpy as a sourpuss—and the werewolf headed down the front porch and to the sidewalk. We all stood behind the open door, watching him go.

"What's wrong, Roderick?" I asked him. The stony smile on his face slipped as he looked up at Draven. "Were you just checking up on me?" He was, at his core, supposed to protect me, I supposed. Though I felt responsible for bringing him to life, and he was child-like, so *I* also wanted to protect *him*.

Then again, he'd been an integral part of the battle against Isadora and her witch sisters. Just like Draven had been.

"You remember Draven," I said, gesturing to the sullen vampire beside me. They'd seen each other at my birthday party and around town, but I wasn't sure they'd ever acknowledged each other's existence.

Neither of them said anything. They just stared at each other.

I felt the need to fill the silence that hung heavily before the still-open front door.

"Um, so Draven is sad," I said, my language going simple, even though it seemed as if Roderick had no issue following conversations. His silence and child-like demeanor just made me turn on a "kindergarten teacher" persona around him a bit. "And I was visiting him to see if I could cheer him up."

Scoffing, Draven stuck his nose in the air.

"Well, I *tried* anyway," I mumbled. "He's lonely," I added.

Roderick looked up at the long, languid vampire who towered over him. Then he looked down at the handheld game still beeping its music in his hand, then back up at the vampire.

Roderick handed Draven the video game system.

His stony eyes were so sweet, so disarming, even Draven had trouble keeping up his ice-cold attitude. "For me?" His features softened as he pointed a finger at his own chest.

Roderick nodded, the stone skin of his neck grinding.

Draven took the game system and held it gingerly in long, pale fingers. "Thank you," he said softly, his gaze focusing on the screen.

I wondered if he knew what it was. We hadn't played any video games in the Spooky Games Club.

"Like *Pong*," he said, then he brought it closer to his face and squinted at it. The artificial light was a bit bright and he flinched back. "Only more sophisticated."

Well, video games had gotten even *more* sophisticated since this system had been released, but Draven didn't need to know that.

Chances were, he'd lose interest quickly—if he figured out how to play it at all—and go back to wallowing in the darkness until sunrise and his return to his coffin.

But at least, until then, he'd have some sense that *someone* with whom he wasn't angry had felt bad for him and had wanted to cheer him up.

Leave it to Roderick's enduring, cute innocence to show the brooding vampire with just one small, silent gesture what I hadn't been able to convey at all.

$\mathcal{M}$om's old cuckoo clock, which hung in my bedroom, usually woke me in the mornings, even though I had no particular task to complete.

Sure, I would often practice my enchantments and potions so I could become a better witch who'd be of better service to my community. And so I could hold my own better in a fight against my grandmother if it came to that again. But it was strange not to have that goal, that routine I'd once had. Trying every potion in my mom's book to try to break my curse from sunrise to sunset, while cramming in some socialization and a good deed before another stone scale grew.

Now I realized the curse was just a part of me— and I could control it.

My left arm was particularly fleshy this morning, no trace of stone scale left.

As Mom's cuckoo clock chirped, Broomie's head lifting up from the end of the bed, where she'd curled up between my feet, a steady knock on the front door made me shoot up and whip the fluffy, black faux fur comforter off. Broomie rustled her bristles indignantly as a corner of the comforter whapped across her, so I apologized as I slipped my robe on.

"Did Lien and Broomhelen ever come home last night?" I asked her.

Broomie lifted her brush head and tilted it, as if listening for signs of her fellow broomstick. She shook her head from side to side.

The knocks continued. I padded down the hallway, glancing inside the smallest bedroom, which I'd given to Roderick. A small boulder sat in the middle of a crisply made bed. He preferred sleeping in rock form, it seemed, and the rock never needed tucking in under the covers, even during cold, winter weather.

"Coming!" I shouted as the visitor knocked on the door again.

I opened it to find Goldie Mahajan, one of the owners of Vogel's general store across the street, buried in a long, puffy pink coat, a pastel pink knitted cap over her head, her brown cheeks dried and windburned.

"Goldie! Come in, come in. MRAW." I cast the warmth enchantment over her without permission, a reflex from my need to see my friend—a woman who was like an aunt to me—no longer suffering.

"Thank you, dear," she said, rubbing her bare hands together. "Oh, how cold it is! I never thought I'd miss the dry heat."

"You forgot your gloves," I pointed out, leading her toward my floral-patterned couch. Broomie flew in groggily, her brush head drooping, but then she perked up, flying in circles around Goldie.

"Oh, I… Yes. I was just in a rush to get over here." She didn't *seem* to be in a rush or anything. Goldie gave Broomie a pet as the store owner removed her coat and took a seat. "Good morning, Broomhilde. No cornhusks today, I am sorry. Corn is out of season."

Didn't Broomie know it. Her bristles rubbed together in a sighing-like manner as she sat on Goldie's lap.

"We'll import some, don't you worry," said Goldie. "It's just that Jeremiah is no longer bringing us the fresh crops."

Jeremiah was Luna Lane's resident farmer, who lived on the outskirts of town on the other side of the woods dividing Luna Lane and Creekdale. He had a hothouse for winter—and I could whip up some enchantments to make anything inside it grow, really—but he also needed the time to focus on just livestock and give himself a semblance of a break for a few months.

"Can I get you anything?" I asked Goldie as she took off her hat to reveal slightly messy black-and-silver hair pulled into a bun. I headed toward the kitchen separated from the living room area by an island. The cottage was rather cramped, and I hadn't hosted a single session of the Spooky Games Club when the vampires, the Vadases, the Mahajans, and Milton had much more space.

"No, thank you, dear. I won't stay long. Arjun needs my help at the store, you know. I just wanted to check on you." Goldie had swapped her usual sari for a wooly, white Nordic sweater and khaki pants. Even after all of these years in Luna Lane, she tended to get a bit colder than most in the winters.

"Check on *me*?" I looked at the clock. I hadn't slept in or anything. And even if I had, I might simply have been practicing my enchantments at home.

"Where's little Roderick?" Goldie looked around, as if he might appear somewhere between the couch and the cauldron across the house in the room over, the one with my summoning etchings carved into a rune circle on the floor, as well as my fireplace, flasks, ingredients, and everything I needed to craft potions and practice enchantments.

"Sleeping." I waved my hands at the coffeemaker, mumbled an enchantment under my breath, and a pitcher started filling with water under the sink, coffee grounds scooping themselves into a filter. Faine made better coffee, but I needed a jolt to wake up now and see what had brought Goldie here so unexpectedly. She *did* visit from time to time and often brought Broomie treats, but with no cornhusks in hand, I was still confused about her sudden arrival.

"Where's Lien and Broomhelen?" Goldie asked. She narrowed her eyes as she looked around. Almost like she didn't want what she said to be overheard.

Lien hadn't exactly won over the majority of the townsfolk.

"Out." I took hold of the mug just as the coffee-making enchantment finished up. "Goldie, why did you rush over here to check on me?"

She took a deep breath. "There was a murder in Creekdale last night. Dale—the man who brings our papers in—told us. Hasn't made the print papers yet, of course. Happened too late. But it's all over the news this morning."

A murder in Creekdale? They didn't get those often. "That's awful. And too close to home for comfort."

Sipping my coffee, almost forgetting the heat would burn my tongue, I searched out my phone, which was where I'd left it on the table near the front door. I swapped the coffee for the phone.

"LAEH," I muttered as I gestured at my face,

healing the burnt tongue. The phone took a while to turn on. Things were faster with magic.

Goldie gave me the details while I waited. "A nun. A *nun*, of all people! But what was she doing out so late at night, Arjun wondered? And I said, well, nuns are free to come and go as they please, aren't they?"

"I think so," I said. My phone screen displayed the provider logo now, but it was still cranking along, taking its time.

"Well, in any case, still, I wouldn't want my grown sons out alone that late at night, let alone my daughter-in-law or granddaughter. Women have to be more careful." She shuddered. "Human women, at least, but that doesn't mean you should let your guard down, either." She tossed a stern look over her shoulder at me. "Especially with all those witches and witch hunters after you."

"I don't think the witch hunters are *after* me..." At least no more than they were any other witch of my kind. Lien had assured me we needn't worry about them, even though she'd invited one into our circle and *worked* with him and hadn't realized he'd still wanted her dead. Of course, he was the one who'd ended up six feet under.

The phone screen was loading now. Which screen button was it Cable had told me would show me the news?

"Did they arrest whoever killed her?" I asked.

"No." Goldie's voice cracked and Broomie offered a sympathetic cheek rub, rustling her bristles. Goldie pet her absentmindedly. "And they won't discuss the cause of death, either, other than to say there were signs of foul play."

My phone was lighting up with notifications that kept getting in the way of searching for more news. A text message from Cable, some updates, a bunch of notifications about savings and special deals. The front door of the cottage burst open.

Lien walked in, dark bags under her eyes, Broomhelen held tightly in one hand.

Goldie and I both screamed, and Lien flinched as Broomhelen poked her shaft out and shut the door behind them. My fellow witch reached immediately for the mug of coffee I'd left on the table by the door and started sipping from it, without even asking what it was or who it was for.

"Where have *you* been?" I asked.

Goldie laughed nervously. "Good morning, Lien."

"Morning," Lien said when she came up for air between gulps of black coffee. She sounded the furthest thing from chipper.

"You said you were checking out Creekdale *two days* ago," I pointed out. "Goldie was just telling me there was a murder there last night! I don't know if you should be staying out all night by yourself—"

Lien grunted. "I know about the murder. I

didn't catch the fiend in the act, but I saw the police investigating it afterward."

"Oh, my," said Goldie.

Lien narrowed her eyes at my human friend, as if she found even the small outburst disrupting somehow.

"So it was a human killer?" I ventured, hoping. Not that it mattered either way—a poor woman was dead—but if it was purely a normie matter, I would just have to let the normies handle the investigation.

"Unfortunately not." Lien threw back the last of the coffee and slammed the mug down back on the table. I glanced inside the mug at the slight froth left over. Maybe I'd wind up at Faine's café after all.

Wait. She'd said it *wasn't* a human killer?

Lien stormed past me and to my potions workbench.

"What are you doing?" I put the phone down on the table and followed her. Broomie flew over from the couch to settle in beside Broomhelen, where Lien had leaned her against the wall beside the fireplace. The two rubbed their bristles—Broomhelen's furry, Broomie's like twigs—together, either in greeting or in some form of conversation.

When Lien didn't answer, just sorting through my stash of concocted potions and potion ingredients—without asking, I might add—I kept prodding. "Was it the witches?"

"No," said Lien gruffly. She picked up a bottle with a dark-red substance in it and examined it, then wrinkled her nose as if she found it disgusting, putting it back on the shelf. That was the leftover vampire venom Draven had gifted me a couple of months back. She *better not* use that. It had taken a lot out of Draven to provide it for me. "That's why I didn't witness it. I was too busy tracking their energy forty miles north."

"North of Creekdale?" No wonder she'd been gone so long. "So they're still waiting," I said.

"Still waiting for you to slip up and leave the confines of my enchantment around this town, yes." Lien grabbed a vial of riverwood sap and set it down, shoving aside other bottles, clearly looking for something in particular.

"Why do you think it was paranormal, then?" I asked.

Lien paused long enough in her riffling to shoot me a sarcastic look. "A woman drained of blood? A human murderer would have had to have transported a lot of equipment to the park she died in to manage that. Besides, there are shops right across from where she was found. Equipment like that— the time necessary to drain a human body of blood —would have been noticed."

Completely drained… of blood?

"Oh, dear," said Goldie standing and wringing her hands as she hovered at the edge of the room. "Not another vampire."

No, no. My heart thudded wildly inside my chest. Lien didn't pick up on my distress, moving over to the table where my mother's potions book rested and flipping through the pages.

"But when Ravana killed… She drove the victims blood mad first. She didn't just drain a victim dry in one attack," I said.

"Who's to say the woman wasn't blood mad?" Lien ventured. She stopped flipping pages and her finger slid down the text in front of her. "I don't know anything about her. Besides, blood madness isn't a prerequisite for a vampire-caused death. A vampire is quite capable of killing in one feeding." She glanced over at Goldie. "Your previous villainess vampire was probably more interested in keeping her work low-profile and wasn't feeding a violent, insatiable urge like some vampires experience. And it worked, clearly. No normies here suspected her."

My back straightened as I felt the urge to defend my friends. "Neither did any of the paranormals."

Lien grunted again and focused on the page in front of her.

"Vampires can't be the only paranormals who drain blood," I started. Qarinah and Draven were the only vampires within hundreds of miles, as far as I knew. I couldn't have Lien accusing them of something I knew them to be uncapable of.

"A werewolf transformed might manage it, too." Lien *tsked*. "Except the full moon was last week."

She really was going to accuse the whole town, wasn't she?

Lien leaned back and tapped a finger across her lip. "A spiderwoman tends to suck the marrow more than the blood, but she *could* be motivated to change up her diet to cover her tracks. That is, if she's willing to drink from a woman when men are usually her prey, but there's nothing to *stop* her from changing it up." Now she was accusing Spindra. She really *was* going to go through the entire town!

"No one in Luna Lane could have done this," I said firmly. "No one here kills."

Broomie let out a little bristly moan and Lien's attention snapped toward our broomsticks.

Actually, a number of Luna Lane paranormals had killed before—long ago. And I had, too, far more recently. My gaze darted down to the rune circle. I still hadn't summoned Eithne. Weeks and weeks had passed since her death, and I could no longer summon my mother, so she was my only option for guidance. And there were questions she needed to answer. But I still couldn't do it.

"Your mayor mentioned a murdering ghost," Lien pointed out. She knew about Eithne, but she, thankfully, didn't bring it up.

"Oh, poor Virginia," Goldie said. She put a hand over her heart. "Oh, Zashil. That whole mess…" It had been during her son's escape room test that her son's business partner had been murdered.

Perhaps deservedly, though, since he'd murdered

Virginia—Ginny—in the first place and gotten away with it.

I stuck my nose in the air. "That was different. That was justice."

Goldie gasped. Well, maybe my thoughts on murder had evolved a bit ever since my aunt had *forced* me to put an end to her in order to save all of the people I loved in Luna Lane.

"Besides, Ginny's gone." My voice cracked. I missed her, despite everything. Despite her pompousness and the deed she'd committed. It had hurt Zashil, too, traumatizing him and sending him back away from Luna Lane.

Lien crossed her arms and leaned against the potions table. "Well, a vampire is really the simplest explanation. We'll hear from the Vampire High Council soon enough if I'm right."

"We will?" Goldie asked. The High Council had only once appeared in Luna Lane, as far as I knew, and that had been to collect Ravana in her coffin and bring her home to Transylvania for her trial. She'd been sentenced to a hundred years' confinement for murder and for driving so many victims blood mad, which went against the Council's laws for vampires who chose to reside amongst humans around the globe.

"Two incidents involving vampires within such a short distance." Lien shook her head. "One might be explained away by a rogue vampire. Two might mean a whole bloodline is tainted."

Ravana's "whole bloodline" meant Qarinah and Draven. Neither of whom had killed before.

"It *wasn't* our vampires," I said more emphatically.

"And that's what the High Council will want to find out." Lien turned around and frowned, staring at my stockpile of potion ingredients. "Your stock is truly lacking."

"You haven't been shopping for any ingredients in weeks," said Goldie entirely unhelpfully. "We have a lot of new spices—"

"*Shopping*?" Lien's nose wrinkled. "For witch ingredients? From a grocery store?"

"I gather what I can in the woods, too." I scoffed. "It's not like I can *go find* anything that doesn't grow around town. All but one month of my entire life, I've been confined to Luna Lane."

Lien held her hand out toward our broomsticks and Broomhelen soared stiffly into her grip. "I'll go get what I can."

"Why?" I asked. I hadn't been focusing as much on my potions since getting back from my trip. Lien had been all about me learning to enchant with more of my own power during our lessons.

"We need a good stock of potions," Lien said. "If we're going to be fighting not just other witches, but *other paranormals*—"

"We're not fighting anyone in Luna Lane!"

Broomie bounced the tail end of her shaft against the hardwood floor in agreement.

Lien looked sharply from Goldie to me. "The only reason I'm here is to protect you—"

"I never asked—"

She held up a long, graceful finger. "Without you, Isadora Poplar will never fall. You're not the only witch in the world, and you're not the only one who suffers under her." She swallowed. "In fact, thanks to your mother and aunt whisking you away, you've *barely* spent more than a few weeks suffering under Isadora Poplar."

I didn't know what to say. As if I'd asked to be on my grandmother's hit list! My mother and aunt had hidden me for a reason. True, they'd kept the truth from me so I could enjoy my youth. But I didn't hold that against them. Not really.

"I'm going to be brewing a lot more potions over the next few days," Lien said. "You can either help or stay out of the way."

Goldie raised a brow and Lien brushed past us both to the door. Opening it, she waved her free hand over her body. "MRAW."

And then she slid on Broomhelen's back side-saddle and took off to the skies.

"Well," said Goldie, shivering despite the enchantment I'd cast on her as we gazed out the open door. "Perhaps someone should alert the mayor."

"And the vampires," I said. "Lien may not know everyone here like I do, but she's not wrong. If a vampire is found to be responsible, the Vampire

High Council will look to Luna Lane for the culprit."

Broomie's bristles swished softly in a sad, little sound.

But there was nothing to worry about. I'd clear their names by the time of Qarinah and Roan's wedding in four days.

Chapter Six

Just as Goldie was about to leave to return to her store—I promised I would spread the word to Mayor Abdel and Sheriff Roan so she could get back to work—Roderick, in his stony, squat gargoyle form, walked down the hallway with plodding steps. He rubbed his eye with his fist and looked from Goldie to me and back.

I froze. I knew he was supposed to be my protector, but he was also a child. I didn't want him following me around as I spread the word about a murder and investigated things a bit to be sure no one accused any citizens of Luna Lane of this crime that had taken place a whole town over.

"Good morning, Roderick," said Goldie in a singsong voice. She had her coat on but had left it open and carried her hat in her hand. My warmth enchantment was still working on her, but it would wear off soon enough. It got a bit annoying to remember to cast it on myself, which was why I didn't really often do it until the depths of winter got to be too much for me.

Roderick nodded at Goldie and waddled over to her. Broomie sprung from my hand and gave him bristly cheek kisses, which made a slight smile appear on his face as he leaned into her brush-head touch.

Goldie's face lit up at the sight, and she clapped one hand against the knit hat in the other. "Why don't you come with your Auntie Goldie and help at Vogel's today, huh, son?" She looked at me for confirmation. I nodded.

Roderick's head turned, the sound like grating stone. His brow furrowed.

"Please, yes, go help your uncle and aunt," I told him. "I have a few boring things to do in town today —I'll be sure to pick you up later."

"Or we can close up shop early and meet at Hungry Like a Pup when the other children are out of school," Goldie suggested as she held a hand out to him.

"That sounds nice. You'd like some cake, wouldn't you?" I asked Roderick.

The gargoyle boy frowned, and Broomie gave him another kiss. His rumbly, grating laugh echoed out into the room and he took Goldie's extended hand.

"We'll see you around four, then?" Goldie offered.

"Sounds good. And thank you." I sent a wink the gargoyle's way. "I'm sure Roderick will be a good little helper today."

He chewed his bottom rocky lip, a stone fang protruding as they turned to go. But he went, watching me over his shoulder all the while.

Gargoyle guardians were supposed to obey royals. I wondered if my gentle cajoling had seemed more like a command to him.

I took a deep breath. But in any case, I didn't want to drag him around today.

I dashed into my room and waved my hand at my closet, rapid-firing "NEPO," "SSERDNU," "NAELC," and "SSERD" enchantments in succession so my closet door opened; my robe and nightgown flew off; I cleaned myself of oils and odors and dirt; and my trademark black dress, winter lace-up boots, and black shawl for the colder months all covered me up. Grabbing a brush, I quickly ran it through my long hair as the clothes wove on and around me, then I stopped by the bathroom before meeting up with Broomie at the coat rack near the door, grabbing my black conical hat with purple belt and affixing it to my head. The magical energy all around me grew stronger the moment the channeling hat settled on my scalp. A witch's hat was a must for performing complicated or long-lasting enchantments.

I hoped I wouldn't need either today.

Just in case, though, I stopped over by the finished potions in my cabinet. Just one little power boost potion in the pouch at my belt for luck.

Broomie glided us through the chill winter air and down to the top of the short staircase leading to town hall. The heels of my boots clicked across the cement as I let myself into the hub of governance in our small town of three hundred people.

Mayor Abdel's booming voice carried out across the petite, open space. There was a desk for greeting visitors, at which sat Erik, a short, rotund man with an amber complexion in his mid-forties who had a wife and a teenager at home.

"Hello, Dahlia," he said. He was busy straightening a pile of papers on his desk. "How can we help you?"

"I was hoping to speak to the mayor," I said, clutching Broomie upright in one hand. "And the sheriff, if you've seen him. I swung by the sheriff's office on the way here and it was empty." Not locked—because who would steal anything from law enforcement in Luna Lane? Just empty. Roan had no other deputies or assistants.

"Sheriff Birch is in with the mayor right now. There's all those details about the wedding to plan, you know." His voice grew quieter and one eyebrow arched. "And registering as a paranormal citizen."

Just then, Ryan, a human man roughly my age who'd moved to Luna Lane a few years back after an encounter with the paranormal in his hometown, appeared around the corner, carrying a file. He cupped the file to one side of his face, as if whispering, but his voice barely lowered a register. "We still don't know if he's going to change into a vampire. His license is provisional." He lowered the file and smiled at me, his bushy, red beard jostling with his broad grin. "Hello, Dahlia! Exciting, isn't it? We haven't had a wedding in…" He looked to Erik. "Well, I don't know how long."

"Twenty-six years," Erik said, still sorting through his papers. He held up his left hand. A solid-gold band gleamed off his ring finger in the overhead lights. "When Cara and I got hitched."

Had Luna Lane really not been the site of a wedding in *twenty-six years*?

"You're forgetting Faine and Grady," I pointed out. I'd *definitely* been at my best friend's wedding. Maid of honor and all.

"No, I'm not," said Erik, still not looking up. "They had a second ceremony here, but they legally tied the knot up in Canada, in the werewolf hometown. Way they do it in their culture, you know."

My stomach flip-flopped. I wasn't sure I'd known that. Had it mattered? It had felt like a real wedding to me. Both Faine's and Grady's parents had made the trip, as well as a few extended wolfy relatives. It was just… Well, if Faine had wanted to get married in the town in Canada to which her parents had moved, I wouldn't have been able to attend. Trapped in Luna Lane and all. Maybe she just hadn't wanted to tell me the truth.

"A wedding is still a wedding, paperwork or not," said Ryan curtly. "I just wish I'd been here to see it. Werewolf marrying werewolf, and now vampire marrying human—"

"Or maybe a vampire," Erik pointed out.

Roan's laughter was louder than Abdel's now. My heart softened. Roan wasn't an overly dour man, but it was rare to hear him quite so cheery, especially outside of the pub. He took his job seriously, even if there—usually, at least until recently—wasn't much for him to do.

The door to the mayor's office opened at the back of the wide, open space and Chione stepped out first, a pen and notepad in hand. The dark-skinned model-like beauty with sharp cheekbones and long legs was dressed in dress pants, a blouse, and blazer, as usual, her color of choice today a deep lime green. Beads were woven through the braids in her black hair, and they clicked softly as she made her way to her desk, a smile on her full, red-painted lips.

Roan stepped out in tan uniform, complete with sheriff's gallon hat, two hands on his belt beneath his slightly protruding belly.

Mayor Abdel's business suit was sleek and perfectly-tailored—as anyone living in Luna Lane's clothes ought to be, considering the presence of Spindra, our tailor—his bandage-covered hands and face poking out from beneath the sharp attire.

"Roan!" I cried out. I hadn't returned to First Taste last night or otherwise sought him out to congratulate him.

"Little Lia," said Roan as he and Abdel neared. I was hardly "little" anymore. In fact, I was probably slightly taller than him. His grin widened as we neared each other and embraced. "Just the girl I was hoping to see."

"Oh?" I asked as we pulled apart, only for Broomie to get in between us for a bristling kiss against the stubble on his cheek. Roan laughed as he gave her a pet like one might a dog. "I was also looking for *you*," I said as Broomie leaned back into my grip. "First off: Congratulations."

Roan's ruddy cheeks grew three shades darker as he scratched a cheek. "Oh, no need for all that."

"On the contrary!" Abdel said, wrapping an arm around Roan's shoulder and patting him with a bandage-covered hand. "A wedding in Luna Lane is always cause for celebration!"

"Qarinah and I both aren't looking for much of a fuss," Roan said. "I don't have family from out of town, and well, she pretended she'd died rather than let her human family back home know about the existence of vampires…" He crossed his arms as

Abdel went over to Chione's desk to confer with her about something. "Thing is, so that means, it's down to you and Draven."

Broomie cocked her brush head, echoing the confusion I felt.

"What is?" My gut tightened.

"Being our maid of honor and best man, of course!" Roan leaned toward me, his voice lowering. "Well, it's really best woman and lad of honor, should we say? Qarinah picks him and I pick you, but however you want to do it."

My mouth opened into a puckered "o." That was the last thing I'd been expecting when I'd searched him out this morning. Sure, the thought of being paired with Draven even in this innocent sense made me a bit uncomfortable, especially knowing the mood he was in, but there were more important matters at hand.

"Of course!" I said, wrapping my arms, and Broomie, around him again. "I'll be your best woman, groomsmaid, whatever you want me to be!"

"That's what I was hoping to hear!" Roan patted my back. "I'm only sorry we didn't throw this together before your beau had to leave."

"Qarinah said he'd video in."

"So he shall. Told the lad last night. Qarinah told me she'd told you and had sent you over to speak with Draven…"

"Yeah. Not sure I helped any, though, really."

"Well, we both appreciate you trying. Skies

above know you've done more than enough for that vampire." Roan had kept his mouth *mostly* shut while I'd dated Draven, but I could tell back then he hadn't been happy with the match. That had been after I'd lost Mom, and it wasn't like I'd talked *a lot* about it when I'd summoned her spirit after that, so he'd been the only parental figure I'd had to express any sense of disapproval. Goldie and Arjun had just been happy I'd been dating *anyone*, even if it wasn't their son like they'd hoped.

"Hey, Roan," I started, ready to discuss the bigger issue. One that I had to consider, too, if Cable and I were to have a long-term relationship. "Qarinah mentioned she was hoping to turn you into a vam—"

"Get the mayor on the phone!" shouted Mayor Abdel, which made Roan and me both do a double take. The mayor speaking of another mayor in such a panicked tone could only mean something bad.

"Bananaberries," I said under my breath. I'd nearly forgotten what I'd come in here for.

"What is it?" Roan adjusted his belt as Chione and Ryan were sent into a frenzy, turning on computer screens.

"Murder in Creekdale," I said. "A nun killed last night. According to Lien… All of the victim's blood was drained."

The news might have drained the blood right out from Roan's face. "Qarinah was at First Taste," he said softly, as if he knew what came next. An accusation. "I stayed until two in the morning. Then I left to get some shut eye, but I know there were other customers who stayed." He bit his lip. "Draven wasn't on duty like he was supposed to be."

"Wallowing in pity at his house," I said. Then again, I'd left his house at around seven. Maybe earlier. I didn't know what he'd been up to the rest of the night.

"What was that you said about blood draining?" Mayor Abdel slipped in front of me. "This wasn't a human-on-human murder?"

I took a deep breath. "Lien didn't think so. Though she was north of Creekdale at the time."

"Where is she?" snapped Abdel. "If she's responsible—"

"She's not," I said, though in fact, I didn't know that, either.

I had no idea who could have been responsible —and why the nun had been targeted. Assuming she hadn't been a random victim in the wrong place at the wrong time.

"What about the other witches after you?" Abdel asked.

"She says she was chasing their energy forty miles away." But she hadn't said she'd caught sight of them, had she? A paranormal murder right outside the barriers prohibiting them from being able to reach me?

What if it was just a message? To me?

What if someone had *died* at random because of me?

"Send that witch to speak with me," said Abdel. "The news is reporting 'unusual circumstances.' I wanted to connect with the Mayor of Creekdale, see what he knows, rule out any paranormal involvement." His thin lips, mostly obscured by the cream-white bandages, grew into an even thinner line. "But if there *is* reason to suspect paranormal involvement… It might be time to fess up. He doesn't know about us. He thinks I just have a skin condition." Abdel gestured to his mummy bandages.

That would be one wallop of a skin condition.

"You never want to call in county for things like these," Roan said.

"Of course not!" Abdel nearly shouted. "The high percentage of paranormal residents in Luna Lane is a closely guarded secret. But if *our* secrets are spilling out into other towns, we might not have a choice." He looked grim. "Where *is* that witch cousin of yours?"

"She went off to gather potion ingredients," I replied. "I don't know how to reach her."

Chione picked a smartphone off of her desk. "Call her?"

Of course, I'd left mine at home on the table by the door. I *still* wasn't used to that thing. "I don't remember her number. And I doubt she'd pick up anyway. Once she gets an idea in her head, there's no distracting her."

Abdel frowned and looked around at all of the heads turned his way in the room. "Well, I'm sure this will all be explained. We *know* no citizen of Luna Lane could do such a thing."

Erik *tsked* gruffly. "Except that a ghost and a vampire who walked amongst us were both outed as murderers during the past few months."

Ryan sent Erik a disapproving look, but the slightly older man shrugged. "I'm not wrong."

"Doc Day!" said Roan, drawing all heads to him. He bristled and adjusted his belt again. "Doc Day managed to lure Lazarus out of hiding for the first time in ages. Well, she and her Creekdale doctor friend—"

"Corbin," I supplied. I'd never forget his name because he was absolutely necessary to sign off on the inhuman levels of healing that took place in Luna Lane when I lent a hand.

"Right," said Roan. "They were still there when I left First Taste. Planned to spend the whole night there discussing all those morbid things they find so exciting about surgeries and embalming and so forth. I'm sure they could serve as Qarinah's alibi."

Abdel stared at Roan. "No one was accusing Qarinah." But his voice cracked.

"What about Draven?" said Chione even quieter. The woman had nearly lost herself to blood madness once. Ravana had been to blame, but it had taken some time to wean her off the vampire venom. Vampires were sure to be a touchy subject with her.

"Draven, uh… Well, I was with him at his house until around seven," I said. Broomie nodded her agreement. "Grady and Roderick can attest to seeing him there, then, too."

Ryan looked at his computer screen. "It says the estimated time of death is around three in the morning."

All eyes turned to me.

"I don't know what he got up to after that," I admitted. "But it couldn't be Draven. It just couldn't be. I came here to tell you all what Lien said, but also that we need to prepare the vampires as soon as they wake tonight, gather all the evidence we can about their whereabouts during the crime—"

"*Gather evidence?*" said Abdel, inhaling a sharp breath. I wasn't even sure the mummy still breathed. "Was that what Lien suggested? That we'd need to prove their innocence?"

I picked at a single bristle in Broomie's brush head. "Well, no. She seemed almost certain someone in Luna Lane was responsible."

Chione let out a hiss and Roan grunted.

"A vampire in particular," I said softly. "She said, though it was possible another type of paranormal could have been responsible, it most likely was a vampire." My voice grew hushed.

"But did she mention that the Vampire High

Council might think so, too?" Abdel touched a hand to his forehead. "Oh, goodness, and they're on their way. They've been informed about this marriage. About Roan's…" He looked to the sheriff, as if waiting for permission to say more. Roan was too busy staring at his own feet, his forehead dotting with sweat. "They'll be sending a representative regardless."

"Is that bad?" I asked.

"It means Luna Lane's vampires will be the primary suspects," said Abdel. "At least until they can both be cleared."

"And with their sire being a proven breaker of vampire law," added Chione softly, "the whole bloodline might already be on thin ice."

Abdel shook his head. "If either is responsible, it doesn't bode well for the other, innocent or not."

My knees grew shaky, and I reached for Roan's hand to give it a squeeze. His palm was sweaty.

As if he were nervous enough to believe… that if it hadn't been Qarinah, then it had to have been Draven.

But he was wrong.

"Didn't you tell us Draven had been willing to kill that man, that…" Chione snapped her fingers as she tried to think of whatever it was that was on her mind. "Karter Wattana? A suspect in Virginia's murder?"

My jaw dropped as I looked at Roan. He'd been going around telling people that? "Draven and

Qarinah were about to *die* when he suggested that!" I said, dropping Roan's hand and shaking my head. Ginny had wanted Karter dead, and the man's death would have freed us all from the escape room in which she'd trapped us, which would have saved Qarinah and Draven both. "He didn't *mean* it! He was just desperate."

Roan frowned. "Still, he was willing—"

"And yet he didn't! We all solved the puzzles and escaped in time—which we might not have been able to do, by the way, and failure would have meant Qarinah's death, too." Vampires being so close to a large source of para-paranormal for nearly an hour had been slowly proving fatal to them.

No one had a reply to that. In fact, I couldn't seem to catch anyone's eye. Not even Roan's. Had he condemned the vampire already?

Even if he was the town's sole detective, I'd show him he was wrong.

Chapter Seven

There was no waking the vampires while the sun was still out, so I'd have to work on gathering the facts of the case—and discovering the vampires' whereabouts during the previous night.

Roan and Abdel could work together to prepare for the Vampire High Council representative's arrival and to smooth over the details with the Creekdale police.

I would focus on protecting our own.

I'd checked with the day shift at First Taste and they were no help—both men hadn't been anywhere near the pub at the time of the crime and had been sleeping. Both had been alone, though that hardly mattered since they were normies and therefore not suspects. Jamie didn't actually live alone. He was Doc Day's only boarder at the moment, but like Roan had guessed about the doc,

Jamie testified to her not coming home until after dawn as far as he knew, telling him she'd spent a long night catching up with old friends.

It had been unusual for her, especially at her age, but so was the local funeral parlor reaper walking out about town, so Jamie had understood what might have sparked the rare behavior.

Enchanting a straw into a ballpoint pen with a wave of my hands, I scratched out some notes on one of Hungry Like a Pup's dispenser napkins. After exiting First Taste, I'd made my way next door for a late breakfast or early lunch. Faine and Grady were busy with the lunch rush, so we'd only managed to say a few words to one another, but I had an investigation to focus on and I didn't want to distract them from their work. I couldn't leave town to go see the scene of the crime myself, though I had no doubt it was mostly cleaned up by now. So what else could I do before the vampires woke up and could detail their actions the previous night themselves? Doc Day and Lazarus came to the top of my mind, as I assumed Doctor Corbin had gone back home to Creekdale.

That would take care of Qarinah's alibi. But what about Draven's?

I gazed up, over Broomie's sleeping, curled-up form lying across from my plate on the table, and watched Grady in the kitchen, flipping some burgers as Faine worked the malt machine. Most of the people in the café were those I was friendly enough with but not particularly close to. Jeremiah the farmer was waiting on a to-go order. He nodded at me, his hands both tucked into his red flannel coat pockets, his ruddy cheeks and brown beard poking out from under a fur-lined trapper hat. I nodded back.

The Vadases were Draven's neighbors, but they also slept at night when Draven was awake. Still, they might have noticed if Draven had noisily left at any point.

I chewed on my enchanted pen, the tip turning back into the paper straw the Vadases favored at their café. My eyes caught a glance of the half-eaten BLT on my plate. Before he'd left, Cable had gone to the trouble of taking as many old Irish pounds as I could summon out of the dimension Mom—or my aunt Eithne, actually—had stored it all in for my care and exchanged them into American currency. There was probably more money to be summoned, actually, but we'd procured a tidy sum, enough for me to pay all my bills for several years at least. And then he'd set up an account in a bank over in Creekdale for me—well, it had both our names on it, but that was merely to make it easier for him to set it up since I couldn't leave town—and hooked it all up to my smartphone so I could pay my bills that way.

I patted the pouch at my belt. Well, when I *remembered* my phone, anyway. I was too used to telling everyone to put things on my tab.

I wolfed down a few more bites of my sandwich

and stood up just as Faine passed a bag full of food and a single malt over to Jeremiah. My phone would have more information on the murder, too. It was either that or head to the library, but I'd promised Cable I'd be better about carrying my phone around with me, and I'd failed already two days after he'd left.

Faine walked over, wiping her hands on the frilly apron over her navy capri pants. "Leaving already? Things have finally slowed down." She gestured over her shoulder as Jeremiah left. About half the tables were still full of diners.

"It's going to get even busier in an hour," I pointed out. "I'll get out of your hair—but I forgot my phone." I winced. "I'll pay you next time?"

"I know you're good for it." Faine winked.

So I wouldn't be a total imposition, I waved at my plate, utensils, and glass with both hands. "NAELC."

Fewer dishes for her to clean.

She started stacking them up, then noticed my scribbled-on napkin. I tucked that and the pen in my pouch, the pen's origin as a straw allowing me to bend it to fit it in there.

"What's that?" Faine asked, nodding at my pouch. Broomie stirred and stretched her brush head and tail as far as they would go as she unfurled onto the floor.

My eyes darted every which way to see who might be looking. No one was. I lowered my voice and stepped nearer Faine. "Have you heard about the Creekdale murder?"

Faine frowned, nodding as she held the stack of my dishes in front of her. "A nun, right? What a tragedy."

I took a deep breath as Broomie floated over into my hand. "Word is the paranormal is involved."

Faine's eyes widened as she stepped toward the counter, putting the stack of dishes down. She spun on me. "The witches who are after you?"

"Lien doesn't think so," I said. They made the most likely suspects in my book—though I couldn't be sure as to their exact motivations for targeting the victim. "But the thing is… Everyone seems to be suspecting a vampire."

Faine gasped. "But the only vampires within a thousand miles…"

I'd get straight to the point. "Do you know anything about Draven's whereabouts after Grady dropped Roderick off there?"

Faine put a hand on her hip and let a breath out of her mouth, her dark bangs fluttering. "You can't possibly be suspecting him?"

"*I'm* not," I assured her. "But I'm working to establish their alibis while they're asleep so we can move on from this nonsense." I gave Faine the lowdown on everything I knew. The victim's total blood loss. The visitor coming from the Vampire High Council, due for the upcoming wedding.

Qarinah could likely be vouched for by Doc Day and Lazarus. That just left Draven.

"Well, usually, I don't hear a peep from next door overnight," said Faine. "Since the two of them are working. But funnily enough, we did see Draven again after you left. Both Grady and I."

An unexpected tension left my body. "When was that?"

"About eleven," said Faine, tapping her mouth with one finger. "The kids were asleep and Grady and I were about to retire ourselves."

Eleven. Still too early to be an alibi for the time of death. Bananaberries.

"He had that handheld video game system Roderick had had earlier?" Faine said. It was more a question than a statement.

I nodded. "He gave it to him. Out of pity, I think."

Faine smiled. "That's sweet. But, well, it had stopped working. He asked if we had its charger. I told him he needed batteries. We didn't have any on hand. The kids' toys go through them like water, you know."

Broomie and I exchanged a look, Broomie's brush head cocking. "Draven knocked on your door as you were about to go to bed… to ask if you could charge a video game system?" Draven had had a smartphone before I had, so it wasn't too surprising he knew about chargers. But maybe he hadn't been paying attention to video games back in the nineties when Faine, Cable, and I had been kids. If I remembered right, that thing ate through six AA batteries.

Faine nodded. "He looked so… tired, maybe? I couldn't get mad at him, especially since I knew how upset he was about Qarinah. Not that I agree he *should* be, mind you, but knowing him, I figured he just needed to let off some steam and he would understand he was being selfish soon enough."

"So what did he do when you couldn't help him?" I asked.

Someone called Faine's name from the corner and waved a mug of coffee in the air. "Just a second, hon," she called back to him. She swept around the counter, grabbing the coffee pot with the orange handle, her eyes still locked with mine. "Well, I remembered I had that old system from when we were in elementary school, you know? We'd just talked about. It was somewhere in my storage closet. Rather than send him home empty-handed, I sent Grady over with that. The system, the controllers, the one game we could find in the box along with them. I've brought it all out for the kids before, but they like the new stuff better, so I told him Draven could keep it as long as he likes."

"Does he even have a TV?" I asked. I'd never seen him watching one in my life.

She nodded. "Grady said Draven dragged an old set out of his attic. It was the little, chunky kind, with antennas and a built-in stand to raise it off the ground and everything. Draven said that Ravana had followed a 'suds' for a while in the late seventies and early eighties."

"A 'suds'?" I asked.

Faine giggled. "We figured out later he meant a 'soap.' A soap opera."

I laughed. "Could Grady even hook up the game system to a set that old?"

The man in question rang the little bell indicating a finished order. "Order up!"

"Coming!" Faine called over her shoulder. She scooted back around the corner and stood beside me with the coffee pot. "It worked. The system is pretty old, too. Dad bought it for himself and Mom before I was even born."

Nodding, I followed Faine toward the table of the patron who'd asked for more coffee. I hovered back as she got him a refill and chatted with the table, taking a few small plates and balancing them under one arm before picking up the coffee pot again.

"And after that?" I asked once she'd finished. She set everything down on the counter to deal with later as she made her way back around the corner to grab the hot food.

"After that, I couldn't say." Faine stacked the plates on a serving tray. "Grady said he got a game working for Draven, the vampire sat down and picked up a controller, and then Grady left and he and I went to bed."

"Hmm, okay. Thanks." I grabbed my napkin notes and pen out of my pouch again, scribbling down all the info. "I'll get out of your hair. See you for dinner? Goldie's bringing Roderick over here to play with the kids."

"Sounds great," Faine said, heaving the tray up. We walked together as far as the front door. Though balancing four plates on a tray with one hand, she still reached out to grab my forearm before I left. "You don't really think Draven would be capable of *murder*, do you?" She whispered the "m" word.

Perhaps she, like the others, was thinking of Draven's suggestion to kill Karter Wattana and free the rest of us from Ginny's escape room game.

"I don't." I tucked in my chin. "I'll do my best to figure out what really happened in order to prove it."

Faine frowned but let go of my hand, adjusting her grip on the tray. "Another mystery for Dahlia Poplar to solve?"

"Looks like." I stuffed the notes and pen back in my pouch. "As long as *law enforcement* is focused on the wrong direction, I'll do what I can to figure out the truth."

"Just stay safe," she said, turning to drop off the food a few tables away from the door.

I couldn't even leave Luna Lane to learn what had happened over in Creekdale. How much danger could I be in?

Chapter Eight

The clock in the center of town square down the block from Hungry Like a Pup rung out the noon hour. Flying home on Broomie to grab my smartphone and coming back would only take about ten minutes.

But Doc Day's house was so much closer, and since she hadn't been at the café, she was likely at home for lunch. She mostly did house calls, so her medical equipment was all set up at home for times she needed more than she could carry in her medical bag.

With the time difference, Cable was definitely finished with his work for the day. Last night, I'd texted him about Qarinah and Roan's wedding, but he'd likely been asleep. Still, I knew Roan had spoken to him about it. Was I ready to tell him about this latest crisis in town?

He would think Luna Lane was nothing but a den of murderers if I didn't clear this up first.

"Off to the doc's," I told Broomie, sliding on her shaft.

She let out a bristly-friction chirp and we took to the air, the increased chill of the wind breaking through even my warmth enchantment. But it was more aerodynamic for me to grip the tip of Broomie's tail with both hands and lean forward. We plowed over the streets until we reached the colonial-style two-floor that was Doc Day's house. Her kids long ago grown and moved on, she'd opened it up to boarders a few years back. Jamie had lived there a few years.

But neither Jamie nor Doc Day were likely to choose to leave a shiny, black coffin on the front steps.

The door to the doctor's house opened as Broomie took me in for a landing. I noticed the large, rental U-Haul in the doctor's driveway.

"Yes, of course." Doc Day's voice drew my attention as my feet touched the walk leading up to her front door. "But can you get that by yourself? I could call some of the neighborhood men over—"

"No, thank you, madam, I am quite capable of carrying my master myself. As you can see, I've had no issue getting him this far." The voice that spoke was high-pitched, a little quavering, and possessed a French accent.

The man who spoke was bulky, wide shoulders

actually bursting out of his suitcoat, which was ripped at the shoulder seams. Oily, dark hair pasted messily along his forehead, a cowlick protruding off the very top. He put his back to the coffin and crouched down so far, his shins scraped along Doc Day's front porch. Wrapping her white lab coat tighter over her floral blouse with one hand, the mist escaping her lips in the cold air, she stepped out to hold the door.

"Doc?" I asked as I approached, Broomie flipped over in my hand. "What's going on? Who's—"

With a mighty grunt, the man slipped his fingers around either side of the coffin and stood, the coffin shifting into place over his hunched back.

I wove my hands in his direction, my brain hardly catching up to my instinct to save this man before the heavy load crushed him. "ETATIVEL!"

The man let out a high-pitched scream and collapsed forward, the coffin crushing him, and my enchantment waving over the coffin into the air at nothing.

"Oh my!" said Doc Day, letting go of the door. She scrambled forward.

"Let me." I waved my hands at the coffin again.

"Stop! Stop, you witch!" The strange man crawled out from under the coffin, which landed on the porch with a *thud*. He threw himself over the top of the coffin on his back and spread his arms and legs widely. "I will die! *Die* to protect my master from your witchcraftery! Do not think I am unaware of what your kind is capable!" His blue eyes, dark circles below marring pale white skin, roved madly upward.

"I wasn't going to hurt anyone," I said. Broomie's brush head leaned toward me as if to whisper to me. "I don't know what's going on," I told her. "But a coffin…"

"It's all right. Everyone, please. Calm down, Valentin, sir." Doc Day looked from the man to me and back, pushing down the air with both hands as if to mellow us out. I wasn't frazzled at all, but the man clearly was.

Doc Day squeezed her lab coat tighter over her chest again and came over to whisper to me. "This is Valentin. He's the human attendant to Lord Aleksandru, member of the Vampire High Council. As we have no inn, they've asked to stay here while they attend to their business."

It was my turn for *my* eyes to widen. Of course. Why else would someone be dragging a coffin around? Despite the trouble it caused, it was the only sensible way for vampires to travel.

But when, exactly, had Qarinah contacted the Council? How had they gotten here so quickly?

As if reading my mind while that strange Valentin man began singing something like an anthem in French behind her, the doctor explained. "They have a system, Valentin explained, of transporting coffins via airplane and then rental vehicles wherever they go under the guise of burying people in their homelands. They left just yesterday afternoon and are quite tired from their journey. I said there was room enough in my second-largest bedroom. But perhaps, as long as you're here, you could go inside and whip up some enchantments to make sure there's room for the coffin alongside the bed?" Doc Day pursed her lips, her hair hanging slightly out of place over her forehead.

"Sure," I said. I leaned around the doctor and spoke louder so Valentin could hear me. "But I could enchant the coffin up the stairs for you, too."

"No!" Valentin sat up on the coffin and swung his legs. "Never! No hands but mine and my master's shall touch this coffin!" He patted it and looked down, a warm sense of tenderness relaxing his brow just a bit. "Other than the airplane cargo men, of course." He nodded, as if speaking to the coffin itself. "But *no* witches! Never! *That*, at least, I made sure of!" He practically growled at me.

I held my free hand up in surrender and headed toward the door, which the doctor opened for me and kept open as Valentin readjusted himself to carry the coffin on his back.

"First door on the left at the top of the stairs," the doctor told me.

I nodded and headed for the staircase, Valentin's grunts and the sound of him singing in French hard to ignore, even as the sounds drifted off into the distance.

I found the room Doc Day had directed me to —the others were all closed, except for one that led to a bathroom—and waved my hands around at a dresser and bedside table in order to enchant the items closer against the wall to make room for the coffin.

Behind me, Valentin's grunts alternated with his singing. The sounds grew louder, as with a *thump, thump, thump,* the coffin was dragged up the stairs. Then the thumping stopped, only Valentin's singing echoing out into the air.

Finishing my enchantments, I exited the room, but the Vampire High Council member's coffin was entirely blocking the top of staircase, the human assistant nowhere to be found.

The sound of a toilet flushing made me jump, and I turned around to find the bathroom door closed, the sound of running water competing with the man's operatic voice for dominance.

I was just about to get on Broomie's back to fly over the coffin when the sound of running water stopped and the bathroom door whipped open. Valentin hit the light switch in the bathroom and then shot me a glare as we scooched around each other to trade positions in the cramped hallway.

"You are not what I expected," Valentin said.

He'd expected to see me at all? "I'm sorry?"

"Witch." He spat the word.

"Have you met a witch before?"

He grunted. "I do not speak of it."

"Hmm." I stared him down. He didn't say anything about my resemblance to said witch, so I had to assume it wasn't my grandmother who'd drawn his ire. "Are you the only one here? With your master?"

"Yes? And why would I not be?" He straightened up and stuck his nose in the air, picking up the front of the coffin again as he did so.

"Why doesn't the Vampire High Council travel with an entire retinue of followers? It would be easier to carry the coffin—"

"I have served my master for twenty-odd years," he said. "And it is *I* and *I alone* who shall be the next vampire he sires. He has promised me that." His expression grew dark, the bags under his eyes signs of being rather often drunken from, though he was clearly still human. "And promised me. And promised me." He muttered the last few words. "Now *pardonnez-moi*," he said as he dragged the top of the coffin over the last step and in my direction. He was not asking me *politely* at all.

I ducked into the open bathroom, resting Broomie's tail end on the tile floor as the strange man went back to grunting and singing and dragging the coffin down the hall. Every time he reached a corner, his song ended, replaced by more grunts as he shoved and pulled and rolled the coffin sideways. I could only imagine the vampire tumbling about inside.

But I didn't dare offer any assistance.

Broomie let out a soft coo, her brush head pointing at the sink. I looked. On the back of the silver faucet handle was a smudge.

What did she care about that? I glanced in either direction. Another door led off to, presumably, the master bedroom.

"WOLG," I whispered as I waved my hand. I could have turned on the light switch, sure, but some small instinct told me not to draw attention to the fact that I was busy in here as Valentin dragged a coffin outside in the hall.

My left hand glowed and I waved it over the sink and crouched for a better look. It was impeccably clean, as if someone had just cleaned it, but there was that smudge. It was brown-ish, or rather, perhaps a rust red, in the shape of a fingerprint. Like someone had cut their finger, maybe, and had started bleeding as they'd washed their hands.

Someone… like Valentin?

Or perhaps I was imagining things, looking for gruesome explanations where there was no need for them.

Valentin started singing again, the coffin hitting the ground with a great, big *thump* that startled me back into standing upright.

The bathroom light flickered on, and I whipped around to find Doc Day smiling at me.

"I was wondering where you went off to. Was there a reason you stopped by? Other than to, uh, meet the visitors in town?" She gestured over her shoulder.

I hadn't even *known* there'd be visitors. Well, Abdel had said as much, and Lien, too, but I hadn't expected them quite so quickly.

"Yes, actually." I gestured with Broomie toward the door leading to the hallway. "Do you have a minute?"

"Of course," the doctor said, a faltering smile on her face. "I told Valentin I'd scrounge up some lunch for him, and I suppose it's about time I ate myself. Why don't you join us?"

"I already ate," I said, following her down the stairs and to her kitchen. Valentin shut the door to his guest room as we passed, his brows narrowed before he ducked out of sight. "And I should just take a minute of your time." I imagined Valentin wouldn't have been too happy about sharing the table with me.

"Have a seat." Doc Day gestured toward the breakfast bar in her homey kitchen, and Broomie and I slid onto a pair of stools next to each other as the doc opened her fridge.

"I don't know if you heard what happened last night in Creekdale..." I checked over my shoulder to see if Valentin was anywhere nearby. Did I want him to hear? What if the Vampire High Council wasn't yet aware, and they were only here for Qari-nah's wedding?

"Hmm?" Doc Day brought out a carton of eggs.

"Oh, yes, how could I forget? I saw it on the news this morning. What a tragedy." She turned the light on over her stove and heaved a pan up from a drawer underneath the oven. "I wonder if Doctor Corbin knows anything about it? Did they rush the nun to the hospital?"

"I wouldn't imagine so." I threaded my fingers together over her counter. It was bothering me more and more that I hadn't taken the time to research what the news had reported—it was just that I didn't expect the news to be of much help, since most normies were still ignorant of the paranormal. But I was here to establish Qarinah's alibi. My voice lowered as I leaned over the corner and Doc Day cracked an egg into the pan. "Rumor is she was killed instantly. Her blood drained dry."

Doc Day's back grew stiff. But then she cracked another egg, her shoulders softening. "Blood drained dry. As in…?"

"Vampires." I frowned, looking over my shoulder again toward the direction of the stairs, but there was no sign of the strange normie visitor who clearly worshipped the vampire he'd been left in charge of. "What time did you say those two arrived in Luna Lane?"

"Shortly before you came." Doc Day cracked another egg and then another, stacking the empty shells back in the paper carton. "Probably only about ten minutes. I'd just gotten up—long night, you know, and I don't have any appointments today

—and heard the sound of the truck pulling into my driveway. I got dressed and the man was already dragging the coffin up the porch before he'd even knocked on the door. I could hardly turn them away at that point—not that I would have, mind you." She turned on the fan over the stove and clicked on the burner, grabbing a cover for the pan and setting it on top.

"But when did their plane land?" I asked.

Could it have been as simple as that? Had the vampire arrived in time to drain a nun just outside of Luna Lane? Perhaps there was no urgency from the vampire's assistant about heading to the vampires' manor because they *knew* who had committed the crime.

Now that I thought of it, why hadn't they gone straight to Draven and Qarinah's? Neither vampire would have been able to greet them, but wouldn't the lofty vampire manor have suited as a place for the vampire and his normie lackey to stay?

Perhaps not, now that I thought of it. The place would have been fine for the vampire, but there was hardly any food in the kitchen, nor were the facilities kept clean. The vampires had no use of them. It was only when we had Games Club meetings there that the place halfway resembled something comfortable for human inhabitants.

"He didn't say." Doc Day crossed her arms tightly over her chest. "Other than to say they left Transylvania yesterday afternoon."

I brought my napkin-note and pen-straw out of my pouch, doing a quick enchantment to turn the straw back into the pen. Not all of my enchantments wore off like that one, but I'd never been particularly skilled at transfiguration. Unlike my aunt Eithne or the witches who were after me, who'd hidden a large, onyx pike that was their weakness first as a playing card and then a letter opener.

It was stuck in letter opener—or dagger—form back at home. I might need it someday again if the witches crossed Lien's barrier into town.

I made a quick note to look up the length of time a flight took from Transylvania to Chicago. Tapping the pen to my lip, I thought again. Hadn't I been able to track Cable's flight with the Internet? I wondered if there were ways to even find the exact flight, as well as the time it would have landed.

The pan sizzled behind Doc Day and she turned to check it, covering her mouth for a yawn.

"Anyway, about that late night of yours," I said, tapping the doctor's name on my list. "I was hoping you could confirm Qarinah was at the bar all night."

"Surely, you don't suspect…?" Doc Day's gray eyebrow arched.

"*I* don't," I said. "But I think it might help Roan and Mayor Abdel get their heads in the game if we can establish our vampires' alibis."

"Well, Qarinah worked alone last night." Doc

Day stared off over the stovetop at the wall. "But she did leave for a brief time."

I stopped tapping the napkin. "What? When?"

"I couldn't tell you the time." Doc Day turned off the burner and lifted the cover to the pan, releasing a cascade of steam. "I was into my third drink at least by then, and the boys and I were talking…" She shook her head. "All I could tell you was at some point, she let us know she was stepping out and asked if we might just keep an eye on the place, let anyone new who entered know she'd soon be back, but no one else came in while she was gone, anyway. I didn't think much of it."

"But she…" The time she left was *very* important. "You're sure you don't know what time this was? How long was she gone?"

"No, sorry, dear." She opened a cupboard and removed two plates. "If I'd have known what would happen, of course I would have paid closer attention. But it'd been so long since Corbin and I had seen Lazarus. It's always fun speaking to him. He doesn't even really like visitors at the funeral parlor, you know." She grabbed a spatula and started serving the eggs. "Broomie, be a dear and knock on the guest's door? I told him I'd knock when it was ready."

Broomie, happy to be given a task, perked up from the stool and floated past.

"Be careful," I told her. I didn't trust that Valentin—and he clearly didn't like witches.

Hey, *I* didn't like half the witches I'd met. Even the ones I didn't dislike entirely had their moments.

Broomie nodded and soared up the steps.

Doc Day frowned. "I'm sorry. I'm searching my memory of last night, and I hate to admit at my age that it's all a bit fuzzy. She could have been gone ten minutes or two hours, I couldn't say. I don't even remember what we were talking about when she stepped away. She *did* come back, though, I can tell you that much. I'm sure once you ask her, she can explain it all away." She picked up the pan and set it on another burner, then picked up the pepper and sprinkled one of the plates of eggs.

"I could give you Doctor Corbin's number," Doc Day said. "I know you can't go to Creekdale to speak with him—and I know that beau of yours finally got you a phone of your own." She winked at me as she opened up a cupboard and removed a coffee mug. "Maybe he remembers. He might be able to tell you if the nun was brought to his hospital, too. I'm sure she was, even if it was straight to the morgue." She shuddered.

"Thanks," I said. "I'll take the number. What about Lazarus?" I asked as Doc Day told me the number and I wrote it down on my napkin-note. "Do you think he'd remember?"

Doc Day laughed as she turned on her pod-style coffeemaker. "Doesn't get drunk, that one, and he's pretty sharp, so yes, it couldn't hurt to ask. I just don't know if he'll answer when you knock on the door. Had his fill for years of socialization last night, I'd wager." She flipped off the fan over the stove and a knock echoed out from overhead. "You sure I can't get you anything?" She gestured to the coffeemaker as a door upstairs creaked open.

"I'm good, thank you," I said. "Broomie and I should get going. We're meeting up with Goldie, Arjun, and Roderick for dinner, so I want to get all this information squared away before then—before the vampires even wake up."

"I was wondering where that kiddo of yours had gone off to."

"Shoo!" screamed Valentin from upstairs. "Shoo, you feline-turned-abomination! Shoo, and get away from my master!"

I leaped up from my stool and caught Broomie just as she shot down the stairs into my arms. She shook as she curled herself into my grasp.

It was *my* turn to glare at Valentin, who loomed like a specter at the top of the stairs.

"Mr. Valentin," said Doc Day, her stocking feet pounding on the floor. "I will *insist* that my boarders remain respectful in my house. I asked little Broomie to go knock so you would know lunch is ready. Now get down here and eat, but I warn you —*one* more rude comment to *any* of my friends, and I'll have to ask you to leave, coffin and all."

Valentin looked aghast. Perhaps it was the thought of dragging that coffin back down the stairs so soon after he'd dragged it up.

"Thanks," I said, offering Doc Day a brief smile. "If anything else about last night comes to you—"

"I'll be sure to let you or Roan know." She winked at me. "You seem to act as Roan's deputy these days."

"Oh, no." I chuckled softly, petting Broomie's head until she stopped trembling. "I'm just trying to clear my friends' names."

Doc Day let out a little "hmm" and didn't sound convinced.

But I wasn't an investigator, an enforcer of the law.

I was just trying to make sure no one hurt my friends in any way.

And I had a knack, it seemed, for getting to the bottom of things—eventually.

Chapter Nine

roomie's bristles shifted in the cold wind as we headed home. My destinations were there or Lazarus's funeral parlor, and like Doc Day had said, he was unlikely to want company. He didn't sleep, as far as I knew, so there wasn't a good or a bad time to drop in.

Home was where my phone was. And maybe Lien had come back by now.

As Broomie landed on our front walk and I carried her in hand up to the covered porch, I spared a glance over my shoulder. Across the street at Vogel's, Roderick was visible in the front window, stringing up a banner of cut-out red and pink hearts like a stone cupid. He seemed wholly focused on the task and my heart warmed. I supposed it was never too early to start advertising for Valentine's Day.

Though this was my first Valentine's Day with a

boyfriend in years, and he was clear across the globe.

I stepped inside, trying to ignore the sinking in my heart. He was safer away from me, anyway. "Lien?" I asked, but there was no answer, and the house was chilly.

I waved my arms at the thermostat and turned it up two degrees with an enchantment. Yes, I could warm myself, but it was easier to keep the house at a habitable temperature so the pipes wouldn't burst in winter and I wasn't constantly casting enchantments on myself to stay warm, even in my sleep. Broomie slipped out of my hand and took off toward a sunny spot on top of my floral couch, curling up and letting the tip of her shaft hang down like a tail that she flicked about lazily.

I snatched my phone and took out my napkin-note and pen-straw. Now that I was home, I could transfer my notes onto an actual notepad and stop worrying about this pen that wouldn't stop bending. Sighing, I tossed it all on my kitchen table, wondering if I should practice transfiguration next. My eyes flicked to the onyx dagger I kept in a cup at the center of the table amidst a few other pens and pencils. Perhaps at a glance, an attacking witch wouldn't realize I had a weapon that could spell her doom so near at hand.

First order of business was to check out Cable's texts. There was his excitement over Qarinah and Roan's wedding first. I'd texted about it last night, but Roan must have told him to arrange his virtual attendance, as he was talking about that as well. Then there was a quick recap of his day, asking how I was doing, letting me know he was taking some old friends out for dinner.

It was only a matter of time before he found out about the murder in Creekdale. But what good would it do to worry him now? He was safe, happy. Living a life without those kinds of worries. I typed back that I was looking forward to seeing him virtually this weekend and to have a nice time. I'd be busy myself eating with the Mahajans and Roderick, so I might not text again before morning.

There. Perhaps by then, I'd have a story to tell him instead of an unsolved mystery.

Next was the research about the murder. There definitely wasn't anything paranormal in the Creekdale news about it—it had even made the state news and was being picked up by a few more outlets. Nuns weren't often murdered in our country, I supposed. The news seemed more interested in that fact than anything strange about the cause of death, which was not yet known, other than to say the police were confirming foul play.

I wondered who was holding back those details, and what they thought about it. Roan had some friends in county who helped explain away paranormal deaths. Was he calling them right now? Were they the ones examining the victim?

If she'd been pronounced dead on the scene, as

the news corroborated, she was unlikely to pass by Doctor Corbin's hospital outside of the morgue. Not to mention, he'd been in Luna Lane at the time, I was pretty sure. Still, I wanted to ask him about when Qarinah had left the pub anyway. I dialed the number Doc Day had given me, but only a robotic voice explaining to leave a voice mail answered.

"Hi," I said, clearing my throat. "This is Dahlia Poplar, from-from Luna Lane." I was *not* used to phones. "Doc Day gave me this number and said I could ask you a few questions about last night? I'm trying to figure out what happened. Well, you must have heard about the tragedy in Creekdale by now. Please give me a call back? I, um… don't know my number." I thought about it. Nope. Didn't know it. "But I think this leaves a record of who calls you, right? I hope? Thanks."

I hung up. Well, *that* had made me sound intelligent. But maybe if he didn't know how to get in touch with me, he could start by calling Doc Day.

The news reports had been updated during my brief phone call. Comments from the nun's fellow sisters at the Holy Home of Mother Mary had been posted to one report. They'd also added a picture of the victim to the report and revealed more details about her.

Sister Mary Katherine had been forty-four and had joined a convent later in life in a small country in Eastern Europe; her fellow sisters didn't know which. She'd been sent to the Holy Home of Mother Mary just a month ago, as part of an exchange program between the United States and Europe, for those interested in seeing the world during their work. She'd been kind, patient, and eager to teach those in the community, especially those who struggled to learn English or read and write, as she had in her youth.

She was pictured in her full habit, a simple cross necklace over the front of the black material, her hands clasped in prayer in front of her chest so that the necklace was only just visible. Her hair and neck were entirely obscured by the veil and wimple of her headpiece, and her eyes were closed in prayer, so it felt like only a fraction of a portrait of her. But there was something about the angled cheekbones of her pale-white skin, the sunken sallowness of the area around her mouth that seemed familiar. Her lips were full and were pursed as if in thoughtful prayer. She had dark eyebrows that really stood out against her overly wan face.

I searched for more pictures of her, using keyword techniques Cable and Faine had taught me since I'd gotten my phone. That was the only picture any news outlet had released of Sister Mary Katherine of the Holy Home of Mother Mary. And they were all posting it now, over and over.

Outside of just a quick glance of a few walking along the street during my time in New York City— I'd seen all manner of humans there—I'd never otherwise seen a nun in person. Luna Lane didn't have a house of worship, since paranormals would be unlikely to be welcome in most of them. Though some human residents went over to Creekdale for such things, it didn't appear that the Holy Home of Mother Mary held regular worship services for the general public. It was a place for nuns to live, study, pray, and do their charity work around the community.

I jotted down my notes about the victim, after transferring the few notes I'd taken on the napkin so far. There were too many things that stood out to me as strange. The woman had only been in Creekdale a month. And she was from Eastern Europe— exact country unknown, even by her sisters who'd welcomed her from the exchange program.

The victim's history was too vague. Trouble with the witches had begun about a month ago.

But surely, Lien would have noticed if a witch had moved into the convent during her scouting trips over in Creekdale? Then again, she had to cover the nearest towns in all four directions, as she wasn't sure from where the witches might be launching their next assault.

And then there was this strange feeling I'd gotten in my gut at the sole picture of the victim. Why did she seem so... familiar? I'd never met anyone with that face; I was sure of it.

Sighing, I rubbed my forehead with my thumb and forefinger. I wished I could go over to that convent and sneak around. Perhaps Lien could do it for me—but the witch was stretched too thin as it was.

I at least needed to see the scene of the crime, even if the body had been moved.

I found a link to a news report that included a video and clicked it. The video had been shot in the early morning, the sun just barely rising over the skyline, the park behind the reporter, a beautiful dark-skinned woman likely in her twenties, bathed in a sort of eerie, orange glow.

"Police continue to search for clues in the tragic murder of a local nun," she said. No name given. So this had been recorded before more details about the victim had been released—though that had been easy to tell by the fact that it had been recorded around dawn. The time in the corner read 6:32. The reporter's face remained neutral, her lips drawn in a grim line. "They are not yet releasing details about the cause of death or the victim, aside from the fact that she was a nun at the Holy Home of Mother Mary, which you can see behind me in the distance." She looked over her shoulder. To her left was a sidewalk and a line of shops, most of which had their lights off. To her right was the park, complete with police tape around one section of it, and at the far back of the sidewalk was the convent. A large, thin cross protruded from the top of a chapel, the building made of brick and looking like something from a hundred years back or more.

"Sisters report that they're cooperating with the police in the investigation. Mother Abbess Mary Christina provided us with this statement: 'Our sisters don't usually leave the convent alone, particularly so late at night. Short of specific reasons to be out serving the community, nuns at the convent usually keep indoors at night, as it's a time for prayer, reflection, and rest. Please keep our sisters in your prayers.' A statement which begs the question as to what this particular nun was doing in the park long after sunset. Most stores you'll find along this street are closed at that hour."

The camera panned over her shoulder to show a row of shops. Sure enough, all but one had their lights out. The one with lights on instantly drew the eye because the light seemed too bright. It was, I was surprised to find, a video game store. What was *that* store doing open early this morning?

"The one exception," continued the reporter, "is this locally-owned video game store. They were open all night to celebrate the launch of a new game but closed once the police arrived to disclose the tragedy that had taken place nearby. Our sources are saying the police are interviewing the sole employee on duty last night and reviewing any possible security camera footage they may have recorded."

Ah. Helpful human technology, that. I hoped it would show the suspect clearly so the victim could get some justice and my friends could be cleared.

The camera panned back to the reporter, who continued to look dour despite her beauty-queen appearance. "Police are encouraging anyone who might have attended the all-night game celebration to contact police if they saw anything that could help lead to this nun's killer. Early reports indicate it was not a well-attended event, despite—"

The reporter let out a little yelp and ducked on camera as a screeching, chirping shriek echoed out into her microphone, the fluttery thin, black membranes of wings coming just barely into frame, enough to almost skirt the reporter's scalp. Something fell just at the edge of the frame from the sky to the ground. Something small.

But the reporter didn't comment on it.

"Excuse me," she said, standing up and letting the cool, steely reporter expression take over her face again. "A bat just flew by, off into the park." She stared in the direction it presumably had gone.

Then she stared back at the camera, diving back into her report as if she hadn't just been almost clipped by a bat. I paused the video.

A bat.

Heading off in the direction of… Luna Lane. Just as dawn had been about to break.

But if it was the vampire who had drained all of Sister Mary Katherine's blood, why had it still been hanging out nearby the scene hours later, almost until dawn, when the sunlight would prove dangerous for them?

Using my phone, I quickly checked the time of sunrise this morning. 7:14 A.M. Enough time for the vampire in question to make it back to Luna Lane and into a coffin if they were in a rush. Which they must have been. They hadn't even retrieved whatever they'd dropped on camera.

Then again, perhaps it had just been a bat. A normal bat. Carrying nuts or whatever bats might have carried. Big bugs? Fruit? In winter? Rodents?

I chewed my lip. Bats weren't known for carrying things. And that would be one strange coincidence if it had been a real bat.

Practically a pro at this smartphone stuff already, if I did say so myself, I went back to the video and tugged on the little dot on the progress bar to play that part of the video again. It took a few tries, but I paused it before the object fell out of frame.

It was a tad blurry, and I couldn't figure out how to make the image any clearer.

But I could see the "AA" written on the side of the thin, cylindrical object.

I was pretty sure it was a battery.

I knew a vampire who'd just last night been searching for AA batteries.

Chapter Ten

"Why do these have to be… so… big?" I muttered to Broomie as I continued to attempt to stuff my smartphone into the pouch at my belt. "Is *this* why Faine carries a purse a lot of the time?" Well, that and kids, I supposed.

Sighing, I removed the power-boosting potion I'd packed earlier in the day and set it and the phone down on the table by the door. "EGRALNE." The pouch got bigger. Hmm. I nodded, satisfied with myself. Enlarging something was a form of transfiguration, albeit a basic one. But I *was* getting better at it, clearly.

I slipped the phone more comfortably into the pouch and the potion along with it, though the two clicked together with every step.

"Oh, bananaberries! Who said we have to carry these things all around with us? It's ridiculous!"

Then again, I was waiting for a call back from Corbin. I took a deep breath, removed the power-boosting potion from the pouch again, and set it on the table by the entryway before stepping outside, casting another warmth enchantment over myself and sliding on Broomie's back.

"Heading to the funeral parlor," I told her. My insides flip-flopped at the thought of rushing straight to Draven's, but he'd be asleep in his coffin now. I had to wait a couple of hours until sunset. I never thought I'd be so grateful for it growing dark so early.

Broomie's flight was quick and certain, even though we barely ever set foot in Luna Lane's funeral parlor. Even one funeral was enough to engrave the memory of the place on one's soul, I supposed.

The funeral parlor was down an offshoot lane of downtown, a few blocks farther east than the old bowling alley turned defunct escape room. It, like so many things in Luna Lane, had the aesthetic of charming-meets-spooky at a glance, the cobblestone walk and wrought-iron gate around the premises somehow both beautifully antique and borderline dilapidated. The parlor itself was single-story, aside from the basement, an angular building with an iron cross placed to the side of the tall, reedy metal crematorium chimney.

Broomie brought us down on the interior side of

the fence and gate, near the two white-painted wooden front steps.

Taking her in my hand, I stepped up onto the front porch and went to ring the doorbell, wondering if Lazarus would answer the door. Before I could press the button, though, Broomie stiffened and moved her brush head to block my way.

"Broomie?"

She rustled her bristles together in a sort of *shush*-ing noise. The door behind the screen door was opened, and there was something like a little musical *beep, beep* sound carrying out from the darkened parlor entryway.

Opening the screen door as softly as I dared, I stepped inside, Broomie slowly moving her brush head this way and that, though there was nothing much but the darkened hallway to look at. A small, antique green marble-top table was to the side of the door. Atop the table were ancient, yellowing brochures about the parlor's services in a dusty glass holder, as well as a quill and ink beside a big, open, book that visitors were to sign during a funeral, though it was likely just an example, since the yellow pages were blank. Photographs of people from a hundred years ago hung along both sides of the walls atop green, floral wallpaper met halfway up from the ground by cherrywood panels. I glanced at a few—the people, including infants, looked stiff, their eyes closed more often than not—only to remember what Mayor Abdel had told me while we'd been milling about here for Leana Woodward's funeral.

In the Victorian era, it had been custom for humans who could afford it to have their recently deceased relatives pose for a portrait, the better to remember them by. I didn't know why, with all the undead people walking amongst me, staring at a photo of a woman with her dark hair pulled into a bun, her skin so obviously pale even in the gray, monochromatic color scheme of the portrait, her hands folded over her lap, should have sent a chill down my spine. What a macabre design choice, even if the place *was* owned and operated by a walking skeleton.

The flat, electrical music drew my attention from the end of the hallway. *That* was where I knew it from—the game Roderick had been playing! It'd been ceaseless background noise all day yesterday.

Surely, it wasn't the exact same decades-old game, but it was most definitely coming from a retro game of some sort.

I headed to the end of the hallway, my voice caught in my throat as all the photos of dead people on either side of me seemed to be closing in on me. I didn't call out Lazarus's name. Terror gripped my throat for reasons I couldn't explain. There was just something in the air. Though familiar in a strange sense, it felt *cold* despite my warmth enchantment, and the sensation made me think the dead were really here among us, in this place. Just beyond my sight.

I turned at the end of the hall. To my left was a set of cramped stairs that led downstairs to where Lazarus did his work as a mortician, and where he often retreated when his funeral parlor became overfull. Beside the staircase was a lift in the earliest sense, a simple cage that acted as an open elevator to the basement and up again, which allowed him to do his work, but there was a chain and lock over it right now. Safer for the kids visiting during funerals to leave that alone.

To the right was the reception room, its double doors held open with doorstops. Wooden benches lined a walkway in the middle over threadbare brown carpet. Despite an intermittently overcast sky, a sliver of sunlight had burst through the clouds and filtered in through each of the three dusty windows at the end of the room. A coffin was placed at the center of the dais in front of the windows. Probably an empty one for show, a sample for those in need of Lazarus's services. It was black and sleek and—

I'd seen this coffin before.

The *beep, beep* and electronic music was louder in here. Though there was no one in sight.

I took slow, careful steps down the center aisle, as if moving too quick might make someone pop out from between a bench and snatch me like a video game princess in distress.

I'd almost forgotten I *was* a princess, too.

Standing over the coffin, I took a closer look. Dust particles danced in those wayward sunbeams.

Broomie chirruped softly as she bent toward it.

"Draven?" I whispered aloud. What in my enchanted broomstick's name was Draven's coffin doing *here* in the funeral parlor? Who had endeavored to move it overnight?

And *why?*

The electronic music continued, but the *bleeps* and *bloops* paused.

Did that mean he was in there? That he was awake and he'd heard me?

A voice carrying out from behind me in the hall caused me to whip around.

There was a distinct French accent to it.

"Excellent. Excellent. My master will be most pleased."

Lazarus's own voice—unmistakable with its rattling, cough-like echo—answered back. "I endeavor to serve."

Despite the fact that the front door had been opened, I felt suddenly caught red-handed, as if I'd broken into the place. I ran around the coffin and crouched down on the other side, laying Broomie flat on the ground beside me.

Footfalls pounded against stone, as if the two men were climbing up the steps. Whipping my pointed witch's hat off and setting it down beside Broomie, I dared to peek my head up over the coffin, ever-so-slightly.

Sure enough, that strange assistant to the Vampire High Council representative was here, in Lazarus's funeral parlor, and the reaper who eschewed human company for years at a time was chatting with him at the top of the stairs, in front of the open reception room. The lights were still off, but I could make out the distinct glimmer of Lazarus's bones. He looked even more ghoulish in the dark, old-fashioned hallway.

"The mayor assures me the body will be sent through Luna Lane. He's negotiating with the mayor of this Creekdale city, but the attention drawn to the murder has unfortunately meant that some explanation must be made. Creekdale, as I am told, is not fully aware of our kind."

"Yes, most unfortunate," Lazarus replied. He held both hands over the top of his walking stick. "I am prevented from going to collect the corpse myself." He gestured one bony hand at his body. "As I am."

"Understood. Just make sure the body is *dealt with*. There is still a chance she may revive. Botched attempts at turning humans into vampires are tricky, you see. If there is not the distinct desire to save the human, a bond between sire and offspring, most attempts to create a vampire end in murder of the curious kind my master and his fellow Council members abhor. That is why it must be so regulated." His voice got lower, and I strained to hear, especially over the electronic music echoing out from the coffin on which I was leaning. "No one must know, *comprenez-vous*? If she revives on your table. You will contact me *posthaste* if she does." His breath caught sharply. "What was that?"

His head whipped right toward me.

Slick as a whistle, I slipped down, out of sight, my breath sharp. If I revealed myself now, they'd wonder what I'd overheard.

The two of them were clearly speaking of the dead nun. Mayor Abdel was arranging for her transport here? To cover up the paranormal circumstances of her death?

But Valentin had spoken as if the woman might rise again. As a vampire. So there was no doubt, even among the assistant of a member of the Vampire High Council?

"I have a guest," said Lazarus simply.

"You did not tell me. This is *entirely* secret. I do not want even my master to be bothered with the details of this meeting—"

"He sleeps. In his coffin."

Valentin let out something like a *hmm*. "A suspect, then. My master will want to meet him immediately at dusk. I was not made aware of a change in his abode, though."

"It is but temporary. Now, perhaps, we shall see if the mayor has succeeded in arranging for transport? You *do* want me to examine the woman before anyone else does, correct? Since you suspect she may resurrect?"

"Yes, yes. And you must contact me *straightaway*. Remember." Valentin *harrumphed* and thudding footfalls echoed out over the carpet.

I peeked back up over the coffin, my heart about to leap out of my chest. Something strange caught my eye. A stained part of the coffin, still wet with something like sludge. I didn't dare touch it and make any sudden movement. Broomie quietly, carefully, rustled her head. She was wearing my witch's hat.

I just had to wait for the sound of the front door. It seemed as if Lazarus might have been leaving with the vampire's assistant. After a couple of minutes, there was a sound of a car—sleek, like a sports car—off somewhere down the street. Traffic was so light here, any vehicle's engine would have been noticed.

I looked to the coffin on which my hand rested. It was cold to the touch, and there was that strange, large wet spot. I had so much to ask Draven.

But if he was here… what did that mean?

A "temporary" guest of Lazarus?

Lazarus, who was acting so suspicious, discussing this nun with Valentin?

Draven, who'd been in need of AA batteries last night? There'd been the bat who'd dropped one on TV near the scene of the crime a few hours after the murder.

What did it all mean?

"Draven?" I whispered. The *beeps* and *boops*

paused again, just the electronic music echoing out from the coffin. Was he really in there—playing Roderick's video game?

What of the system Grady had hooked up for him last night?

"*Go…*" The voice that spoke now echoed out from the coffin, but it was not Draven's at all. It was eerie, devoid of any discernable accent, higher in pitch than my vampire ex-boyfriend's.

"Draven?" I asked even so.

"*Leave…*" That voice sent shivers down my spine, my warmth enchantment gone with just a word.

Broomie shook beside me, and I sluggishly grabbed my hat from her head and fixed it to my own. I might need it to harness energy for enchantments.

"*Leave now… before it's too late.*" The voice was positively hoarse. A woman's. She sounded ethereal.

Green, oozing goo appeared on the top of the coffin.

The screen door swung open out front and shut, followed by the heavier door to the parlor. There was the sound of a bolt sliding shut.

I leaped to my feet, Broomie sliding in place between my legs, though the ceiling wasn't particularly high in here and it'd be difficult to fly.

My legs shook as I stared at the green ooze dripping down off of Draven's coffin.

I couldn't flee. What if this—whatever this was—was harming him?

Broomie started levitating, and we flew up the five feet or so we had space for above the coffin before my hat would scrape the ceiling.

"Leave!" shouted the voice, louder this time, the ooze practically bubbling over.

I knew what that was. I'd never seen it coming from a vampire's coffin before.

Ectoplasm.

There was a ghost in here. In Draven's coffin. And it was permeating through the solid material in order to get out.

"Reveal yourself," I said, my voice a whisper despite the fact that I'd heard Valentin and Lazarus leave.

How could I be so scared of the dead?

I was a witch!

But still my pulse raced, my jaw grew tight, and my palms sweated as they gripped Broomie's shaft.

I wouldn't leave even so. I needed answers.

The clomp of footfalls from the hallway startled me even more than the oozing ectoplasm, the eerie voice. They thudded against the carpet in threes: *clomp, clomp, clomp.* Lazarus's shoes and his walking stick. He hadn't been locking the door from the outside. He'd been locking it from the *inside.*

"Draven?" the reaper asked.

My mind raced, fumbling for an excuse, wondering if I could just zoom past him overhead and enchant the door open and be on my way without being seen or if I'd need to try to make myself invisible first, but then all plans proved useless. My phone rang.

Lazarus's voice echoed out, his footfalls growing faster. "Who's there?"

"LEAVE!" screamed the eerie voice.

And then, in front of me, emerging from the coffin, was a misty, white form, all menace and urgency and… something familiar.

A glint of red shone in the beam of sunlight.

"KAERB!" I said as quietly as I dared, waving my hands over one of the windows. There was actually a better enchantment—vanish—for that, but I wouldn't have time to hover outside of the window and replace it right after.

The glass shattered.

I leaned forward on Broomie and nudged her bristles with my boot.

We took off, leaving the parlor through the broken window.

Chapter Eleven

roomie zipped us high into the sky and down the nearest alley, my phone still ringing like an old-fashioned corded telephone.

She descended once we'd reached the park off the town square, taking us in for a rough landing between a line of hedges and a large pile of snow some kids—the Vadas children, maybe—had heaved up into a sort of fort.

I shivered, my warmth enchantment forgotten as I pried the pouch on my belt open and looked at the phone. Creekdale Hospital.

It had to be Doctor Corbin returning my call.

"Hello?" I said after swiping to answer it. My bare legs between the top of my boots and the bottom of my skirt were cold on the frozen snow. Broomie crawled into a hole in the side of the fort and ducked inside, shaking. The disembodied voice had spooked her, too.

I definitely wouldn't have resorted to busting out a window like that if not for that voice.

I winced at the thought. I'd need to fix that. Go back to speak to Lazarus. And what, admit I'd been there, sneaking around, albeit unintentionally at first? How else would I know about the broken window? Could I fix it without him noticing?

"Oh, I thought I'd get voice mail by this point," said the deep voice on the other side of the call.

"Doctor Corbin?" I reiterated to be sure. My teeth were chattering. No wonder everyone else wore so many layers in the winter. I hit *speaker* on the phone and set it down on my knee, gesturing at my body. "MRAW."

The snow started melting beneath me, slowly but surely. I grabbed the phone again and stood up so I wouldn't wind up sitting in a pile of soggy mud.

"Pardon?" the doctor asked.

"Nothing. Um, do you have a few minutes?"

"I'm between patients," he said. "You said this had to do with the murder of the nun here in town last night?"

"Right. Um, well, two things." Why was I so flustered? Probably because I barely knew the man and here I was, acting like some kind of professional investigator. That, and everything in the funeral parlor had thrown me way off my game.

"Doc Day told me you were at First Taste with her and Lazarus until dawn," I said.

As if to prove the point, Corbin yawned audibly. "Yes. Well, somewhat before dawn. I had an early shift, so I wanted to get back in time. I know I shouldn't skip a night's sleep like that, and I feel like a bit of a hypocrite, considering what I'd tell my patients, but having Doctor Lazarus's brain to pick like that is an opportunity that comes around so rarely."

Apparently, the reaper wasn't so introverted as we'd all thought. Valentin had gotten him to come up from his basement to discuss something about the nun on his first day in town.

Something suspicious.

"So what time did you leave?" I asked.

"Oh, had to be about four. I wanted to swing by my house before my shift started at six."

Four. So after the estimated time of the nun's murder.

"And both Doc Day and Lazarus still stayed behind?" I asked.

"Oh, yes, as far as I know. Geraldine texted me to tell me they'd stayed until sunrise, and Doctor Lazarus had brought up a few more good points about coagulation during emergency surgery." Geraldine was Doc Day's given name. Almost no one in Luna Lane used it. "But say, what did you want to know about the tragedy here? I thought you might be asking me to look into where the body was taken. Straight to our morgue, I'm afraid. She was declared dead on the scene."

So she *was* in the Creekdale hospital. At least until Mayor Abdel had the body moved.

How much did the mayor know about Valentin's involvement? About the chance that the woman could still resurrect as a vampire?

"Oh, yes, thank you for letting me know," I said, walking in circles in the soggy grass. "But back to First Taste. Was Qarinah there the entire time you were?"

"Qarinah…? Oh, the lovely pub owner. Yes, of course. She kept checking in on us."

"She didn't leave at any point?"

"Leave? Well, not that I noticed. But I was quite absorbed in our discussion."

"Doc Day said she came over to the table to let you know she'd be gone for a bit."

"No, that, I would certainly remember. Perhaps it happened after I'd left."

Perhaps so. But that would mean Qarinah had gone on her mysterious errand closer to dawn than one would think would be comfortable for a vampire. Then again, that would also place her firmly at First Taste when the murder occurred.

But why hadn't Doc Day remembered that Doctor Corbin had been gone when Qarinah had left? She hadn't even mentioned him leaving a bit earlier.

What, was I suspecting our kindly town doctor of something nefarious now? Hadn't she admitted she'd been so wrapped up in her conversation, so buzzed on drinks, the details of last night were all fuzzy?

My mind was muddled in all sorts of ways.

"Hmm," said the doctor over the line. "Qarinah's a vampire, correct? Are you saying someone suspects…?" His voice grew quieter, though I'd assumed he was alone in his office somewhere. "I snuck a peek at the preliminary report. There are signs of puncture wounds on her neck, and she seems to be low on blood. They haven't started the official autopsy yet, though, as there's a note that the mayor is calling in experts. What kind of experts other than paranormal?"

"Yes, I think my mayor and sheriff might be looking into maybe having her transferred here. If a vampire was involved, we have a member of the Vampire High Council in town for a wedding, so I'm sure he'll want to deal with it."

"Ah, yes. I thought you worked with the town sheriff."

"Um, no. Not usually."

"You also help Doc Day—"

"I help most of the town with anything they need, you know? Kind of a witch-of-all-trades."

"Oh, I see. Might be handy to have you help out with some of our serious cases here, too, if you could."

"Injuries, sure. But I can't cure disease. Not even a more powerful witch than I had been able to," I said, thinking of my mom and our neighbor who'd had dementia before Milton. "And right now——"

"You're still trapped in Luna Lane," said Corbin. "Geraldine filled me in on things."

"Yeah…" I stopped pacing and Broomie's brush head peeked out of the fort, looking both ways as if expecting to find a villain around every corner. To be honest, I hadn't been thinking much of the good my enchantments could do if I were free to move about as I pleased. It used to be an excuse of mine —I couldn't do much for the greater good because I was confined to one town—but as soon as I'd been free, I'd just gone on a vacation.

And all I'd thought about since was how I missed Cable. But truth be told, even if I'd been free to move as I'd pleased, I wasn't sure I'd have packed up and moved to Scotland, true love or not.

This was my home… And I liked the quiet life here. Too many unexplained rapid healings in even an only slightly-larger town like Creekdale might draw too much attention to me.

There was a slight pain at the back of my throat at the realization of my selfishness.

But paranormals had to be careful about being discovered, too. Which was why the international attention this murder was getting had so many people flustered, even if it wasn't a central story just yet.

"Well, I'll let you go," I said. "If you can think of anything else about last night that might help us get to the bottom of this attack in Creekdale, please call again."

"I will," he said. "But I've told you just about everything I know."

"Of course. Thank you." We hung up and I slipped the phone back into my pocket, patting the pouch and thinking of the potion I'd left at home. What if I'd *needed* it in the funeral parlor? What if Lazarus, or that *entity*, had proven more than I could handle?

I sighed. I was too relaxed. This was my own backyard, so to speak, and I had Lien's assurances that her enchantment would keep other witches from crossing the barrier, but my grandmother knew where I was now. My mother and aunt had hidden me away for three decades, but that had ended with Eithne's death. And I'd humiliated Isadora Poplar on the train. She'd be back.

And yet, here I was wandering around town as if there were nothing that could possibly harm me.

What did I do now, after running from the funeral home like a criminal? Talk to Roan or Abdel about what I'd heard?

...And admit to the crimes I'd committed. If not trespassing, at least breaking a window?

Did that matter right now, though?

I'd fix what I'd broken. Technically, if Lazarus wanted to press charges, there was bound to be a fine or jail time, but it wouldn't be much, and I just couldn't picture anyone in Luna Lane doing that to one another.

Besides, if he and Valentin were hiding something, would he want to draw attention to the fact that someone had been there to hear them?

I didn't want him to *know* I'd been there. Not yet. Not until I got to the bottom of things. I could admit culpability later.

I checked the time on my phone. Even after the call with Doctor Corbin, I'd been pacing and thinking out here in the cold for far too long. The Mahajans would be bringing Roderick to the café to meet up with me in a little over an hour. Not too long before the vampires could be waking from their coffins from the night.

Sister Mary Katherine's body was still at the Creekdale Hospital, as far as Doctor Corbin had known. Mayor Abdel and Roan were likely busy arranging the transfer still.

And what *had* I heard? Would it be so strange for the assistant of a Vampire High Council member to want to take charge of the body of a victim of a vampire in the area? Allegedly?

They wouldn't want the paranormal aspects of her death to get out.

My heart thudded wildly. I had limited time to kill and so much was still unclear.

What could I do to possibly save my friends at this point?

Though I didn't know what Qarinah had gone

to do during the night, at least two witnesses had testified she'd been in town during the murder.

It was Draven I was most concerned about.

Short of establishing an alibi, the discovery that could release him from suspicion would be proving another type of paranormal had been responsible for the murder. It was a long shot, but hadn't Lien brought up the idea? She hadn't only thought a vampire could have been the perpetrator.

Lien. I'd go home to check in with Lien, assuming she was back by now. Maybe she could tell me more about what she'd seen in Creekdale.

And if she wasn't home yet, well… There was one witch I'd grudgingly call an ally whom I could talk to about the kinds of magic that could lead to such an outcome.

A witch who owed me answers about many things, answers that were long overdue.

If I went home and found the house empty, I just might finally summon the soul of Eithne Allaway.

Chapter Twelve

"Lien?" I called out as soon as Broomie and I stepped inside my house. I'd checked for Roderick in the window across the street again, but he must have been inside and out of sight.

The Valentine's Day display was cute. Hanging cut-out hearts, boxes of chocolates, and a giant Cupid silhouette cardboard stand I could have sworn had been modeled after Roderick himself. I'd have to compliment him later.

There was no answer, no stirring from inside the house as I unloaded the pesky smartphone on the table near the door.

My power boosting potion was gone.

I assumed that meant Lien had been back in my absence and had taken it. But she could have left *something* for me to use myself.

Broomie slid out of my hand and soared toward the room devoted to brewing potions.

The room with my rune circle.

I'd gotten to the end of the number of times I'd been able to summon my mother, as each summoning brought a spirit closer to fully migrating to the realm beyond once and for all.

Now, the only witch spirit I knew I could summon for guidance was my aunt, Eithne Allaway.

I'd spent so much of my life hating her, thinking her responsible for my mother's death.

She'd wanted it that way, to keep me focused on a "simpler" villain than the ones I'd actually face once Eithne's spell keeping me hidden in Luna Lane fell.

She'd even forced my hand to make me defeat her.

She'd threatened to end my friends if I failed to, and despite the fact that I now understood she cared for me in her own way, I believed she would have done it.

Whatever it took for me to defeat her and get ready to face the Queen of Witches who thirsted for my blood.

Broomie used her bristly head to start sweeping around the rune circle carved into the floor. It had been marred by a playing card explosion—weird words to string together, but true—a few months back, but I'd fixed it since, knowing this day would come. The day I would finally use it to summon my aunt.

"I know," I told my broomstick companion. I let out a deep breath. I didn't usually summon without boosting my power, but that was *before* I'd halfway mastered the ability to activate the gargoyle blood that ran through my veins. Before I'd faced Isadora Poplar and her wicked sisters and had gained access to greater power with the death of the heir before me. Eithne's death.

She'd known I'd grow into a greater witch if she fell.

If this summoning didn't work without the potion… then it just wasn't meant to be.

I could live with that.

My pulse quickened in my veins as Broomie floated aside and sat upright, alert and her head held high, on the potions mixing table.

I approached the circle, centering myself near the star symbol, and felt the magic flowing through me, from the tip of my hat down to my toes. I held my hands aloft, focusing on my aunt, though there was less for the summoning circle to confuse her with than there had been with my mom, Cinnamon.

"YAWALLA ENHTIE, EMOC," I chanted. "TNUA YM, EMOC!"

The summoning circle glowed brightly, saturating the room in more light than the fading embers of the late afternoon sky could.

From the center of the glowing symbols, trapped inside my summoning circle, a mist poured out from empty air. And from that mist floated my aunt, Eithne Allaway, riding side-saddle on Broomholly, her all-black broomstick companion, with her even in death.

Eithne smiled and I flinched. I was too used to seeing that wicked glint in her violet eyes, and assuming her amusement had come about from something nefarious. She may have been a better witch than some, but she hadn't been above assisting in a murder or two—and that was just as far as I knew.

She set her purple-booted-toes on the ground first, sliding off Broomholly gently. She made a show of smoothing out imaginary wrinkles on her lavender dress draped over her tall, willowy frame, then fixing her pointed lavender hat straighter. There was a faded quality to her and Broomholly, just slightly, as if they were trapped in a photo that had yellowed and aged.

Broomie shirked as Broomholly neared her at the edge of the summoning circle, but the black broomstick couldn't exit the circle. It was more like she was prowling it, testing her limits. Like a panther, her previous incarnations' feline attributes coming through, Broomholly continued her skulking circle until she settled for swishing back and forth at knee-height in front of her witch companion.

"I've been wondering how long it would take

you to summon me." Eithne spoke with an Irish lilt. She'd grown up at least partially in Ireland, and her father—whom I'd met since I'd seen her last—had been from there. She'd shared a mother with my mother, but not a father.

"How long's it been?" she asked.

"Two months."

"I see. Surprised you're summoning me so early, then. Hard to keep track of time on Earth over there. And I've never been that good at it, really. Seems like I'd blink and half the humans I'd met were six feet under."

"Some put there by yourself," I ground out.

Eithne looked exaggeratedly aghast, but she was clearly trying to keep herself from smiling too widely. "Look at you! Pot calling the kettle black."

"You *made* me kill you!" I shouted. Broomie's bristles rubbed together sadly. She'd had a part in it, too, and in sending Broomholly to the afterlife. I took a deep breath. Each summoning could only last so long, and I hadn't brought her over just to chat. "Never mind. I've met my grandmother. She tried to kill me. I've got questions."

"Wasted no time, did she?" Eithne's smile dropped and her lips went into a thin, tight line. "At least that only proves that everything Cinnamon and I did to keep you safe for so long worked. It was only once you'd won your freedom that the wicked witch showed her face."

For Eithne to think another witch qualified as

wicked, well, that just went to show the depravity of which other witches were capable.

"She roped your father into taking me unawares," I said.

Eithne cocked her head. "There is so much wrong with that statement, dear one. She shouldn't have *caught you unawares*, as I'd warned you she'd be after you. And my father is dead. Long ago." Her eyelashes fluttered. "My mother murdering him is what got me to leave her coven, once and for all."

I decided not to comment on the "caught unawares" bit. I'd failed to grasp the depths of the danger, though I'd done my best to be ready in case, dragging along my father's onyx pike in its unaltered form even on vacation.

"I know he's dead—and I know about his twin brother, too. Isadora kept their bodies around so that—"

Eithne finished for me, realization widening her eyes. "They could be brought back together, one always cursed to perform a task while the other did my mother's dirty work. I'd wondered why I couldn't find my father in the realm beyond. But not everyone's here, you know. Some pass beyond faster than others." Her eyebrows narrowed. "That *witch*."

There was a bit of contempt in her accusing tone.

"Poor Da," she said quieter. "My uncle, too, though I knew he resented me and Da's connection to the witches."

"Yes, well, both tried to kill me—or I supposed it was more personal for your father than your uncle. So my sympathy is at a minimum."

"Oh, Da wouldn't have even been alive—properly—when you were born. It wasn't personal." She fluffed a hand at me.

I rolled my eyes. "He made it *seem* awfully personal. Didn't like the fact that my mom existed."

"Yes, well, he must have thought his own daughter would have become Queen of the Witches someday. I tried to tell him it never mattered to me." She shrugged. "But the idea of being father to a queen was half the reason he agreed to be with my mother in the first place." She frowned. "But I imagine you didn't summon me just to chat about my family. How'd you survive, by the way? This plan my mother concocted to stop you."

"Lien, mostly. And some good luck, a helping hand from a friend—and a boost in magic." Did I tell her about Roderick?

"Lien." Eithne nodded. "Cousin Lien. You can trust her, I think. About as good a witch as you could find in Isadora's circle. Still, Cinnamon and I weren't *certain* she would keep you secret, so we didn't ask her for help when it came time to hide your existence away."

That wasn't exactly a stellar recommendation.

"She's put a barrier around Luna Lane," I told her. "Doesn't let witches in other than her."

"Smart. But that means you're trapped here again?"

"Yes." My shoulders hunched. "But until we defeat Isadora—"

"*Defeat* Isadora?" Eithne cackled and Broomholly stopped her pacing to wrap herself around Eithne's shoulders, letting out a bristly sort of laugh of her own. "Oh, darling, I don't imagine there's hope of that."

I ground my boot into the wooden floor. "But with you and Mother gone, my magic—"

"Ah, yes. Splitting the heir magic over so many, that does weaken it. I figured my death would boost your own magic. But remember, you're not the only heir even so."

"What do you mean?"

"Well, there's Lien, for one. But before her, her mother, and after her, Aunt Sally. Should you fall, Mabel is next in line."

"Your mother told me—when her sisters couldn't hear her, I might add—that she planned to seek a new husband and have another child."

Eithne's eyebrow arched. "Getting a bit old for babies, isn't she?"

I shrugged. "She claimed there was a way to access magic to do it."

Eithne shuddered. "Perhaps the sooner you defeat her, the better."

"You just said I *couldn't* defeat her!"

"Well, I certainly hope I'm wrong." She flicked a

lock of her long, silver hair over her shoulder. "But I'll tell you your best bet: Defeat the other heirs first and gain all the magic you can."

"I'm not *fighting* Lien," I said. Mabel and Sally, I had no qualms about attacking if need be.

I just wasn't sure I could handle them, especially together.

Eithne shrugged. "Maybe my aunts will be enough, then. But you know the other way to defeat a witch."

"My father's onyx pike." I nodded toward the kitchen table. "It's in a smaller form now, but it pierces a witch's skin just as well."

Eithne smirked. "I take it you've tried that. So yes. The onyx pike. But more importantly?"

"Love," I said softly, remembering my discussion with Eithne on this very subject. Her love for me—albeit twisted and perhaps the last bit of love my aunt carried within her—had weakened her enough to be susceptible to the onyx pike.

"Yes, and Isadora Poplar will *never* love anyone. Never has and never will. She thinks love softens one's heart and makes one weak."

"I could tell." It hadn't exactly been a beautiful family reunion.

"So you'll need all the power you can get to make that fatal strike."

I rubbed at the back of my neck. "I'll talk to Lien. I'm sure she'd agree we could aim to take on

Sally and Mabel first. I know Mabel's her mother—"

"There's no love between them, either." Eithne bit her cheek. "Cinnamon was the only Poplar capable of such a thing before you. She softened Lien a bit. Softened me. Softened even a heart of literal stone."

My father. The gargoyle protector.

"Lien seems to want to do everything on her own, though," I said. "She keeps me behind her barrier and goes off by herself."

"Sounds like her. Gets tired of being bossed around by her mother, yet she's a lot like her that way."

"But she can't win without me, right? We have to work together."

Eithne nodded solemnly, patting Broomholly's brush head. "I'm glad she's on your side. Remember she's not like you—she's been alive far longer, and she's done some things I know you'd consider dark. Most witches have. But if you can overlook those *flaws*, she's your best shot."

I scuffed a toe against the floor, thinking. Then I shook my head. I had a few more things to ask.

"Where's my father?"

"I don't know. Truly." Eithne shook her head. "I searched for him a few times out of respect for Cinnamon, just so I could tell her he was out there, fine on his own, despite the grief we knew he'd experienced when he'd thought he'd lost you both. But in all my travels across Europe, I never found him. Did my mother brag about putting an end to him?"

My heart squeezed. "No…"

"Then he's still out there somewhere. She wouldn't have been able to stop herself from telling you if she'd destroyed him, I'm sure of it."

The muscles in my tense shoulders relaxed somewhat. "Did you… or my mother… create him using Ravana's venom?"

Eithne cocked her head. "That's an odd question. Does it matter?"

"I just want to know."

Eithne tapped her finger to her lip. "Yes. I suppose we did. I got the venom from that vampire Ravana right here in Luna Lane, and when it was time for Cinnamon to choose her boulder to turn into a gargoyle protector, she asked me if I'd help her instead of our mother. Mother gets her venom sourced straight from the Vampire High Council, you see."

Was that how Valentin had had dealings with witches? He certainly didn't seem to be happy about whatever had gone down between them.

Eithne was losing more of her color now, the tips of Broomholly's shaft and tail fading.

"I'm-I'm dealing with another issue right now." I didn't have time to explain it all, or how my deeper-rooted connection to Luna Lane, to Ravana, to all sorts of villainous people made me feel. "A human was found drained of blood in Creekdale. Two puncture wounds. Everyone suspects a vampire trying to turn a human and botching the job."

Eithne tittered even as the very tips of her hat and toes were fading away. "My, how this town continues to amuse. Though now the activity is extending out to Creekdale, is it?"

"I just want to know if there's any way any other paranormal could be responsible for it."

Eithne smirked. "That's right. You and that handsome vampire have a bit of a history, don't you?"

"He told me you once asked for a kiss as payment for your enchantments."

She laughed heartily, covering her mouth with the back of her hand. "So I did. He was cute. Shame if he killed a human. The Vampire High Council is unlikely to let that stand." She and Broomholly were at least a quarter vanished now. I had to speak quicker.

"Put Draven aside," I said, my voice packed with urgency. "At least tell me hypothetically. Could any other paranormal pull such a murder off?"

Eithne tapped a finger to her mouth again. "Well, I suppose a witch." That was my first suspect, too. "If I'd been tasked with making it look like a vampire had done it, there are enchantments. Mimic the fang bites. Drain the blood. Doable with enchantments, particularly if the witch is a strong one. The hardest bit to fake, though, would be the venom."

"Venom?" Why would that need to be "faked"?

"The Vampire High Council can examine a body and extract vampire venom, of course. Then it can be compared to a vampire's venom fresh from the fang. There's a distinct signature to each vampire, you know. They'd know if there was a match."

My stomach dropped to the floor. Eithne and Broomholly were almost entirely gone now.

"So it's not *impossible* for a witch to do this, right?"

Eithne's laugh lingered in the air, even as her lips faded from sight. "Cling to your little hopes, darling. It's not impossible. Just highly, highly unlikely. No matter how determined the witch might be. Then again, who's to say, before any venom is extracted, that your Draven is the vampire responsible? *Right*, cous—"

With that last, lingering echo, my aunt and her broomstick companion vanished entirely, the glowing of the symbols comprising the summoning circle fading to nothing once more.

"Why did you summon *her*?"

I jumped and Broomie shot up into the air. We both spun around.

Lien stood in the hallway, Broomhelen's shaft in one hand, a cloth bundle stuffed to the brim against her hip in the other.

Chapter Thirteen

"Lien! I was wondering when you'd be back." I had to take hold of Broomie as Lien grunted and brushed past us and to my potions-mixing table, depositing her bundle as she let go of Broomhelen, who started lazily floating around.

She untied her bundle and started bringing out what she'd had inside of it. All sorts of twigs and berries and dry leaves. Nothing lush, not in the winter season, but not every potion required fresh ingredients.

When she seemed to have nothing more to say, I remembered her question.

"I used to summon my mother and ask her for guidance. I did it often enough over ten years that I can't summon her anymore."

"So you called *her* instead?" Lien looked over

her shoulder, her hands pausing in their quick movements for only a moment.

"I had a few questions for her. And you weren't around, I might add."

She gestured to the array of things she'd brought with her. "I've spent the day gathering these to prepare us for anything."

There were enough things spread out around the table to brew a dozen potions at least.

"If the witches can't get into Luna Lane, you don't have to worry so much," I said.

She just grunted and flipped through my mom's potions book. Broomhelen went over to the fireplace and started brushing out ash without being told to.

"You know, Eithne was no kindhearted princess," said Lien after a bit.

"You don't have to tell *me* that," I muttered. This whole family seemed to be full of people just about the *opposite* of kindhearted.

"Yet you summoned her."

"I also killed her, in case you don't remember the story I told you." She knew I hadn't done it because I'd wanted to.

"Good," said Lien. "We didn't agree on much, but I agree with her idea to toughen you up and pass on her strength to you." She gave me a quick, assessing onceover. "You definitely need it."

I decided *not* to tell her about Eithne's suggestion that I wipe out the other potential heirs next— including her, which I'd definitely intended to leave out of the plan. I wondered when she'd come inside and how much she might have overheard.

"Fire, please," said Lien.

Rolling my eyes, I let Broomie join Broomhelen in sweeping out the last of the ash. "ERIF," I said beneath the hanging black cauldron once they'd finished.

"Where's your guardian?" Lien asked without looking up from the page of the potions book she was studying.

The fire crackled beneath the cauldron, pre-heating it before any potions brewing could begin.

"Roderick? He's with the Mahajans." As if on cue, Mom's cuckoo clock echoed out from down the hall. Four o'clock. "I'm supposed to be meeting them at Hungry Like a Pup."

"Keep plying him with sweets and he's bound to grow soft." Lien grabbed for an empty flask.

"I suppose you'd have me feed him rocks and daggers," I mumbled as Broomie got back into my hand.

"I'd *have you* not feed him at all." Lien frowned at me. "It's all right to let him get out and explore a bit, see what humans and paranormals do, get some exercise in. But remember, he's supposed to grow into a warrior. He's supposed to protect you. And to protect you, he has to be *near* you."

"He's a kid." My grip on Broomie's shaft grew tighter. "And I don't want him involved in serious matters."

"Matters like a war against the paranormals of this town?"

"We're *not* going to war against the paranormals in this town!" I smacked my lips.

"A vampire killed a human right outside of these walls. And there are exactly *two* vampires anywhere near here. I'll give you half a dozen guesses *where*."

I narrowed my eyes at Lien just as she narrowed hers at me.

"You never told me what you saw out there."

Lien looked away, grabbing a mortar and pestle. "You really want to know? Or are you too afraid to face the truth that your beloved Luna Lane could be full of murderers?"

I wasn't going to comment on that, considering both Ravana and Ginny had killed people in this town, and I'd always felt safe around them. I *still* would have felt safe around Ginny. Hers had been a special case.

Broomie's head drooped as I spoke. "If you know something that might incriminate someone, tell me."

Lien sighed, putting down the pestle and taking hold of the table. "Does it matter? Once the Vampire High Council has done a venom sampling on the body—"

"Something I didn't know they could do until Eithne told me," I muttered. Lien could have explained everything she'd known before traipsing off into the forest.

Lien shot me a look. "Well, I didn't sense the death as it happened. That worries me."

My shoulders softened a bit. "Why? You can't be everywhere at once."

"But I *can* sense things involving the paranormal within a reasonable radius. I *should* have been able to sense things." She took a deep breath and stared down at the potion ingredients, then quickly whipped through the pages of my mom's book. "I need to strengthen my senses."

"So that's it? The fact that it happened without you knowing? Is that all you can say about last night?"

Lien stopped flipping through the book and slammed her palm against it. Letting out a breath that sent a stray lock of her hair flying off her face, she left the room and headed to the kitchen, waving her hands and muttering an enchantment that got the coffeemaker brewing.

She grabbed a mug out of the cupboard and turned around, leaning on the counter to face me.

"I saw that Draven vampire, all right? Is that what you wanted to hear?" Though the coffeemaker was still turning on behind her, she lifted the empty mug to her lips as if about to take a sip.

Even *she* noticed there was something off about what she was doing. She stared down into her mug, as if expecting a drink to appear in it. Her one weakness seemed to be drinking any and every hot drink she could find out of nervousness, whether it was hers or someone else's.

She stared down into the mug as Broomhelen came floating into the kitchen, using the tail end of her shaft to take the mug from her witch companion and sliding it under the coffeemaker, as if quite used to her witch doing such a thing.

The spectacle had distracted me to the point where I'd barely registered what she'd said. "You saw… Draven? In Creekdale?"

I *had* seen that bat carrying batteries on the news report.

"No," she said. "But on the way into town."

"You didn't get back until past dawn—"

"I was doing a quick circle around town before heading back into Creekdale for one last look for the night. This was before I knew about the murder."

"But after it occurred?"

"Apparently." The coffeemaker started brewing and Lien stared at her mug. "He was flying as a bat and he popped into vampire form as we reached the edge of town. He asked me for a favor."

"A favor?"

She shrugged. "He wanted me to help transport his coffin from his house—"

"To the funeral parlor!" I finished for her.

She arched a brow as she stared me down, then she grabbed her mug. "You knew?"

"I didn't know *you* were the one who moved him. Though that explains how it was done. I mean,

I assumed maybe Lazarus took his hearse out." I was muttering now, thinking. "But why? Why move?"

Lien took a sip of her coffee and scrunched her face a bit like it had burned her. Then she sipped again and repeated the process. "He explained he was fighting with his sister. He asked me to move a few things with him besides his coffin, but even my goodwill was stretched at that point. I told him I had to get back to doing my rounds. That something was off around Creekdale. I just hadn't known *what* then." She shook her head. "It was probably the murder he'd committed."

"You don't know he did it!" My stomach dropped. Fighting with his sister? But really, moving out before she did? Would they just leave the house empty, then?

Then again, Lazarus had mentioned he was only staying there temporarily…

Lien shrugged. "We'll see."

I let out a deep breath. Had Lien mentioned her goodwill, as if such a thing were often stretched? She was hardly the definition of a do-gooder. It was a wonder she'd done a favor for someone in Luna Lane other than me in the first place. And she only protected *me* because she hated the other witches so much and seemed to think I'd be key to putting an end to them.

Apparently, everyone was counting on me to be

a more successful witch hunter than the average such trained human sworn to defeat us.

She'd already *tried* going the witch hunter route, though, and that had ended poorly.

My brain racked itself for more clues in what she might have said. "So what time was this?"

"When I ran into the vampire? Had to be around 6:00."

And Sister Mary Katherine's estimated time of death had been 3:00.

How long did it take a bat to fly from Creekdale to Luna Lane? He'd flown dozens of miles and caught up with a speeding train fairly quickly before.

Some tightness in my neck loosened. That was long after he'd have been back if he'd gone out for a snack that had gone disastrously wrong and he'd wanted to hide from it. What would he have been doing the full three hours afterward? He could have moved his coffin on his own in that time.

Wait a second, though. The news report with the bat and the battery had been filmed around 6:30. How many times had Draven flown into Creekdale? And how quickly had Lien worked?

"When did you finish moving his coffin?"

Lien shrugged. "I don't know. It didn't take long. Maybe fifteen minutes. I told him I didn't have all morning to help him out." Fifteen minutes. So had Draven then rushed into Creekdale after and managed to get filmed just fifteen minutes after Lien had last seen him? He was fast, but *that* fast?

"What else did he want you to bring to the funeral parlor that you didn't grab?"

Lien cocked her head, as if wondering why that would matter. "I actually don't remem—oh, a television set. And a box with wires and little rectangles at the end of the wires."

"A game system?" It would have been a wonder I'd put that together, but I *was* getting the knack of sleuthing these days. That, and Faine had mentioned Grady had set one up in the vampire manor late last night. "Video games?"

Lien offered a blank look. "I try my best to blend in, but I haven't been as attuned to human society as you have for the past few decades. I recognized the TV, but… Oh, and a red chair. And a portrait. Frankly, I cut him off then. I told him it would have to be the coffin alone or nothing at all. I was busy." She bit her lip and went to drink again, making a choking sound as the coffee hit her closed mouth and came right back out. I didn't comment on her quirk.

"He wanted you to help him set up the video game system. At the funeral parlor."

Her tongue poked into her cheek. "He wanted me to move all that stuff, anyway."

And the portrait. Probably the one of his mother.

"How did he seem?" I asked. What in the world had been going through this vampire's mind?

"Agitated, frankly." She set her mug down on the counter and took a deep breath. Broomhelen patted her shoulder with her brush head. "I should have known something was wrong."

"Draven was upset last night," I said, my cheeks coloring in his defense. "It makes sense he was agitated—"

"Upset enough to make a grave mistake?" Lien whipped around. "Maybe, as you say, Draven is not the type of vampire to maliciously murder humans, or to attempt to turn them without the Vampire High Council's permission. But is he the type of vampire who might get… emotional? Lose his sense of control?"

"I, uh…" I thought about it. Maybe she was right. Maybe it had been a horrific accident. Maybe the nun had seen him all depressed—in the Creekdale park, in the middle of the night, of all places—and had approached, asking how she could help.

Maybe he'd somehow convinced her about vampires and instead of making the sign of the cross, which actually would have had no effect on him, and heading for the hills, she'd offered to let him drink her blood. To feel better. The nuns were active in helping the Creekdale community, after all.

Though I couldn't imagine a human's *first* reaction to discovering vampires existed would be an act of charity.

But the scenario sort of fit. Because then maybe, just maybe, tired and exhausted and jealous and lonely and hungry, Draven had… taken things too far.

But no. He wouldn't have just come back home and strong-armed a witch he hardly knew into moving his coffin and video games to the local funeral parlor after that.

Unless… he hadn't known the nun was dead. Maybe he'd thought he'd drunk just enough and had flown away, before she'd collapsed.

Ugh, I wanted to scream. It just couldn't have been Draven. It couldn't have been!

"There's one other thing." Lien strode across the room and back to the potions-brewing table, gathering some ingredients she'd ground down and tossing them into the cauldron.

"Yes?" I asked, wondering if she'd forgotten what she'd started to say.

"I've seen the news reports about the nun since then," she said, looking at a list of ingredients and walking over to my cupboard filled with excess items. She didn't stop in her mad dash to start brewing. "And I've seen the nun's picture."

"Me, too." It hadn't exactly been detailed, but there'd been only the one image.

Lien tossed a bundle of pine needles into the cauldron and then stopped for a moment, a hand on one hip. Broomhelen floated over to the table and started grabbing things to add to the brew.

"I thought I'd seen that face before," she explained. My heart thudded. How? True, the nun had come from Europe, and Lien had spent her whole life in Europe, as far as I knew. But that would have been a strange coincidence, her path crossing with this murder victim's. "Where?"

"In that painting in Draven's house. The one he asked me to move."

The nun… resembled Draven's mother?

Chapter Fourteen

Of course, I'd assured Lien that couldn't have been the case. Draven's mother had died centuries ago.

My witch cousin hadn't known the portrait had been of his mother in the first place, but that was what had struck her once she'd seen Sister Mary Katherine's picture.

I'd seen them both. The more I thought on it, the more I thought… Maybe?

That was all she'd had to offer me, other than to instruct me to go get my gargoyle guardian and come back to help her prepare more potions.

I agreed with the first part. The Mahajans were expecting me by now.

I had too much else to do to simply come back and help her brew portions.

Especially if she expected to use them for war.

The sun was barely an ember glow on the horizon. If I was to catch Qarinah and Draven early after they awoke, I'd have to be fast. But I'd tell the Mahajans what I was up to first.

Broomie landed us in front of Hungry Like a Pup. It was only open for another hour or so, so the Mahajans were the only patrons inside, aside from Roderick and the three Vadas kids, all of whom were gathered around a table for four next to the Mahajans, each holding a handheld video game system.

A much newer model than the one Roderick had been playing with yesterday, by the looks of it. They were identical in shape, though Roderick and Flora both had gray units, Falcon a bright yellow, and Fauna a pale blue.

"Dahlia!" said Arjun, waving me over. He had a tuna sandwich and fries on a plate in front of him. Widow's-peaked and with a slight cherubic chub to his cheeks, he had warm, dark eyes and a kindly smile whenever anyone crossed his path. "I hope you don't mind that we ordered."

"No, of course not. I know I'm running a bit late, and I apologize." I stood next to Goldie's chair and leaned Broomie against one of the open seats. Broomie curled up on the seat but kept her brush head tall to sort of sniff at Goldie's plate. It was a salad, complete with corn, but naturally, there weren't any cornhusks.

Goldie winked at her and waved her fork in her direction. "I told her to bring out a plate of cornhusks when she saw you. Don't you worry about a thing, girl."

Broomie shook her brush head in excitement, practically wagging a stalk-clump "tongue" up at me. Broomhelen's more dog-like nature was wearing off on her.

"Roderick," I called to my gargoyle guardian, my hand on the back of Broomie's chair. "Did you have fun today?"

He looked up, a slight smile on his stone lips. Then Flora shouted in what appeared to be frustration and he turned his attention back to the screen.

"He was such a good helper," said Goldie.

"And he even helped a new customer, didn't you?" Arjun asked.

"New customer?" Luna Lane didn't get a lot of visitors. That left precisely one guess as to whom it may have been.

"A Frenchman," Goldie said. "Said he was here with a member of the Vampire High Council. Of course, we'd have to wait until nightfall to meet his esteemed patron." She said the last few words as if they'd been fed to her by the man himself.

They probably had.

"What was he shopping for?" My gut tensed a bit. Him coordinating the retrieval of Sister Mary Katherine's body with Lazarus made sense if it was on behalf of the Vampire High Council, but there was still something about that exchange that weighed heavily on me.

"Oh, different odds and ends," said Arjun. "What was it Roderick had trouble finding?"

"Oh, yes. It took us a while to figure out what he was saying, but he's *such* a good communicator when he tries. Reminds me of Zashil."

"I rather thought his eagerness reminded me of Hitesh."

The Mahajans were always reminiscing about the days their sons had been growing up in Luna Lane.

I had to get them to focus. "What was it that Valentin wanted?"

"You've met him?" Arjun asked.

I chewed my lip. "I… ran into him at Doc Day's. He's been busy today, it seems."

"He was looking for eyedrops."

"Eyedrops?" His eyes had seemed fine to me. Though I supposed I hadn't looked too closely.

Arjun made squeezing motions with a thumb and forefinger. "Yes. Been a while since we sold any of those. We actually had some in stock, but I saw they were expired when Roderick brought them up to me for the man to check out. He said he didn't care, though." Arjun shrugged. "Of course, now we're checking the whole medicine aisle before tomorrow so that doesn't happen again. Expired medicine doesn't usually *hurt* anyone, but it just doesn't work as well. Yet he was so insistent he'd buy them."

"I told him what Doc Day can't treat, people in

town usually go to you for." Goldie chuckled. "You could take care of dry eyes like that." She snapped.

Arjun cleared his throat. "He wasn't too happy about the idea of going to a witch for help, though."

"Yes…" Goldie bit her lip.

I could only imagine what the man had said to make their brows crease so.

"When was this?" I asked. "Approximately?"

Goldie twirled her fork in the air, as if thinking over my question, though Arjun regarded me curiously. "Not too long ago. I'd say around three o'clock? I remember because Roderick seemed to want to know when we were going for dinner, and I checked the clock right before that man came in."

So after I'd happened upon him at the funeral parlor. Maybe about an hour later. I would have been coming back from the park around then, yet I hadn't noticed the man across the street.

"Chione gave him a lift." Arjun took a bite of his sandwich. "I remember seeing the mayor's car idling out front for a bit. Though it was a while after I first took note of the car that the man entered the store, if I recall, and she didn't stay to give him a lift back into town."

A while…? Had he been discussing something with Chione in the car before he'd come inside the store, then?

The door to the back of the kitchen whapped open and Faine came out with a plate bursting with cornhusks.

Broomie's bristles shook so quickly together, they might have been part of a pompom.

"Hey, Broomhilde! Dinner is served." Faine set the plate in front of Broomie with a big smile and a wink. "We're adding tamales to the weekly special rotation, so I made sure to special-order plenty of cornhusks."

Broomie slurped up the cornhusks. Where they actually went within her bristles, no one knew. It wasn't like she actually digested anything.

"What can I get you?" Faine asked. Her eyes flicked to the kids' table. "Oh, I hope you don't mind. All that talk about video games with Draven last night... Grady went out this afternoon to Creekdale and bought *four video game handhelds* for the kids. Including Roderick."

Grady popped his head out from behind the window leading back to the kitchen. "I didn't want to disappoint the little guy if I just brought back three."

Faine let out a deep breath. "We didn't *need three*, even! The kids could share!"

Almost as if on cue, Falcon giggled and Fauna let out a little cry.

Flora leaned over to look at her sister's screen. "Guess Falcon stole your monster, huh?"

"That's not fair! He doesn't even know what he's doing! He just got lucky!" whined Fauna. "That monster is mine!"

Falcon and Roderick both laughed.

"Share, huh?" Grady smirked. "Besides, they each have to have their own systems to play together like that."

"*And* their own copies of the game." Faine rolled her eyes, a hand on her hip. "Games were never quite so tricky to play together when *we* were kids. Do you remember how each system *came* with a game?"

"And sometimes even a second controller." I nodded.

Faine fluffed her hand in the air. "Now the kids have got their Internet games, playing with people around the world. And they still have to pay extra just to play with each other across the table."

Faine watched her kids and Roderick play for a bit, and my gaze followed suit. Roderick looked so happy.

Lien was wrong. He wasn't meant to protect me *all the time*. He could be a kid, too. And I'd protect him just as much as he protected me.

The street beyond the wide window taking up most of the wall flicked to brightness as the streetlight turned on. It was dark outside.

"Say, do you have something I can just eat real quick? On the go, preferably? A bagel?" I looked to Broomie, and she nodded up at me, though that didn't stop her from slurping up her cornhusks. In fact, she started gobbling them faster.

"A bagel? You sure that's enough?" Faine cocked

an eyebrow and the Mahajans looked up at me, their expressions curious.

"You'll have to forgive me," I told them. "I can't stay for dinner. I'll take Roderick with me if you want—"

"He can stay with us and the kids." Faine turned over her shoulder. "Toast Dahlia a bagel, would you, dear?"

"On it."

I shook my head. My gut was churning with all the confusing things I'd learned today. "But yes, thank you, Grady. Faine. I'll pay you back for Roderick's games."

"Don't worry about it."

"It had to be expensive."

"It's fine. You and Roderick are family." She turned to Arjun. "Can I get you more water, hon?"

"Yes, please." Behind Arjun, the music coming from the kids' video game systems was far less electronic than the music in Cable's old system had been.

Faine left to grab the pitcher behind the counter. I'd keep arguing with her, but I had other things to worry about just then. Maybe I'd slide her a few-hundred-dollars-tip at some point with the payment app Cable had set up. Those games *had to be* expensive.

Those games. From Creekdale.

"Grady," I said, approaching the counter after a minute and leaning toward the window leading to the kitchen as Faine passed by me with the water. "You said you went to Creekdale for those?"

Grady's head popped back up. "Yeah. After the lunch rush. There's a game store at the edge of town. Right across from the park and the…" He wrinkled his nose. The murder this morning.

I'd heard about the place on that early-morning TV report. "It was supposed to be closed for investigations," I said. He held up some butter and some cream cheese. "Cream cheese, thanks." He grabbed a knife and presumably started to spread. "The news said they were open all night for a game launch and the Creekdale police were looking to see if their store security footage had caught anything."

"They were open by the time I went." Grady shuddered. "I still saw the police tape and everything, though."

Faine came back to the counter with her water pitcher half-full.

"Did they say anything about what happened?" I whispered.

Grady put a plate with my bagel up for Faine to grab and hand to me. I was too focused on him, waiting for his answer, to start eating. Besides, it was probably still hot.

"Well, you could tell it had *been a day*," Grady said, leaning over the window. "Poor woman was working by herself all night. Was still there. Said my big purchase made it all worth it, though."

Faine rolled her eyes as she poured a glass of

water and slipped it my way across the counter. "You keep telling yourself it was nothing but benevolent of you to do without asking."

"*You* suggested playing video games sometime with Spooky Games Club." Grady didn't often join us, unless the meetings were held at his place. It was an adults-focused social club mostly, and someone had to stay behind to watch the kids. Games were more Faine's thing, anyway.

"And what, the kids are going to let us *borrow* their systems? I doubt that." She gestured at them, all wholly focused on their handheld games. "I was thinking more of the system we lent Draven. Two at a time, a kind of tournament for high scores."

Faine was often thinking of new and fun ways to spice up Games Night.

"There won't be Club this weekend, though. This Saturday is Qarinah and Roan's wedding," I told her. "If… If it even goes forward at this rate."

The three of us all went quiet and looked solemn for a moment.

I chugged a drink of water and dug into my bagel, eager to finish it and go after the vampires. For their sake. For Roan's sake. For all of Luna Lane.

The bagel *was* a bit hot. "LAEH," I muttered at my tongue as I gestured at it. Slight burn.

But I didn't slow down. "So the woman who helped you was there last night," I said between chomping bites. "Did she tell you if she saw anything strange?"

Grady leaned back and scratched his head through the hairnet over it. "Well, I didn't want to say anything…"

Faine put a hand on her hip. "Grady? You told me the woman didn't want to talk about it."

"She didn't. I mean, she told me the police told her to keep everything quiet, you see, until they were sure what was important to the investigation and what wasn't."

"But she couldn't keep herself from hinting about something?" I mumbled through the last few bites of the bagel.

I grabbed a napkin and wiped my lips down, staring at Grady. Together with Faine, the two of us got him to crumble under pressure.

"She just said she'd planned this all-night game launch party for months and so few people showed up. She thinks a store in Chicago offering tons more freebies at their party must have attracted most of her customers."

Chicago was a bit of a drive away. Must have been some really good goodies.

"How many people showed up?" I asked.

"Just three. All night long."

Faine *tsked*. "Poor woman. Hardly worth keeping the place open overnight, if she sold just three of those games."

"Only one," Grady said. "Only one customer

asked for the game the store was staying open all night to celebrate."

"That's weird." I finished off my water and shook my head, resting my hand over the top of the glass when Faine sprung up to refill it. "What did the other two do, just wander in?"

"Well…" Grady frowned. "See, she thought something was off about the both of them."

Faine shook her head. "Seems like she was *hardly* tight-lipped about the matter, whatever the police told her to do."

"She didn't go much into detail," Grady protested. "She just said one asked if she had any games from a video game system that was thirty years old—and no, of course she didn't. And the other one at least actually bought something. But it was just batteries."

I gasped, my brain running wild. But he was speaking of these customers as if they'd been two different people.

"A game system thirty years old, huh? Like my dad's old system?" Faine frowned. "Draven was one of the 'off' customers, wasn't he?"

"That was my guess," Grady said. "He's the one who didn't buy anything, then."

But then… who had bought batteries? And turned into a bat? And why, then, if not Draven for Cable's old handheld game system?

"That's not all," Grady said, pulling me from my thoughts. "That was all she said about her 'disappointing' customers, but the one who actually came for the game in the middle of the night, long after the party was supposed to have started?"

Faine and I both leaned in closer, me practically sliding across the counter, hanging on every word.

"It was the nun," he said, each word a harsh whisper. "Visited the store in habit and everything. The owner had never seen her there before—and she'd definitely remember if she had."

Sister Mary Katherine had bought a copy of this new-release video game in the middle of the night?

"That explains what she was doing out so late," said Faine, her breath hushed. "Did the owner say what time exactly?"

Grady shook his head. "She mentioned it was well after midnight, though."

"Was she a passionate gamer?" I asked. "Otherwise, couldn't she have waited until the next morning to buy it?"

Grady shrugged. "She said she'd never seen a nun in her store before. Maybe she didn't want her convent to know."

"The news didn't say anything about her being found with a game on her person," I said.

"Law enforcement doesn't always leak details like that to the press," Faine pointed out. "At least not so early in the investigation."

I leaned back from the counter. "This raises more questions than it answers, really. But look, I've got to go. Thank you for the game system and for watching Roderick." I glanced at him. I'd have to explain where I was going and also thank the Mahajans again and apologize for bailing on them. "But I have to find Qarinah and Draven, especially since that member of the Vampire High Council is bound to wake up at any minute—"

Before I could finish, the door connecting Hungry Like a Pup to First Taste, the neighboring pub—Grady and Faine often made some dinner selections in advance for hungry overnight pub customers, purchased in bulk by Draven and Qarinah—burst open.

A long cape flowing behind him, a pale, harsh and sunken face towering over a willowy frame.

Black hair focused into a widow's peak over a sharp, gleaming forehead.

It was a vampire, no doubt. It had to be Valentin's master, the visiting member of the Vampire High Council.

Chapter Fifteen

From behind the vampire lord appeared Valentin, walking with a sort of hunched-over glee, cutting out from behind his master and getting on one knee, then lifting both hands back up toward his patron as if in worship.

"May I present, simple townsfolk, the one and only, the *excellent* Lord Aleksandru the Intrepid!"

I exchanged a look with Faine and Grady. Behind us, the kids' video game music played softly in the otherwise-quiet café. A round of tepid applause from the Mahajans' table startled me.

"That's quite enough, Valentin." Lord Aleksandru spoke with a thick, Transylvanian accent, but more strange was the fact that his words practically came out wheezing, as if he were about to croak at any moment. His head turned sharply toward the kids' table as Valentin jumped to his feet, continuously bowing. Only Flora and Roderick had looked up from their games to look at the visitors. Lord Aleksandru's lip curled.

"That leads to the café next door, my good man," said a familiar voice as another figure approached from behind the vampire and his assistant. Mayor Abdel came through from First Taste, followed by Chione. It was the mayor who'd been speaking.

"I can take you to the vampires' manor," Mayor Abdel continued. "But I assure you, at least one of them, if not both, will appear at the pub at any moment—"

"No need." Lord Aleksandru glanced over his shoulder at the mayor. "My assistant has informed me of everything that transpired during my absence. The most important thing shall be for us to examine the body. If a vampire was responsible, we have our ways of finding out exactly who."

Flora yelped and Faine whisked into mom mode, dashing around the counter to walk toward the kids' table. She stood between them and the sight of the visiting vampire and his town welcoming committee, speaking to them in soft tones.

"Roderick," I called. The gargoyle had not had the same reaction as the young werewolf. He hit a button on his new video game system and trotted over beside me, the system at his side gone quiet, the screen dark, as the mayor and Lord Aleksandru continued their conversation, Chione and Valentin hanging back quietly.

"Roan assures me it's on its way," Abdel said. "It took a great deal of finessing with the Mayor of Creekdale, I must say. He seems to know *something* is different about Luna Lane, but he can't quite bring himself to ask. It took the urging of both our sheriff and me to convince him to give 'our medical examiner' a chance to offer his expert opinion on strange, inexplicable cases, but—"

Lord Aleksandru's dark, red-rimmed eyes turned to me. "You have a witch in town." His gaze flickered to gargoyle Roderick at my side. "Couldn't she have enchanted him, made it gone smoother?"

I crossed my arms. "I don't manipulate people with my enchantments." I wasn't even sure I could. Since I'd never even imagined trying. Though I was sure Eithne or even Lien might have been able to.

"Hmm," said Lord Aleksandru, crossing his arms over his abdomen. They were long, pale, and spindly. Like a corpse's. "Pity."

"We keep our resident witch here. At home. Best way to help Luna Lane." Through the hole in his facial bandages, Abdel winked my way. So he wasn't telling the vampire I was *stuck* here in Luna Lane. At least then I wouldn't have to answer any questions on that matter.

Chione turned around, something through the open inner door to First Taste drawing her attention. Her stern look melted and a smile hit her face. "Qarinah! Qarinah is here!"

"Ah." Mayor Abdel gestured for the vampire guest to retreat back into the pub. "As I said. Shall we?"

Chione frowned. "No Draven?" she asked inside the pub.

No, Draven was at the funeral parlor, last I knew.

Lord Aleksandru straightened his shirt. "She is the one who summoned me here. I suppose a cordial greeting is in order." He turned to Valentin. "And then we must take a venom sample."

Valentin nodded vigorously and dug into his overly large coat, producing a small, corked bottle from an inner pocket with a *clink*.

"But then we must examine the body promptly," Lord Aleksandru said to Abdel as he swept past him and into First Taste after Chione.

Broomie flew over from where she'd been slurping down her food and into my hand, her brush head looking to me as if to ask what I planned to do next.

I glanced at Roderick, whose questioning gaze seemed to ask me the same thing.

I had questions for Qarinah, but she was bound to be occupied by the Vampire High Council for a while at least.

I knew where Draven was due to have woken up. And it was the same place where Sister Mary

Katherine's body was due to be brought, if Abdel had indeed managed to convince the Mayor of Creekdale to send it over.

The funeral parlor. Where I'd sort of trespassed and busted a window.

And where Valentin and Lazarus had been discussing some shady secrets.

"Faine, can you watch Roderick?" I asked, heading toward the door.

"Sure, but—"

I froze as I reached the door, a quick tug at the back of my skirt practically ripping me back.

Stumbling, I caught my footing and looked down. Roderick frowned and held my skirt tightly with one stone fist, his video game system in the other.

I looked to Faine and her kids, blissfully back to playing their games, then back to Roderick.

He was a kid, but somehow, he sensed that things were about to get serious.

He wanted to protect me.

"Never mind," I said. "We'll go together. Thank you again!" I waved and nodded at Faine, Grady, and the Mahajans in turn.

Roderick let go of my skirt and we stepped outside.

"I was heading to the funeral parlor," I explained to him as we started walking in that direction. "I'll fly ahead and once you get there, you can hide outside, watch for anything I should be wary of—"

Broomie let out a little moan and shook her head. Roderick frowned up at me again and grabbed my skirt. Right. He wouldn't know *where* the funeral parlor was.

But there was no time to waste. Lord Aleksandru and the others were probably headed to the funeral parlor as soon as they were finished with Qarinah.

Though if they were to collect a venom sample from her… I remembered the one time Draven had supplied some of his venom to me for a potion. It had taken him some time to extract from his fang and had caused him a bit of discomfort.

I still had a bit of that venom in a vial at home among my potions ingredients, actually. Vampire venom was used in a number of complicated potions. Though not the kind I attempted to craft often.

Roderick's little stone wings flapped, and I realized he could probably keep up.

I mounted Broomie. "Follow me," I told him, and we all took to the skies.

The flight to the dark alley with the funeral parlor didn't take long, and Roderick, despite his weight, didn't straggle far behind. When we reached the right alley, I spotted the sheriff's vehicle toward the curb and a hearse out front of the parlor,

Sheriff Roan and Lazarus in the walkway leading up to the parlor.

The presence of Roan caused a swell of confidence to rise up within me. I settled for landing right behind him beyond the gate, shouting, "Heads up!" as I went to land.

Both Roan and Lazarus looked up as I approached.

"Lia?" Roan asked. "What are you doing here?" Roderick's stony wings echoed out like shifting gravel and then the gargoyle boy landed beside me. "Hey, buddy."

Roderick nodded once, then brought his video game system back up, turning on the screen. Perhaps Roderick's defenses were lowered with the presence of Sheriff Roan, too.

"Good evening, Dahlia. Little gargoyle child. Broomhilde." Lazarus put two bony hands over his cane and turned his hollow eyes toward each of us. There was no way for the reaper to have expressions, but I felt a strange sort of accusing glare from the nothingness of his skull. Like he knew who'd busted his window earlier.

"Evening," I croaked out.

"Law enforcement business," Roan said, gesturing toward the funeral parlor and then the hearse behind him. "Had to borrow this from Lazarus to go get…" Roan lowered his voice, his gaze flicking to Roderick. "To go get the body of that nun. We loaded her into Lazarus's basement for autopsy. But I promised to wait until Abdel and the member of the Vampire High Council arrived."

"They're on their way," I explained. "They had to ask Qarinah a few questions before they came."

Roan looked at me thoughtfully, perhaps wondering how much I knew about the situation. He said nothing, though. Maybe he was used to me sleuthing my nose into his business these days. And good thing I did, too, with all these paranormal incidents.

"I came to, um, see Draven," I said, not willing to let Lazarus clue in on the fact that I might be investigating this murder on my own. Not after his hush-hush meeting with Valentin about the nun's body. Lazarus tapped his cane against the cobblestone, and I realized he'd likely wonder how I knew about Draven being here, too. Rookie mistake.

"Draven?" Roan asked, puzzled. So *he* hadn't noticed the vampire when he'd helped Lazarus bring the body inside?

"Lien told me," I said quickly, thinking on my feet. It wasn't a lie. Just not the whole truth. "She, um, ran into him this morning and he asked her to move his coffin here." It was my turn to glare at Lazarus. "For some reason."

Roan scoffed and took hold of his belt under his puffy, black winter coat. "Let me guess. That reason being his sister's and my wedding?"

Lazarus's skull head tipped upward slightly. "Draven was here. He spent the day in his coffin, naturally. But as soon as night fell, he told me he was sure his sister would have left the manor by now, and so he returned to it to collect more of his things."

"Real mature." Roan rolled his eyes. "She's going to move out of the manor at the end of the week."

"He doesn't want to speak to her," Lazarus said simply, as if that were an entirely understandable position.

Roan tossed his hands into the air. "I've known the man longer than he's known Qarinah! What does he have against me marrying her?"

"It's not that," I said softly. "He just… feels abandoned."

"Well, that's a real selfish point of view if you ask me." Roan rubbed a hand over his moustache, which I realized was getting a bit frosty. "As if *I* don't know anything about being happy for a woman when *she's* happy—even if that means she's not happiest with you."

My mother. His longstanding, unrequited crush. My eyes flitted guiltily to Roderick, as if he'd known about my family history. He'd only been born last month—he never would have met my father, even if they were the same species.

"MRAW." I motioned my hands to warm Roan up and then myself and even Broomie, as she was known to appreciate a good fire. Roderick and Lazarus wouldn't need the assistance.

"Thanks, kid." Roan smiled at me, and I thought I caught just the smallest glistening of tears pooling in his eyes.

"Perhaps you should escort the esteemed member of the Vampire High Council here, Sheriff," Lazarus suggested. "I'll prepare the room for the autopsy." He shifted slightly to me. "You will tell Draven there is going to be a bit of a ruckus here for a while, will you not? Perhaps it's best he stay put."

Roan shoved his hands in his coat pockets. "I should check in with Qarinah, anyway. Say, why don't you ask Dahlia to fix that window of yours?" Roan leaned toward me. "Says a bird crashed into it."

A bird…? I looked to Lazarus. He had to have known that had been no bird.

"In due time." Lazarus tipped his hat at me. "There are more important concerns right now, and I've blocked it with some boards. But do tell the warm-blooded among you to dress warm. It's cold in the basement regardless."

With a *clink, clink* of his walking stick against the cobblestones, Lazarus approached his parlor, climbing up the few steps and heading inside.

"Can I give you a lift anywhere?" Roan asked. He gestured over his thumb toward his own vehicle.

Broomie's head sunk, her bristles rubbing together in a sort of pout. She hated the idea of me riding in cars when she could take me. Roan held up both hands in surrender. "Just offering, girl. You take her to the vampire's manor and knock some sense into that old man, why don't you?" Roan chuckled. "Does me good to remember he's so much older. Even less reason for him to be acting like a big baby."

"I'll do my best." I grimaced. I made a show of climbing onto Broomie's back and she and Roderick both took to the sky, Roderick's game in sleep mode and hanging off from his side again.

We flew to the end of the alleyway, opposite of the direction Roan was heading in. "Just a sec, Broomie." We floated in the air, Roderick catching up and flapping his wings beside us.

I watched as Roan's pickup took off and turned out of sight.

"Roderick, head to Draven's," I said.

His stone lips frowned, a pointy tooth sticking out.

"He likes you more than he likes me right now," I pointed out. "Keep him there. I'll be along as soon as I can. It's all right." Roderick hesitated. "*Please*. I know you want to protect me, but protecting me means protecting my friends, too."

Roderick chewed on his stony lip, then nodded, flapping his wings in the direction of the vampire manor.

Broomie perked her head to the side, as if to ask what *I* would be doing.

"You and I, girl, we're just a couple of window-busting birds. Lazarus *knows* it was us, I'm pretty sure. But he didn't tell Roan to try to get us in trouble for it—maybe he didn't want to call attention to the fact that we may have caught him having a secret meeting with Valentin. And he was keen to get both Roan and us out of there for a moment alone with the body before the rest of the cavalcade arrives."

I narrowed my brow. "We're going to sneak in there and see what he's up to."

Chapter Sixteen

ack on the front porch of the funeral parlor, Broomie and I slunk against the wall to peek through the windows of the reception room. The lights were off, so it was difficult to see inside, but I could vaguely make out the shape of an open coffin, the lid propped up.

There were several planks of wood over the window I'd broken earlier. "If I hadn't panicked, I could have just done this," I told Broomie, though she'd know as well as I would.

"WODNIW HSINAV," I said to the window beside the one I'd broken. The glass pane disintegrated at the edges, vanishing into nothingness.

I stuck Broomie in first and then climbed in after her, landing with as soft a *thud* as I could on the other side. Flinching, I looked around, but there was no sign of Lazarus. I expected him to be in the basement regardless.

A soft breeze of chilly air ruffled beneath my shawl. I turned around to enchant the window back into place, but then I wondered about the need for making another hasty exit. Then again, wouldn't a completely vanished window make the local witch more of the suspect?

"WODNIW EROTSER," I whispered, waving my hands in front of the pane. The window rematerialized, as if it had never been touched. I supposed it hadn't been.

Not that I thought Draven was still here, even with Lazarus acting suspicious, but I took careful, quiet steps toward the open coffin. No vampire inside. No sign of whatever spooky ghost had scared me away from here, either.

There *was* Cable's old video game system, though. I picked it up and hit the power button. Nothing happened. I thought back to the little *bleeps* and *bloops* I'd heard when I'd snuck in here earlier today. Surely, Draven hadn't stayed awake all day in his coffin, playing this game instead of resting, had he? But if he'd successfully gotten batteries last night, then, if I remembered right when thinking about these old systems' terrible battery life, a full eight hours or more of play might have drained it again.

But what was it Grady had said about the visitors to the special release party at the video game store last night? It hadn't been Draven who'd bought batteries.

But then what other bat would have been carrying them? Perhaps the video game store owner had just gotten her memories mixed up, and the "strange" customer who'd asked about games for a thirty-year-old system had also bought the batteries.

Broomie let out a quiet rustle of her bristles to remind me that everyone was due to arrive soon, so our time to sneak around was limited. "SEOHS TEIUQ," I tried with a wave of my hand at my boots. I'd never tried that enchantment before.

It seemed to have worked, though, my footfalls near silent as I made my way down the aisle between the benches and to the hallway of the funeral parlor. I peered both ways, shuddering again at the creepy portraits all over the walls. The hallway was dark, too. No sign of anyone.

A dim light trickled up from the door leading down to the basement, which was shut but not quite all the way.

I snuck over, my back hunched on instinct, as if that alone would stop me from being spotted, and as quiet as I dared, I opened the door just enough to slide Broomie and myself inside. Grabbing for the handrail, I took the first set of steep, circular steps downward. Each time my foot dropped, a jolt of vertigo made me sure I was about to tumble down the stairwell. No wonder there was an elevator, too, though that didn't seem particularly sturdy by the looks of it.

The lower I went, the louder Lazarus's

humming got. I hadn't pegged him for someone who hummed when alone.

"Just a drop," he sang, the humming changing into a song. Broomie and I peeked around the corner. He was hunched over the body, only the back of his skeleton head visible beneath the top hat, the white of his bony hand glinting as it lifted into the air. "A drop or two will do," he sang again, and with a flourish, his hand went downward then into the air once more. He was holding something small and long, his bony forefinger and thumb squeezing the rubbery tip.

"Shame. I would have liked to have seen an undead rise from my table one day." Lazarus leaned over toward the body's head, as if to whisper to it, but his voice didn't lower in volume at all. "Purely a scientific interest, you see?" He laughed, and the sound was like the clattering of teeth.

He hummed again, using the item in his hand like a conductor's baton. I squinted my eyes, too afraid to use an enchantment to get a better look. It seemed to be… an eye dropper?

Was that something morticians or medical examiners typically used?

I supposed I didn't know.

He was at a table aligned with various shiny, silver tools, rearranging everything and dipping some tools in alcohol solution. I took a look at the body. It was mostly covered in a white sheet, but for the head.

Without her nun's veil and wimple, it was clearer to see. Her long, brittle white hair hung off the sides of the silver table. Hadn't she been only in her forties? She was pasty, her eyes closed. At the side of her neck were two bright red holes. One even seemed to ooze in dark red blood.

But I thought she'd had all of her blood drained. Had that been an exaggeration? She *did* appear rather shriveled, though.

Lazarus picked up a flask on his table and put a stopper in. The flask was empty, though there were traces of a dark color to the glass.

Then he walked with it in hand to the crematorium furnace, opened up the wrought-iron door, and tossed the flask inside.

Why would he do *that*?

A little yelp of surprise escaped my lips as the glass shattered inside, thankfully covered by the sound of Lazarus flipping the switch and turning on the flames that would burn the contents inside.

"Who's there?" Lazarus asked, craning his skeleton head. His teeth chattered together, but it didn't seem to be from amusement. "I will tolerate a lot from the citizens of this town, but I will *not* tolerate anyone intruding on *my* solitude!"

Hugging Broomie to me tightly, I whipped back around the corner, taking shallow breaths. There was something about his voice that frightened me, and it was more than its usual spookiness.

"Quick. You must leave."

That spectral voice I'd heard earlier today, this time coming from up above me in the darkness of the stairwell.

"He stays alone during the preparations for a funeral for a reason," the voice continued.

Soft. Feminine. Melancholy, but somehow… familiar, too.

A glint of red shone in the darkness.

The *clink, clink, clack* of Lazarus's cane and booted feet made it clear he was approaching—and faster than he often moved, too. Yet my feet were affixed to the floor. I was stunned. I didn't know why, but I couldn't move.

"Come out, child," Lazarus cooed. "Come out and meet the reaper of your death."

My heart thudded, but I couldn't move.

"It's too late!" screeched the ghostly voice. *"He's struck you with fear."*

The red glint grew brighter, surrounded by vague, white shadow in the dark, and then it surged down the stairwell with a *whoosh*.

"Broomie, you must take her!" The voice was clearer now.

The form in front of Broomie and me turned distinct.

It was Ginny Kincaid, the ghost we'd once considered our friend. The ghost I'd never thought I'd see again.

"I'll hold him back," she whispered, no trace of her fake Southern accent. She was wearing clothes from the last couple of decades, too, her straw-colored hair, washed out in white though it was, hanging down in waves over her shoulders. "But, Broomie, it's up to you."

Broomie grew stiff in my hand and I realized I couldn't even budge my grip on her shaft. I was paralyzed, not just with fear, but truly unable to move.

"Your death awaits," said Lazarus, his voice louder than ever.

Broomie shot into the air, screwing up her brush head and flailing but nonetheless lifting me up by the arm alone. We took off through the narrow, dark stairwell, my limp feet scraping against steps along the way.

I looked down. The mists of Ginny's form blocked the end of the stairwell, but through her transparent sheen, I could see Lazarus.

His skeletal form crackled with black flames of fire. The sunken eye sockets in his skull flickered with bright-orange flames.

He looked up through Ginny and he saw me, being dragged upward by one limp arm.

"No!" said Ginny, her ghostly white arms wide. "It's not her time. You will not pass!"

"I knew it was you, Dahlia," he cooed, ignoring Ginny entirely. "You will regret coming down here! You invite death early, and I have no choice but to accept your invitation."

"Lazarus, be yourself!" Ginny shouted. "You are

not the reaper of death today!"

Broomie burst through the door, sending it flying open wider, heedless of the sound it made. No sense in keeping quiet anymore.

All of a sudden, my feet could move. I dragged them across the hallway carpet, trying to get my bearings and swinging my free hand toward the front door. "NEPO!" The inner and outer door both shot open.

I took a running start and then heaved myself up and swung my leg around Broomie's back, the both of us, for the second time, taking to the skies from this place soaked in death.

Chapter Seventeen

B roomie and I got as far as the end of the alley, and I gently yanked on her to stop. Floating up above the street, I looked down, glancing each way for the sheriff's pickup or Mayor Abdel's car. "Ginny! That was Ginny." I wiped my sweat-covered brow with my forearm. "But what about Lazarus? We have to warn them before they show up for the autopsy. Is that really how he prepares every body that goes through his home?" I shuddered. He'd always insisted on working alone.

Broomie's bristles trembled behind me, too.

"I know, but we can't—"

From out of the chimney of the smoking crematorium emerged a spectral figure, soft white in the darkness.

Ginny floated up and over, lingering a few feet in front of my face. The wind got sharper, the cold penetrating my warmth enchantment.

"It's all right now," she said, her voice a bit timid and unlike the haughtier Southern belle I'd known her as—falsely—almost my entire life. She rubbed a ghostly hand over her bare arm. She was wearing a tank top even in winter, but I supposed that didn't matter to a ghost. "He calmed down. He's very volatile when dealing with death, you see. Brings out every reaper instinct in him. But he's calm now and he'll be calm for the autopsy when the mayor, the sheriff, and the member of the Vampire High Council arrive."

"You're up to date on everything, aren't you?"

She shrugged. Although it seemed impossible, there was a glint in one transparent eye, as if she were about to cry. "I've mostly been hanging out with him since October. He always scared me before, so I rarely visited. But since I... Since I became a killer..."

Slowly, I nudged Broomie to descend, and Ginny trailed after. I landed on my own two feet on the sidewalk, flipping Broomie over to hold her brush head upright. "Ginny, we've been over this. Eithne worked on your anger, your need for justice and—"

"Convinced me to murder a man."

"Convinced you to murder *your murderer.*" My voice cracked. "If you've been around all this time, then you know I-I've killed now, too."

"Eithne." Ginny nodded, her lips drawn down.

"She gave you no choice. I heard all about it afterward."

"From *Lazarus*?" I hadn't seen the reaper since Leana Woodward's funeral before all of this.

"I go out and wander around town on occasion," she said. "I just make sure no one sees me." She pinched the red-jeweled brooch transformed into the pendant of a necklace over her clavicle. My mother had given her that as a ghost—to keep her grounded, so to speak. Probably trying to stave off her intense need for revenge—the very thing that had kept her as a ghost on Earth to begin with. But then Eithne had gone and let her anger loose again. I supposed her murderer showing up in town, coincidence though it may have been, had been the final tipping point in that. Even a strong witch's enchantment could only do so much.

"How are you still here?" I asked. "I thought you'd moved on, after justice was done for your death."

"That's just it." She shook her head. "Guilt has replaced my need for justice. I'm not even sure what I did *counts* as justice."

"You let Karter go," I said softly. He'd had a hand in covering up her murder and she'd definitely considered killing him for it, but she'd let the law take care of his sentence instead. He'd admitted it all, pled guilty to several heinous crimes, and was awaiting sentencing last I knew. Zashil had told his parents, who'd reported the news to me.

Ginny didn't answer.

"If you've been here all along, why haven't you shown yourself before?" I reached out as if to hug her, but though she'd learned to solidify parts of herself or ghostly items she'd fashioned, I wasn't sure she'd be solid now. My fingers curled back in awkwardly.

"I'm ashamed." She stared downward. "Lazarus… He made me feel better. Death is just one part of a journey. He would know. He's a reaper."

I looked over her shoulder, back toward the funeral parlor. "I have to warn everyone before they show up—"

Ginny waved a spectral hand. "It's fine, I promise. He's told me a lot about himself over the past few months. I knew about his darkest reaper tendencies, but I hadn't seen them. There hadn't been a body kept in his parlor since before I started spending time there."

I arched a brow. "And you think he's got control of himself now?"

"The issue was he didn't invite you in," she said. "He'd unleashed his connection to the realm beyond, doing what he needed to do to prepare the body for its farewell voyage, and that… that harnesses a lot of dark energy. It's not unlike witch's magic."

"Oh?" I cocked my head. I'd been practicing

witch's magic my whole life and I'd *never* felt so dark and unable to move in sheer terror.

"Well, not yours. But you're an unusual witch, he tells me." She smiled. "Oh, yes, he told me all about the places he's been, the other paranormals he's met along the way. Witches with darkness in their hearts are connected to the realm beyond for their worst and wicked deeds, you see. He's heard their voices, pretty much every time he prepares a body for a funeral or an autopsy."

"Their voices?" My breath caught in my throat. "Here? In Luna Lane?"

Ginny nodded. "It's always been that way. Since the dawn of time." She fluffed off this strange revelation with a flick of her hand. "And in any case, he's calmed himself now. If he were to see you, he would apologize, not…"

"Kill me?" I suggested, remembering how he'd said my death would come early.

"That was the darkness," she assured me. "Dark energy channeling through him."

Sighing, I rubbed at my forehead with my free hand. "All right. I trust you."

"You do?" Ginny perked up at that.

"Of course." I offered her a flittering smile. "But I still need to warn everyone."

Ginny straightened her ghostly self up. "I'll do it."

"Do what?"

"Talk to everyone when they arrive. Explain to Mayor Abdel and Sheriff Birch that I've been here all along, warn them about Lazarus—everything. Though I *promise* you he's fine now. He's just sitting in there, waiting for his invited guests. See, that's the important part. If he knows people are coming—*people*, that is, not spirits with one foot in the realm beyond like I have, you see—he'd never open the connection. It's this innate sense that lives in reaper bones—"

"Ginny," I said, gently interrupting her. It was nice to see her as her talkative self again. I just didn't have time for it at the moment. Not until I got the bottom of what had happened to that nun in there. A thought occurred to me. The ghostly, vague form. The red glint—Ginny's necklace. "You warned me to get out earlier today, didn't you?"

"You were uninvited," she said. "I was worried as soon as that man Lazarus had allowed to come in had left, he might… Well, I'd worried for nothing. Lazarus explained his reaper trance, as he calls it, it only becomes uncontrollable when he's opened his connection to the realm beyond, and he only does *that* when he's preparing a body. He asked who that had been, breaking his window—"

"You told him it was me." I winced.

"Well, not too many people it could have been, really." Ginny tossed her long hair over one shoulder. "He would have figured it out anyway. He did wonder why you were there, why you were hiding. I had no idea myself."

"I had just meant to talk to him, and then I saw Draven's coffin, which surprised me."

Ginny rolled her eyes. "Yes, I witnessed the whole exchange. Lazarus told him it was a bad idea to try to avoid his sister rather than work through their problems, but he agreed to let him stay. Just until he got his head clear. But what does the vampire do? Just crawl into that coffin of his and play that little handheld game of his *all day*! The man didn't sleep a wink!" She shrugged. "I may have poked my head in and spied on him a few times, just to see what that racket was. I had a game system just like that one…" She looked off into the distance, growing a bit wistful. Despite her changed appearance, it was still strange to hear her talk about being alive in the *latter* half of the twentieth century.

"I may have whispered a tip or two to him to beat the game," Ginny admitted. "But he was *so* engrossed, I doubt he even heard me. Never thought I'd see a vampire with *bloodshot* eyes. They always have that red ring already, you know? But this is worse."

Draven. I'd sent Roderick to him, and he was supposed to be keeping him at the manor for me to check on. I bit my lip and looked over my shoulder, in the direction of the manor. "I need to go check on him," I said. "But maybe you can help. You saw him move his coffin into Lazarus's last night?"

"Well, I saw your witch cousin do it." Ginny

chewed on her lip. "She moved him in before Draven had even asked Lazarus permission!" Before I could ask how she knew about Lien, Ginny continued. "Yeah, I got the gist of who she was and why she's here—why you're still in Luna Lane despite the fact that Mr. Cable Woodward—er, *Cable* left." She used to refer to everyone by their proper titles. Part of her "I died a proper lady in the early twentieth century" disguise.

"Yeah, that's, uh… A lot has happened in the past few months. But do you know what time this was that Lien helped Draven come over?"

"No. I don't really keep track of time. Sorry." She shuffled a leg about a foot off the ground sheepishly. "Time has no meaning as a ghost."

Was I trying to have someone else confirm Lien's story? Did I doubt Lien, even though she was here to protect me?

I didn't know. I didn't know *who* to doubt. It seemed like there could be logical explanations for almost all of the strange behavior I'd witnessed.

"I asked Lazarus all about it later," she said. "Draven bumped into Lazarus on the way home from First Taste—Lazarus was on one of his rare evenings out with colleagues, and I encouraged him to do it." If I wasn't mistaken, her cheeks darkened just slightly, as if blushing, and she clasped her hands together in front of her abdomen. "And when he found Lazarus on the sidewalk, he told him he'd already moved in. Caused me quite a fright, I must say. Draven just showing up out of the blue with that other witch floating his coffin inside. But I knew he must have gotten permission as soon as Lazarus returned home with the vampire in tow. He wasn't panicked at all as Draven crawled into his coffin in the reception room. The reaper has a thing against *uninvited* visitors." She narrowed an eye at me as she said that. "And you know why now."

"Wait a minute." My brain went over the stories I'd heard from both doctors, though I hadn't spoken with Qarinah just yet. "Draven and Lazarus met outside of First Taste? About what time?"

"I didn't ask. But they got here shortly before dawn. Cutting it a bit close, that vampire."

"Do you think Lazarus would know what time he ran into Draven?" Could he act as another witness to establish Draven's innocence? Then again, if this had happened near dawn, the point was moot.

"Maybe." She shrugged. "He sort of has one foot in the world beyond at all times, too. Time doesn't mean much to him. He never sleeps, for one."

"Could you ask for me?" I cleared my throat and took a look over her head at the funeral parlor. My insides quivered at the thought of going back in there just now, even if Ginny would be with me. Broomie must have sensed my thoughts and felt the same because she shivered, her bristles catching in the cold, night air.

"Of course. Does this have to do with that poor dead woman? Lazarus told me about her even before her body showed up."

"Yes… And I have another question about that. What was Valentin doing there with him this afternoon, do you know? The human assistant for the member of the Vampire High Council."

"Well, I'm not entirely sure. Lazarus was a bit close-lipped at that. Er, closed skeletal jaw," she added quickly. She huffed, a bit of her Southern belle personality shining through. "Not like him to keep secrets from me these days. I thought we were friends!"

"He wouldn't tell you?" That seemed suspicious.

"Well, it's not like he told me *nothing*!" Her chest swelled with pride. "It only made sense he'd make a point of greeting any member of the Vampire High Council who came to town, regardless of any… unsavory incidents. Reapers have a deeper history with vampires, you know." She spoke as if anyone who was *anyone* would know such things, but reapers were notoriously enigmatic about their origins. "There are some stories that say when vampires die, they wither to bones that keep moving. Of course, Lazarus has no memory of being a vampire. He doesn't *know* how reapers are created. Isn't that strange?"

Strange, indeed. "So he invited Valentin over to greet him? As Lord Aleksandru's assistant?"

"Well, he didn't know he'd arrived. As soon as

he realized who the man knocking on his door was, he of course invited him in. They went downstairs, discussed some things… Then a certain *Miss Nosy* showed up and I followed her around the parlor instead.”

I grimaced. “I guess I can go ahead and fix that window for him now, right? If he knows it was me.”

“Why of course you should. But it’s no rush. Laz and I don’t get cold.”

‘Laz?’ Broomie tittered beside me, as if giggling.

I didn’t comment on that. “You were listening to their discussion at first? What did they talk about?”

“Well, a lot of boring, theatrical greetings and such at first. That Frenchman can *talk*,” she said, rolling her eyes. I had to stop myself from giggling, too. I’d never met anyone who could outtalk Ginny. “But yes, he filled him in on the murder in Creekdale, and to tell the truth, just the thought of someone getting murdered in my hometown… I didn’t want to be there anymore. Didn’t want to think about it. Floated upstairs and then there you were, sneaking in like you were about to rob the place.”

“I was not!” I said. “I just got this dreadful feeling, like… Like…”

“Ghosts were among us?” It was Ginny’s turn to giggle.

“All right, ha ha.” I sighed. “So you don’t think Lazarus will tell you anything more? I heard Valentin say the woman might *come back to life*.”

"If a vampire killed her by draining her blood, it's a possibility," Ginny said matter-of-factly. She glanced over her shoulder. "But it doesn't seem like the poor lady will be resurrecting, does it?"

"No, I suppose not." Then again, I'd never seen anyone transform into a vampire before my eyes. Perhaps they seemed like a drained husk for hours beforehand.

"So Valentin thinks it was a vampire for certain." It wasn't really a question. I knew Lord Aleksandru was taking vampire venom samples.

Vampire venom samples... Draven needed to know what was going on!

"Ginny, do you promise to warn everyone?" I asked, flipping Broomie around and getting on her shaft. "I need to talk to Draven."

"You do that," she said. "Talk some sense into him. I eventually tried talking to him, first in his coffin and then once he woke up, tried to get him to open up about why he was being so sullen, but he barely batted an eyelash at me appearing in front of him. He said he was a busy man and had 'no time to trifle with fickle ghosts.'" She'd tried imitating him during those last few words. "I *never*! I wasted too much time talking to him, I tell you that much. Not even Lazarus could get the vampire to open up. The surly vampire practically *ran into* the poor reaper in the parlor hallway at dusk as Laz was headed back down to the basement and Draven was on his way out."

Ginny cocked her head at those words, as if thinking over them. I was busy wincing on Draven's behalf.

"Though why was Lazarus coming back from the front door around that time? Sheriff Roan had swung by earlier to borrow the hearse, but he wasn't back yet. Then again, I was entirely occupied with that rude excuse for a vampire. And *he's* supposed to seduce victims?" She scoffed. "Lazarus told me he had work to do to prepare for the arrival of the body and that I should wait by the door for the sheriff and alert me as soon as he arrived, and not too long after that, Sheriff Birch showed up with the hearse and the victim. I suppose we've been having a parade of guests *all day* here."

If I didn't leave now, Ginny was liable to talk all evening. "Don't forget," I said, taking to the air at last. "Warn everyone Lazarus might be out of sorts."

"You can count on me, darling. Dahlia." She smiled sheepishly.

"It's good seeing you." I offered her a smile. "You don't need to hide anymore, okay? We've all done dark things here. Almost all of us paranormals."

"Thank you," she said quietly. "I wasn't sure I deserved a second chance."

"If you don't, then none of us do." I adjusted my witch's hat to affix it tighter across my head. Then I took off to the skies on Broomie's back.

Chapter Eighteen

The vampire manor was dark as I approached, though that wasn't a strange thing even on a normal night. Vampires flourished in dim light.

Still, there was something foreboding about the place as Broomie and I descended and landed on the front porch steps. Through the drawing room window, there was a bright, artificial light. That was off for a vampire, who generally avoided that kind of stark light almost as much as they would the sun.

I knocked on the door, popping open the bat door with my hand preemptively. "Draven?"

The flutter of stony wings preceded the appearance of Roderick's face through the bat door opening. He was frowning. I'd never seen him so irritated. The door opened, Roderick pulling it back by the handle.

"Hi, Roderick," I told him. "Did you find Draven?"

His free hand, no longer holding the newer video game system Grady had bought him, gestured behind him into the drawing room, bathed in the bright light.

He took off, and I followed him. That light bursting out into the darkness was harsh enough to even cause *me* to squint, let alone a vampire.

My eyes adjusted to the otherwise dark room as Roderick flew up to the mantelpiece over the lit fireplace, perching above the piano and looking down sourly.

The decades-old TV, complete with rabbit ears and a thin-leg stand, which Grady had mentioned bringing out from the vampires' attic, was now in front of the high-backed red chair Draven had chosen to slouch in the last time I'd been here. Only instead of finding Draven in his vampire form, his bat form was flapping its wings and floating slightly over the chair cushion, his long, spindly, furry fingers pushing buttons on an old-fashioned video game controller as a little sprite jumped and dodged obstacles on the flickering TV screen. At one point, the digital man punched a fireball. With his bare fist. But it worked, and the fireball exploded. The game was vaguely familiar.

"Draven?" I stood beside the setup, Broomie in hand.

With a grinding stone sound, Roderick shook his head from atop the fireplace.

Bending slightly, I examined the TV. Draven was still playing. I was sure I'd played this game with Faine when we'd been kids. Little sprite bird enemies were flying down at a generic pixelized man, and the man kept leaping up different-sized platforms, avoiding getting dive-bombed by the birds with a kick or a punch. At the top of the platform awaited a giant, pixelated owl who swept down at the digital-man, causing him to make a little pained face and flash in and out of existence, landing on his rear end. The owl dove again.

Draven was still playing, even though I was right there, clearly in need of his attention.

I waved my free hand in front of the bat. "Draven? Hello? Feel like becoming something that can talk to me?"

The bat squeaked, his little membraned fingers still pushing buttons. I checked the screen. The pixel-man jumped up—once, twice—and punched the owl's white belly, causing the owl to flash and look pained.

I turned back to Draven and waited a moment. No wonder Roderick was frustrated. The vampire was *addicted* to this video game.

I stood between the chair and the TV, my boot catching on one of the wires connecting his controller to the TV set.

The bat's wings flapped harder, his squeaks louder and more shrieking than ever.

Broomie's head swiveled behind me to the TV, then to the bat on the chair, and back. Then, with what could only be called a wicked sort of bristly cackle, she flexed her shaft and slammed it down on one of the cords we'd stepped over.

The power cord.

The TV's display turned to static, grinding and piercingly loud in the cold darkness of the vampire manor.

The bat's shrieks and wing flaps were at war with the TV's static. Even Roderick's stony wings and arms were grinding as the gargoyle moved to cover his pointed ears with his hand. I turned around and spun the dial, shutting the TV off entirely.

The bat flew up off the chair and, with a *poof* and a *blam*, turned into Draven in his vampire form, his feet landing roughly on the wooden floorboards.

There was no mistaking the flaring nostrils, the bags that were even darker than usual under Draven's eyes. He looked… tired. If that were possible for a vampire.

Tired and angry.

"Broomhilde!" His voice grew louder, then his sharp teeth ground together for a bit. "I was about to beat my high score!" He stared down my broomstick as if he were looking for some twigs to serve as kindling.

I pulled her back out of his reach and she slipped out of my hand, flying over toward Roderick and wrapping herself around his shoulders.

Draven's eyes followed her. I stepped between him and her warily, though Draven's expression softened when he looked at where she'd landed. "When did you all get here…?"

"Roderick's been here at least an hour," I said. "Broomie and I just came in."

"An hour…?" Draven cradled his chin thoughtfully, as if thinking. "It can be difficult to tell when I'm in my chiropteran form."

Roderick's stony head shook back and forth, his own anger still present on his face. He must have been frustrated over being ignored. Roderick took off, Broomie still around his neck, and flew in bobbing motions out of the room and to the dining room, where he seemed to have left his modern video game system. He snatched it and sat down on one of the chairs, bringing another bright screen to life in the darkness of the vampire manor.

He must not have sensed any danger from the vampire, even if he *was* tired and grumpy.

"Draven, can we talk?" I turned back to the vampire and held my hand out to his shoulder, softly directing him toward the piano bench so we could sit side by side. My eyes were adjusting to the darkness now, the flames of the fire just enough to guide my way. I wondered if Roderick had started the blaze or if Draven had.

Draven moved numbly, allowing himself to be seated at the bench. He hugged himself and rocked back and forth.

He looked exhausted. But there was more to it than that. Something was eating at him. Something like... a feeding gone wrong?

No. It just couldn't have been.

"So close," he said, mumbling to himself. "Almost broke my record..." He looked back and forth. "Where's the handheld?"

Back at the funeral parlor, but I didn't want him to rush over there, which he might have done in the mood he was in. "Draven, have you slept at all? Were you playing games all night?"

Draven chewed his lip and faced forward. "I wanted to keep playing that one"—he nodded toward the TV—"but I knew I couldn't fit it in my coffin. But I ran out of batteries for the handheld. And I knew Qarinah would be coming..."

"You decided to move into the funeral parlor for the rest of the week, didn't you?" I asked. "You moved in and *then* asked Lazarus—"

"You're the one who told me he'd ventured outside for the first time in years." He sighed. "It put the idea in my head. That way, I wouldn't have to talk to Qarinah."

I resisted the temptation to *tsk*. Avoiding the vampire like a sister to him because she dared to leave him to get married? And not even leave him to go far. She'd still see him at work every day.

"Saw her anyway," he said gruffly.

"Who? Qarinah?"

Draven had no qualms about letting out a *tsk*. "She texted me with her smartphone to ask to meet. To talk. I ignored her, but she ran into me anyway when I was hovering near First Taste, waiting for Lazarus to exit. I didn't expect her to leave before he did. Smartphones, they have video games!" He looked around. "Where is mine? Did I leave it… I must have left it in my coffin." He cursed under his breath. "Where's yours?" He perked up. "Your lover boy bought you one now, too, yes?"

I realized with a start, that as was too often the case with me, I'd left it at home. I'd taken it out before I'd left to meet up with the Mahajans and Roderick. But even if I'd had it, I wasn't about to hand it to him to let him get engrossed in a game. "Draven, focus. This is important. What time did you bump into Qarinah?"

Draven fluffed his hand in the air. "I don't know. I was anxious to get back to the games, but I knew I only had so long to arrange this move to avoid her." He bit his lip. "She caught me before I moved my coffin, which just made me want to speed things up and move in, even before I got Lazarus's permission." So he *had* attempted to get permission first.

"You spoke with Qarinah?" My heart fluttered.

"Yes, well, I…" He rubbed the side of his nose and leaned forward, clutching his hands together over his lap. "I'd had a long night. I'd gone to Creekdale—"

"To look for a game for Faine's old video game system," I finished for him.

Draven narrowed his eyes on me. "Yes… The normie there, she said they hadn't carried such games *anywhere* since before the store existed." He fluffed his hand in the air. "She told me to check the Internets, the online bay stores. I told her I had no time to fiddle with such things. I was there for a transaction of money for goods, and if she could not help me, I would not come back. Not ever."

I was *sure* the video game store owner would feel the loss of his patronage.

"What time was this?"

"I don't know." He sneered. "Why would you ask me that?"

So he wasn't aware of the murder?

"Around one o'clock," he said gruffly. "Maybe closer to two. Two-thirty?" He cocked his head.

The vampire had no idea. And some of those times put him near the site of the murder at far too close to the right time.

"I flew home. And then I realized… I could have bought batteries. *Those* at least are not extinct." He tossed his hands in the air. "They were *right there*! At the counter! And I was too annoyed by her suggestions I go fish at the bay on the nets that I completely forgot about them."

"You didn't… stop at the park afterward?"

He leaned back and stared at me. "No, I did not *go for a stroll in the park*. Why would I do such a thing? I had the idea about moving my things, and I was eager to get started on it. I waited outside of First Taste for Lazarus to exit and that's when I got the text from Qarinah. I didn't think ignoring her would cause her to *come outside* or I would have replied to stall her."

"Wait, so let's back up… Or go forward in the story, I suppose. Qarinah clearly wanted to talk to you. When you didn't reply to her text, she decided to seek you out in person, leaving the pub unattended, from what I hear." At least now I knew what had drawn her away, even if no one could tell me *when* this had been. It was my turn to look around for Draven's smartphone, but it was nowhere in sight. I was just getting used to the things, but didn't they keep track of when messages were sent?

I'd look at that later.

"You can imagine I was flustered when she stepped outside to find me hovering nearby."

"Flustered? Around *Qarinah*?"

"Yes, well…" If Draven could blush, I wondered if he'd be doing so now. "I knew it would be awkward. I knew I had said some things that were… unkind."

"Oh?" I let that comment hang there in the air. Now wasn't the ideal time to get the two to make up. And even if Draven was clearly in the wrong, the last thing I needed was to have him on the defensive.

"So I… I told her I would talk more only if she did me a favor."

I arched a brow, still leaning my elbow against the top of the piano. "What kind of favor?"

"To go back to Creekdale, where the video game store was due to be open all night—I learned that on my smartphone, when I was looking for the nearest such specialty establishment—and buy—"

"You some batteries!" I practically squealed. Yes, that made sense now. The video game store had had *three* strange visitors last night. A nun and two vampires. Then it had been *Qarinah* who had dropped the batteries in the park on live TV. That put her there around 6:30 in the morning. Long after the crime had occurred, and if Doc Day and Doctor Corbin were right, that was the only length of time she'd been gone.

So Qarinah's venom would likely clear her of culpability, assuming they found venom on Sister Mary Katherine's body at all.

A small sense of relief flowed inside me, though I'd never been too worried about Qarinah being accused of the murder.

Not as much as I'd been worried about Draven.

"And what happened when she brought them back?" I asked.

Draven shrugged, but at least he had the decency to look down at his feet and appear a bit sheepish. "By then I had run into Lien and asked her to move my coffin. Lazarus, of all people, had some batteries at his parlor. I found them in his basement before I went back to meet him outside of First Taste. Even though I knew I'd be cutting it close to dawn, I wanted to be sure I killed some time—that I didn't run into Qarinah outside of the pub again. I put them in my handheld system and placed it inside the coffin."

"You sent Qarinah all the way to Creekdale—"

"Just to get her out of my hair." He ran a hand through his wavy, golden locks and sighed. "I am a terrible brother. I know that." His gaze flicked to the TV. "These games… They make my brain numb. They make me feel busy, and not so angry."

"I don't know. You got pretty angry at Broomie."

Draven looked over toward the dining room. "That was because of my high score. I only… Is that another video game system?" He grew straighter, perking up.

Broomie was leaning over Roderick's shoulder, nodding along at the bright light as Roderick stuck his stony tongue out and mashed the buttons on the screens.

After seeing Draven and now this, maybe I'd have to start worrying about Roderick and video game addiction. Maybe we *could* just make it something the kids played while we had our Spooky Games Club meetings. Maybe we could all play them together, make the games a big event to look forward to and not something kids and vampires squeezed into every spare second of their day. But that was a concern for another time.

I leaped to my feet and stood between Draven and his view of the dining room.

"Draven, you were angry last night. Angry at Qarinah. At me. At every person who ever…" My gaze flicked to the painting of his mother on the wall. My heartbeats grew louder. It was true there was quite a resemblance between this woman and the nun I'd seen on Lazarus's table, but it wasn't a perfect match.

Could the differences be explained by the fact that the woman in this panting was healthy, the woman on the table deathly pale and drained?

"Yes, I am aware." Draven crossed his arms and legs. So he wasn't softening on any of that quite yet.

"Then you were angry at the store owner for not having the games you wanted."

Draven *tsked* again. "Faine only had this one game, you see, and I *have* gotten to see its appeal, but it's just that Grady had mentioned something about a *vampire* game set in castles and it sounded quite interesting. I hoped to try it. Though he tells me the vampires are the *villains* in that one."

That actually rang a bell. I wondered if one of the Mahajan boys had had *Castlevania*.

"In any case…" I gestured at him. "You haven't been feeding enough lately.

He crossed his arms even tighter and looked away. "I manage. I'm on a diet."

"Is it possible your hunger and anger got the better of you?" My voice grew soft, a terrified whisper. "That as you flew over the park, you spotted a nun and—"

"A *nun?*" Draven whipped around to look at me, his facial expression twisted. "Is this some sort of setup for a joke? I was there in the middle of the night—"

"And so was a nun." I took a deep breath. "Draven, there's a member of the Vampire High Council in town."

Draven flicked a hand in the air and looked away. "Yes. For the wedding. Because perhaps Qarinah will change Roan into one of our kind." He made a disgusted sound.

"Yes, well, right now he's more concerned about solving a murder. A murder of a feeding gone wrong, a dead nun in Creekdale."

What little color was left on Draven's face seemed to drain further as he stared up at me. His jaw dropped open just slightly. "There's been another vampire murder? This time in Creekdale?"

"A nun was the victim. She went to that video game store and then was attacked in the park."

"I never… She wasn't at that store when I was." His voice grew quiet. "I did not feed. I have not fed in days—"

A pounding on the front door drew our attention. Even Roderick jumped up, putting his game down on the table.

The door opened with a frightening, drawn-out creak.

"May I present His Excellency Aleksandru!" said an accented French voice that could only be Valentin's.

With a loud, heavy set of footfalls, Lord Aleksandru himself walked in, spotting us both in the drawing room almost immediately. "Draven, Son of Ravana!" His voice boomed across the empty space. "You are to submit to a venom sample immediately! Vampire venom has been found in a murder victim's body, and the sample supplied by Qarinah, Daughter of Ravana, has cleared her name." His red-rimmed eyes practically *burned* in the dark as they narrowed on Draven at the piano. "That leaves only one suspect, and I have a feeling I know how the sample matching shall go." He turned slightly to Valentin, who clambered up beside him. "Arrest him at once!"

Valentin rubbed his hands together in front of him. "With pleasure, my master."

Chapter Nineteen

"Wait a minute," I said. "You can't just assume Draven committed a crime—"

Through the open door, behind Lord Aleksandru and Valentin, in walked Mayor Abdel, Chione, Sheriff Roan, and then Qarinah. Their faces were all in various states of distress, Qarinah clinging to Roan's sleeve between two long, delicate fingers, as if needing him to serve as an anchor. Roan held a corked flask in one hand. It had a dark, blood-red liquid in it, though just enough to fill about a tenth of the small bottle.

"Yes, I agree, Lord Aleksandru." Mayor Abdel straightened his tie as he walked farther into the foyer. "We simply must have proof before you accuse one of our citizens."

Roan grimaced and held up the bottle. "Once we extracted this venom sample from the corpse, we compared it to Qarinah's venom sample and she was cleared. I know that means Draven's the only vampire who lives in town left. But process of elimination just won't stand. Frankly, Qarinah and Draven aren't the *only two* vampires in town at the moment, are they?"

Valentin gasped, so loudly, he could have knocked me over. Lord Aleksandru simply turned his head, but it was such a deliberate movement, his thin, blood-red lips in such a dour line, it was clear he intended to convey his intense disapproval.

Qarinah dropped her grip on Roan's shirt and stepped between her fiancé and the visiting member of the Vampire High Council. "What Roan means is—he's a man of the law, and the law must have evidence. He means no offense, of course." Her gaze flickered over my shoulder, and I turned to find Draven there sullenly leaning against the doorjamb leading to the drawing room. His red-rimmed eyes flickered to the floor at Qarinah's gaze. She straightened, tossing her head back. "You won't arrest my brother without proof."

"Very well." Lord Aleksandru waved his fingers at Valentin. "Of course, proof would have been gathered in due course. I was merely attempting to allay any attempts at the fugitive fleeing."

"He's not a fugitive!" I shouted.

"I'll not flee." Draven stepped forward. Roderick shuffled into the room behind him, his game system forgotten, Broomie still on the gargoyle's shoulders. Draven's mouth widened, revealing a gleaming fang, as he stepped toward Valentin. "Take the sample."

"Draven, but you couldn't have—" started Qarinah.

"We shall see," said Lord Aleksandru brusquely. "Valentin, you may take a sample from me as well." He stuck out one gleaming incisor of his own.

Valentin gasped, one hand holding his overly large coat open, the other gripping a few flasks he'd pulled out from within a deep pocket. "I could *never!*"

"You will and you must." Lord Aleksandru's dark eyebrow arched as he glared at our sheriff. "That way, no one will object to any arrests because *all three vampires* in the vicinity of the crime have been thoroughly examined for a match."

Roan nodded glumly. I wondered what was going through his head. Was he jeopardizing his future with Qarinah by offending the representative from the Vampire High Council?

Qarinah went over to Draven and whispered softly to him. He shook his head.

Valentin mumbled and fished into the inner lining of his coat, withdrawing any number of flasks from seemingly endlessly deep pockets. I caught a glance of a strangely small-shaped blue one—complete with some kind of label on it, the only one of his little bottles with a label—and another with a tint of pink that gleamed in the flicker of firelight from the neighboring parlor, and finally, he produced two empty flasks. "Is there somewhere private we may extract the venom?" he asked.

I remembered when I'd asked Draven for some venom for a potion, how he'd insisted on having some privacy. The process had been slow-going and had drained him of energy. I studied the vampire's face now. He looked already far too drained of energy.

But didn't that mean he couldn't have gorged himself on blood? Wouldn't he have, at the very least, looked healthier?

Draven stepped past Qarinah, offering her a brief nod, and gestured upstairs. "This way."

Roan stepped forward. He looked to Abdel and nodded. "I'm afraid there will have to be witnesses to the extraction and the matching again."

Lord Aleksandru's eyes narrowed. "Extracting a vampire's venom is one of the most intimate things—"

"I'm sorry." Abdel straightened. "We must insist. We witnessed the comparison of Qarinah's venom to the sample at the funeral parlor. We shall witness this as well."

Did Roan and Abdel not trust the Vampire High Council, then? Were they hoping to stop any attempts to swamp the samples?

Good.

"Very well." Lord Aleksandru strode toward the stairway, which was covered in dust and cobwebs.

The vampires had little use for the bedrooms upstairs. "But the rest of the Vampire High Council will hear of this. Luna Lane is building *quite* the reputation abroad for its heinous crimes."

My hand clutched into a fist as the five men ascended the stairs single file. Chione moved closer to Qarinah and me as Broomie soared over into my hand and Roderick shuffled over to stand at my side.

"I am sure this will clear his name," said Chione, though she worried at her lip a little.

"But it had to have been *some* vampire," said Qarinah softly. "We both saw the body."

So the party had managed to safely examine Sister Mary Katherine's corpse—and come to the conclusion it had to have been a vampire responsible.

"We saw Ginny," said Qarinah softly to me. "She told us she ran into you, explained about Lazarus's transformation scaring you away."

"She's back." Chione shook her head.

"She never left," I said. "She was just ashamed to come out."

"He's not wrong, you know," said Chione. "Luna Lane… A lot of terrible things have been happening here."

"*This* murder was in Creekdale," I protested, fully aware that I had emphasized "this."

Both Qarinah and Chione looked down at that.

I supposed the location of the crime didn't matter if the accusing glares all centered on Luna Lane.

"I was glad to see her," Qarinah said.

"Me, too," admitted Chione quietly. "She seems… sweet on Lazarus?"

"Yes." Qarinah let out a little giggle despite it all.

She did? Some sleuth I was.

"Qarinah," I said, eager to tie up the loose ends of my amateur investigation, "I've been trying to piece together everyone's movements last night. Draven told me you texted him to talk."

"Yes." She *tsked*.

"What time was that?" I asked.

"Five-thirty, thereabouts. I bumped into him about quarter to six on the sidewalk outside of the pub."

I supposed I didn't need to check their smart-phones for the time stamps, then, if she remembered. Unfortunately, that still meant there were a couple of hours of Draven's time unaccounted for. Even if we could find out exactly when he'd shown at the video game store, that didn't mean he hadn't been in Creekdale's park in the hours between then and when Qarinah had run into him.

Most likely, he'd been alone playing video games here in the manor at that time. Which would mean he had no alibi.

Bananaberries.

Qarinah continued. "I left First Taste for at least an hour, since he sent me on a wild goose chase."

Chione arched a brow, as if wondering if actual geese had been involved.

"Long after the murder," I said. "He asked you to get batteries for the game system Roderick had given him, correct?"

Qarinah nodded. "It seemed a silly enough task, but I was desperate for him to give me a chance to talk things out. If games were soothing his jealousy and irritability, then fine, I would help. I did notice all the ruckus around the park, but I tried my best to avoid witnesses and get back quickly."

"I think you lost a battery," I said, explaining about the bat on the news report.

"That was me." She sighed. "I wasn't thinking clearly. I was very stressed, and there were so many batteries to hold in my little bat feet." She flexed her hand, as if to demonstrate. "It didn't matter that I was one short, though. He'd moved his coffin out by the time I got back." She swallowed, looking around, as if witnessing the very memories of this place unfold before her eyes. "I knew what he was like, but I didn't think he'd react like *this*. And now, with this crisis… I don't know if we'll get married this weekend."

"Don't be ridiculous." I patted her shoulder. "The sample-taking will clear his name. And then we'll figure out what really happened long before this weekend."

I hoped.

We made our way back toward the dining room, where Roderick picked up his game and slid back on one of the chairs at the table. Qarinah sat next to him, looking over his shoulder, speaking to him softly.

"What do you think of the visitors in town?" I asked Chione.

She grimaced. "I don't think I should say. As a member of town hall, it's my duty to welcome all paranormal visitors." She nodded, as if to convince herself.

"I heard you chauffeured Valentin around town earlier today?" I wondered if he'd been annoying the entire time.

"I gave him a ride," she said. "After we met him at town hall. He asked to be taken to the funeral parlor for Vampire Council business regarding the victim's body if it were indeed to be moved there and then to Vogel's for some shopping. But I didn't wait for him to finish at Vogel's. He said he would take a while, so I left."

Take a while…? To buy eye medicine, was it? I thought back to the man's wild, wide eyes. They hadn't appeared dry, but then again, perhaps he'd been using the medicine he'd found. The expired medicine.

That had been the little bottle with the label on it in his pocket, surely, now that I thought about it. It had been right next to something… I couldn't quite remember what I'd remarked upon then. "You didn't give him a lift back downtown, then? Or to Doc Day's, where they're staying?"

Chione shook her head. "I don't know how he got back. Walked, perhaps. My grandfather needed me back at town hall anyway. And I was not about to argue with that man if I didn't need to." She shuddered. "He said something… that didn't quite sit right with me."

"What do you mean?"

"Well, he treated me like a servant the entire time." Her eyes narrowed. "Which I didn't appreciate. But Grandfather was insistent I treat him as an honored guest, so I said nothing. That is… until we pulled up in front of Vogel's."

"When he told you he would take a while to do his shopping?"

"Yes, well, that's just it. He insisted I wait for him at first."

And he'd changed his mind? "But you didn't want to?"

"No," she spat. "But I was willing to. But then he saw your house and he asked if a witch lived there."

What had he been doing looking at *my house*? And what about my house was particularly witchy? I'd taken care of the flora overgrowth some months back.

"I told him you did, but that you were most likely not home, as I'd just seen you earlier that morning. If he wanted you for an enchantment, he could tell Abdel, and we'd arrange something——"

"I have *no desire* to perform an enchantment for that man."

"He said he had no wish to work with *you*." She chewed on her bottom lip. "I didn't like how he talked about you. He got out of the car, then told me I could go, that he would take too long shopping to have me idling there waiting."

"And then you left?"

"Immediately. I saw him standing on the sidewalk in front of Vogel's, watching me go." She winced. "And then I didn't see him for several hours."

"I guess I don't want to know what he said exactly, right?"

She shook her head. "I do not like people like that man." Then she crossed her arms and started to take mindless strolls around the downstairs rooms.

Her story about Valentin's rudeness didn't surprise me. Though I still found it odd he'd pinpointed my house at a glance.

What had it been? The enchanted, floating Christmas lights? But I could have enchanted those for anyone.

Still, I may have been the last one in town to still have her holiday lights up. Without any other neighborhood lights for them to blend in with, they could be like a beacon that said, "A witch lives here."

We kept waiting. At one point, Roderick handed Qarinah his video game system and she smiled, slouching against the back of her chair and holding the system between both hands, her arms outstretched across the table. The bright light danced off her wan skin as she pushed buttons, her chin flat against the table.

Something about vampires and video games didn't seem like a great combination. Or maybe it was just the thing they needed to empty their minds of stress.

Roderick waddled up to me after a while. I stared up at the portrait of Draven's mother in the parlor as Chione took a turn through the room.

"Chione," I said, calling her over. "Do you notice anything about this woman?"

Chione cocked her head and strode closer. She looked up. In the firelight, I supposed it was a bit hard to see. "WOLG." I waved my free hand toward the portrait. My hand let out a soft, illuminating glow.

Chione immediately recoiled. "Why, she's… But no. She can't be. Qarinah!" she called over her shoulder.

Qarinah shuffled into the room, Roderick's modern video game system in one hand at her side. She looked drained—not as badly as Draven, but I wondered if she'd had a rough day trying to sleep alone in this house, even before she'd found out about the murder. "That's Draven's mother," she said simply. "His *human* mother from the very old days. She——"

She went quiet, her jaw a little dropped.

"She looks like Sister Mary Katherine?" I supplied for the both of them.

They exchanged a glance and nodded.

"Not perfectly," Chione said quickly. "Why, I think *that* woman's nose is thinner."

"It could be the effect of a sunken face," added Qarinah quietly.

"But it can't *literally* be his mother. He said she died a human," I said.

Or was that just what he'd *thought* had happened? Hadn't he said himself she'd fallen off a cliff and he'd never been able to bury her?

Didn't that seem suspicious?

But why would she turn into a vampire, despite telling her son she never would, and then not contact him for hundreds of years? It made no sense.

"She could be a descendant," Chione pointed out.

There was that, too. Occasionally, doppelgängers sprung up in family lines. It was a real, borderline paranormal phenomena.

"It still can't be a coincidence she transferred to Creekdale just a month ago." Quickly, I filled them both in on what the news reports had said about the mysterious nun.

Mysterious, indeed. Even the victim's own

convent hadn't been able to fill in the blanks in her history entirely.

"And she liked… video games." My eyes darted to the game at Qarinah's side. "Of course, a nun might be interested in such a thing, but to the point of attending a middle-of-the-night release party without letting her sisters know? Why hide her hobby?"

"Perhaps the convent doesn't approve?" Chione suggested.

Qarinah lifted the video game system and stared at the screen, suddenly tapping buttons, her nose practically pressed up against it. "Nonsense. Many games are harmless fun."

Harmless, indeed. But I'd now seen *two* vampires addicted to video games at inappropriate moments.

Maybe the games really did calm them.

But did that just help prove that Sister Mary Katherine had been a vampire? It would explain her having been hundreds of years old.

"Can vampires die of blood loss?" I asked Qarinah.

She didn't look up from the game. "We have more venom than blood left in our veins," she murmured. "That's why we can't feed off each other."

"But then… If the nun was a vampire, no other vampire could have fed off her!" My voice rose, my knees bouncing. Broomie nodded her brush head emphatically. "It wouldn't have been some hungry vampire not thinking straight and taking too much blood from a nun, whether she gave her consent for a feeding or not. It would be *outright*, first-degree murder."

The word hung heavily in the air, just as a series of harried footfalls broke out at the ceiling.

Waving my hand, I undid the *glow* enchantment.

"I am innocent!" Draven's voice shrieked out from the stairwell.

All of us rushed to the bottom of the stairs, Qarinah setting Roderick's video game system atop the piano as she passed it.

Draven was being escorted down the stairs, his hands behind his back, pinched together tightly by Valentin, who grinned so devilishly, it looked like his smile might break his cheeks.

Behind Valentin strode Lord Aleksandru, his leathery nose in the air.

"Now hold on. Surely, we can still call for a local trial," said Sheriff Roan, tumbling down after him. "It's a local matter."

"A matter concerning vampires requires Transylvania jurisdiction," said Lord Aleksandru. "I simply will not budge on this. Draven, Son of Ravana, is to be confined to his coffin immediately until we can arrange transportation back to the old country."

"*What?*" I said as Draven reached the bottom stairs.

Lord Aleksandru passed Draven and Valentin to hold the front door open.

Valentin attempted to drag Draven out, but the vampire fought back enough to stand in front of me on unsteady feet.

His lip trembled as he looked at me. "I didn't do it." His voice was hoarse. His gaze flicked to Qarinah. "I am so sorry, Qarinah. You are my dearest sister, and I wish you every happiness. Please forgive my selfishness! I swear I did not commit this crime, but I did… I did hurt you! And for that, I am sorry!"

"Enough," spat Valentin. He wrestled the taller, thinner vampire toward the door. "We are aware you moved your coffin in an attempt to escape justice, but we know where it is and we shall bring you there at once!"

"It wasn't to *escape justice*!" Draven protested, but Valentin shoved him out the open door, Lord Aleksandru on their heels.

"Draven!" cried Qarinah, reaching a hand toward him.

Roan slipped in to stop her from following after them, Abdel hurrying down the stairs and Chione rushing to join him as they followed the parade out to the front porch. "You must allow us some more time." Abdel's voice carried back through the open door. "Confine him, yes, but—" The rest of what he had to say went quiet.

"Draven!" screamed Qarinah again.

Broomie let out a soft, bristly coo and rubbed my cheek as Roderick leaned against my thigh. I reached my free hand to pat his head, nudging my broomstick with my head.

"I don't believe it," I said. "None of us do." I spoke for my quiet companions, and they didn't protest.

"Neither do I!" said Qarinah.

"Qarinah. Lia." Roan sighed and let go of his fiancée, taking off his hat to run a forearm over his temple peppered with sweat. "Abdel and I witnessed the collection and comparison ourselves. There is no doubt. The sample venom taken from the body of that nun—which I never once let out of my own hands—it matched Draven's venom. Perfectly."

I shook my head, stumbling backward.

There had to be another explanation.

"Perhaps he was just too hungry to think straight," said Roan quietly. "Too upset—"

"No." I'd determined the "feeding gone wrong" theory just couldn't have explained things. Could it have?

There was only one way to find out. Taking a deep breath, I flipped Broomie over and took a seat on her shaft. I exchanged a look with Roderick, and he nodded his stony head, as if he understood my intentions.

"Lia?" Roan asked. "What are you—"

But I didn't want to explain myself and have him try to stop me. I shot through the open door and took off into the sky on Broomie's back, Roderick fluttering his stone wings behind us.

We were headed to the Holy Home of Mother Mary. In Creekdale. Beyond the safety of Lien's barrier around this city.

It would keep other witches out—but it wasn't supposed to keep me in.

Lien had just counted on me being sane enough to stay within the safety of her protection.

But I would never be sane enough to prioritize my safety over the freedom of a friend.

Chapter Twenty

s I flew through the frigid air of the crisp, winter night, the moonlight bouncing off the fallen snow and brightly lighting the way, I went over everything I knew and everything that felt off to me.

Sister Mary Katherine had only arrived in Creekdale a month ago, and her past was a mystery, though she was from Europe.

She may have been a vampire, or at least related to Draven in some way.

Most vampires came from Europe.

If she was a vampire, that explained—at least to me—her love for video games, now that I'd observed a couple of the fanged paranormals losing themselves in such games. And if she *was* a vampire, whoever had drained her of her venom-blood had absolutely intended to kill her.

Still, she could have just been a normie who'd loved games. But I didn't think so.

Some other things were off. Draven's venom being found on her wound. I *knew* he was innocent, so there had to be a different explanation. People I trusted had witnessed the venom being extracted from the victim's wound, and from both Draven's and Lord Aleksandru's fangs for comparison.

And between the venom being extracted from the wound and arriving at the funeral parlor, Roan had kept charge of it. I trusted him not to pull any tricks.

So much for the hope that Valentin had done any sleight of hand and swapped out a different venom sample to compare to Draven's in that overly stuffed coat of his full of bottles.

Still, there was a lot off about the vampire's assistant. Perhaps even more so than Lord Aleksandru himself.

Could the assistant be working without his master's knowledge? To frame Draven somehow? How? *Why?*

Well, I couldn't rule out the Vampire High Council being in on the ploy, either. But Lord Aleksandru had had a lot less opportunity to mess with things since the murder, being stuck in his coffin at daybreak. Still, he could have ordered his assistant to do any number of things.

Of course. Who else would Valentin listen to, other than his master?

And there was that smudge on the bathroom faucet at Doc Day's house after Valentin had used it this morning. Did that have anything to do with this?

Why was the man a vampire assistant, anyway? Did he hope to become a vampire someday? Did he love feeding his master, feeling that sense of euphoria that came with the ritual when performed just shy of blood madness?

Flying outside of Lien's barrier around Luna Lane was a bad enough idea on its own. Flying outside of it without my father's onyx pike transformed into a dagger—one of the few things known to hurt witches—was downright suicidal.

But if I went home to get it, I knew Lien would stop me from enacting my plan.

Besides, what were the odds the witches were ready to pounce the moment I flew outside of the town? Lien had been snooping around Creekdale for weeks and still hadn't caught sight of them, just sensed them nearby.

Broomie's brush head shivered from behind me as we reached the edge of the woods where I knew Lien's barrier ended.

"I know, Broomie," I told her, my words turning to mist in the air. "But we won't be long. We'll find out whatever we can to help Draven, as fast as we can."

Without slowing down, I nudged her through. I could feel the barrier as if it were gossamer threads in the air, tendrils of the enchantment sticking to my face.

I looked over my shoulder to make sure Roderick didn't have trouble getting through, but he hardly slowed down as he pushed through the invisible barrier. It was just supposed to repel witches, after all.

Broomie shook her bristles again, bringing up, I realized, an important point.

"I know," I told her. "There's no way Lien didn't sense that. She'll come find us as soon as possible—which means we don't have long to investigate before she starts trying to drag us back."

Roderick's stony brow furrowed and he picked up the pace. We flew off over the remainder of trees, the faint lights of downtown Creekdale twinkling into view just beyond. Creekdale wasn't a metropolitan area or anything, though it was larger than Luna Lane. Still, the lights weren't numerous at this time of evening, and it was more the fact that they bounced off the surrounding snow that gave the place the illusion of sparkling in the moonlight.

A strip of stores and restaurants surrounded a block-wide park, easier to see in detail with the bare branches of trees in winter offering little cover for the trails. Tracks through the snow of a little hill on one side of the park showcased countless children's boots and sleds having trodden through. On one corner, though, there was a wide, billowing plastic barrier of yellow tape denoting a crime scene, across from what was clearly the video game store I'd heard so much about—closed, like most of the stores around this area in the midst of the evening, though there were some pubs and restaurants still open. I flew toward a towering pine tree for cover from prying eyes when the door to a pub burst open and a couple of people headed toward a car parked at the end of the block, clutching at the fronts of their jackets as if to hold them together tighter against the cold.

I landed on one of the pine tree boughs and waited for them to leave, Roderick landing beside me. His eyes darted eagerly to the video game store, but his face sunk when he noticed it was closed.

"We'll get you more games," I promised him. "But right now, there are more important things to deal with."

Roderick locked eyes with me and nodded, his eyes growing laser-focused on the scene below.

The sound of the car's engine starting up, the car driving away, signaled it was okay for me to peek out. I noticed barriers at the nearest entrance to the park and wondered if there were other barriers all around the park and if that accounted for the lack of other people here, or if the later hour on a week-night was enough.

I slid again on Broomie's back, hovering over the murder scene alongside Roderick, neither of us touching foot to the ground so as not to disturb the snow.

There was an outline of a human figure, complete with what I imagined to be the flap of fabric from the nun's veil beside where her head may have been.

What there wasn't—and it would have been immediately noticeable against the pure-white snow, even with the scores of footprints that had to belong to investigators—was blood.

"WOLG," I said softly, making my hand glow. Copious amounts of blood would have been impossible to miss, even in just the moonlight bouncing off the snow. But I couldn't find any. No small dots, no rusty brown or bright red.

"Could a vampire have really drunk *that much* blood without making a mess?" I asked Broomie and Roderick.

Broomie's brush head grew stiff and Roderick stuck his stony tongue out. I realized I was being rather grotesque. Perhaps Roderick was still too young to be dealing with these things, paranormal creature or not.

Then again, how fast did they age? How many years could my gargoyle father have walked this Earth before my mother had fallen in love with him?

Best not to think about it.

Lien had insisted most gargoyles sprang to life as full-grown men. Always men, too. Roderick appearing as a small boy had something to do with my lack of control over my power.

But Lien and I had been practicing, and Roderick was my gargoyle protector. I'd need him here since I was so determined to come here on my own.

I floated over the site, continuing to wave my lighted hand over the scene. There were so many footprints that it was hard to even tell which ones might have belonged to Sister Mary Katherine and which to the perpetrator. Roderick flew over toward the path nearby that wove its way through the park and pointed down.

I headed over. It was a footprint. Long but thin, and beside it was two little lines in the snow, just about an inch apart. The similar footprint beside it was just the same. They led to the path and back to the outline of the body. I looked back and forth, following the trail.

"They'll have marked the important stuff," I said. "Good eye." The little thin lines were probably where the yellow rectangular markers human investigators used to mark important clues to a crime scene had once been. They'd likely gotten all of their photographs and taken the markers away by now.

These seemed to mark Sister Mary Katherine's footsteps. Or another average-height, thin woman.

But there were other larger shoeprints, too, that were still thin enough and might have belonged to a woman. Those hadn't been marked with the lines. "A policewoman's?" I ventured.

Though it'd be odd for one to be wearing wedge heels.

I looked down at the sole of one of my own lace-up winter boots. It wasn't too far off from something like this.

My mom had worn these boots once.

Lien had similar boots, only in burnt orange.

Lien would have told me if she'd been on the ground investigating, right?

Or would she have? I checked over my shoulder, as if I might be able to see her zooming over on Broomhelen already. She did a lot of things alone. The most she ever talked to me was to help in my training or otherwise berate me and my town.

I floated around, still searching for blood. However the woman had died, there should have been some, right?

Unless the cause of her death had been internal.

But even normie doctors wouldn't have missed that, right?

Checking both ways for witnesses, I floated upward a bit. Down the road was the rounded steeple of the chapel that was part of Holy Home of Mother Mary, and not far beyond that was the Creekdale hospital Doc Day would take our patients to for some extra care whenever necessary. It was rather large for a fairly small town, but I supposed it was the closest hospital for miles in any direction, as far as I knew.

I wished I'd brought my phone with. I could

have tried calling Doctor Corbin again, even if it was getting a bit late. But did I expect him to know there'd been some sort of mistake—or cover-up? He hadn't filed the initial report, only told me what the file had said.

Still, if he'd known to snoop around a bit and take a closer look, might he have found something off about the report?

I guided Broomie closer to the snow, searching for men's shoeprints marked by the lines indicating the police had considered them evidence. No other shoeprints besides the ones I'd pegged as the nun's had been marked at all. And all the ones that seemed to belong to men's feet, well, none were the fancy, punk-rock patent leather shoes I knew Draven to always wear. They all had treads.

True, even he'd admitted he'd been a bat for the trek back and forth to Creekdale. But if he'd fed—if *any* vampire had fed—there would have been suspicious shoeprints around the body in at least *one* place. More if the victim had fought back at all, surely.

The snow was disturbed around the body's silhouette, but that seemed to be largely from investigators poking around. There weren't any indications Sister Mary Katherine had rolled around, fighting off her attacker.

I tapped a finger to my lip. "Let's assume she was a normie and she knew about vampires—or just was so holy and kind, she didn't care much when she found out they exist," I told Broomie and Roderick. "A vampire asks for a snack." I gestured at my neck. "She obliges. She's still for a moment to allow the vampire to bite her neck." I floated toward the marked footsteps looking for where she might have stood still. There. Right in front of the body's silhouette. Like she'd just... fallen backward.

"The vampire drinks..." I muttered, trying to think it all through. "And drinks so quickly, she just faints? So cleanly, there's no blood splatter anywhere?"

I tapped my neck, floating in circles around the footprints and body print. There was that mark from her nun's veil again. Her nun's veil... The sole image of the nun that had been shared on the news popped into my mind.

She'd had to have taken off her veil and wimple for a vampire to get good access to her neck. It covered her neck entirely, from front to back!

"Say she took the habit off, tucked it under her arm or something. She would have been carrying a bag. She'd bought something at the game store." I searched around for a mark in the snow that might have been a bag. There, beside the figure's right arm. Perhaps. It was hard to tell. "So why is the mark from the habit up here by her head, not her arms or the bag?"

Roderick peered down, examining everything in the shadow of the light.

"Because she wasn't bitten last night," I said. "Despite the fang marks found on her neck."

I gazed off in the direction of the shoeprints. "Let's go confirm whether or not the mysterious Sister Mary Katherine was already a vampire before she died."

A vampire wouldn't have offered herself up for a bite.

A vampire who looked *a lot* like Draven's mother would have certainly been a sight that would have affected Draven. I knew him. He wouldn't have been able to keep that secret—let alone the fact that he'd killed someone. Video game fugue state or no.

"Let's go," I said, pointing in the direction of the Holy Home of Mother Mary. It was the only place I had to investigate the video-game-loving European nun.

And, judging by my occasional spotting of more of those familiar wedge-heel boot prints, it was also the direction the second presumed woman had gone, though the shoeprints disappeared once they hit the sidewalk along the edge of the park. I shook out my hand and dismissed the enchantment lighting it up. Careful to not be seen, I shot up along the nearest pine tree, Roderick on Broomie's tail.

We flew high above the park and headed for the convent.

Chapter Twenty-One

There were a few candles burning in some of the windows of the Holy Home of Mother Mary, but for the most part, the place was dark. Taking a quick look around for signs of any human presence and finding none, I landed Broomie in front of the door leading to the chapel and flipped her around in my hand. Roderick's stony wings grated as he came down in a circular path, landing beside my feet. Before I could even think twice, Roderick had taken hold of the door's handles and opened it. The door opened without protest. Perhaps it was a policy of the nunnery to keep their doors open for those in need or those who wanted to pray.

We slipped inside, pushing the door as little as we dared, and I shut it closed behind us. Even softly, the door made some noise.

A candelabra lit up the pulpit at the end of a

long, stony path between rows of benches. It was an echo of the reception room in the funeral parlor, though grander, with ceilings that could have allowed Broomie and Roderick to comfortably play catch while soaring through the air.

There was a dark figure bent at the pulpit, hands clasped together. She turned. A nun. "Who's there?"

Roderick froze for a moment, then did a little spin in place and actually transformed into the human-looking boy he'd been when I'd first transformed the boulder and summoned him into being.

All this time, and this was the first time I'd seen him take that form.

Only problem was, he was entirely gray from head to toe. The gargoyles the witches had brought with them on the train had looked human, complete with natural skin tones and soft-looking clothes.

Roderick resembled a statue of a boy carved out of rock, complete with stone shirt and slacks. No wings, of course, either.

"Good effort," I whispered to him. I gestured at my pointed hat with Broomie's head. "But I can't really explain this away to most normies, anyway. Let's go. ELBISIVNI." I gestured at the three of us.

Now we shouldn't be seen. For as long as the enchantment would last. Which might not be long, considering this was a fairly new enchantment for me and I hadn't imbibed a power boost potion today. If only I'd kept mine in my pouch and not put it back on the table by the door at home. Then Lien might not have grabbed it for whatever kind of potion stash she was putting together.

"Come on," I said. "I'm looking for her room. I don't know if we'll find anything in here."

Even my whispers were louder than I'd expected in this place.

"Hello?" The nun stood up, grabbing a candle by its stand and holding it nearer her face. "All are welcome here, but please do come into the light. You'll give an old woman a fright."

I reached out and felt Roderick's stony back, pushing him toward a wooden door in the corner. Judging from the layout of this place, that would lead to other buildings.

Roderick's feet clinked against the stone floor, making quiet movement impossible.

"Hello?" the nun said again. She was headed toward the same door we were.

"ETATIVEL," I said under my breath, gesturing at the pulpit as we neared it. It flew into the air.

"Oh!" cried the nun. "My Lord! My Lord, is that you?"

I didn't wait to see if my distraction would go down in history as a sign of communication to normies from the realm beyond. Perhaps it'd be dismissed as one nun's account, late one evening, when she might have been seeing and hearing things in the dark.

I took hold of the door and swung it open, waving my hand and timing the closing of the door with the release of the levitate enchantment. The falling pulpit echoed out into the church with a greater thud than the door closing.

The nun let out a scream.

Wincing, I shuffled down the hallway revealed behind the door. I hoped I hadn't given her too much of a fright.

"Mother Abbess?" called a voice from ahead of us.

The hallway was more of a walkway between buildings, another stone path and windows in an arch like an elongated hothouse. Moonlight bouncing off snow illuminated the way in a pale blue light. A couple of nuns approached from the opposite end, one carrying a candle, the other a flashlight.

I reached out to find Roderick, his form cold and smooth to the touch, and yanked him against one wall to allow the nuns to pass.

The door to the chapel shut behind them, three voices becoming an indistinguishable flutter of conversation. It was a relief to hear the original nun we'd encountered speaking, as that meant I hadn't frightened her too much. Satisfied they were distracted, I stepped forward.

The invisible enchantment on all three of us retreated. I flexed my hand. My energy was getting a bit depleted.

It'd been a long day.

"This way," I whispered to Roderick, sitting on top of Broomie once more and gliding down the rest of the way. Roderick followed behind with stony steps, his brow furrowing, and then he transformed back into his diminutive gargoyle form. At least he *could* turn into a more humanoid boy. That was progress.

As a gargoyle, he flapped his wings and soared behind Broomie and me.

The other end of the hallway opened up into a larger building, a series of wooden doors going both ways.

A stony finger tapped my shoulder and I turned, Roderick pointing down the hallway at a door decorated with flowers, crosses, and burning votive candles.

A vigil.

Perhaps in front of Sister Mary Katherine's room.

I nodded at Roderick and we headed that way.

I wasn't sure at first how I was going to open the door without disturbing the memorial. Then I remembered my trick with the vanishing and reappearing windows back on the train and funeral parlor.

"ROOD HSINAV." I waved a hand at the door. It faded into nothingness.

First Roderick and then I floated inside, setting

my feet down. "ROOD EROTSER." The door appeared behind us once more.

It was a wonder what I could do with enchantments when I wasn't panicking.

Roderick flew over to the small cot, a thin comforter tucked tightly against the unslept-in bed. The room was small, humble. There was the bed, a wooden desk, a dresser, and a closet, and the whole thing was smaller even than my bedroom at home. The floor was stone, but it had been covered with a plush carpet with floral designs. Religious symbols and paintings decorated the stone walls, and there was just one small window. I peered outside. The window overlooked a nearly empty, snow-covered courtyard, at the middle of which was a white marble water fountain, though no water appeared to be flowing.

"WOLG," I said again, illuminating my hand over the room.

What was I looking for?

I knew from my time spent with Draven that not every myth about vampires was true. They could appear in photographs, though their images in reflections were hazy. It was as if the magic in their bones didn't account for something invented centuries after they'd come into existence. There was no immediately apparent mirror in this room, but that could be explained perhaps by a nun's modesty, too.

As I approached the desk, Broomie slipped out

of my hand and curled up beside Roderick, keeping her brush head up and focused, as if looking for clues.

There were crosses on the walls of this room—of course, explicable by the nun's occupation—but Draven had never been at all affected by those, either.

Another rumor.

What *did* apply to vampires?

I opened the first drawer. There were papers inside, neatly stacked. Vampires didn't like disorder—which wasn't quite the same as them preferring cleanliness. Dust and cobwebs didn't turn their eyes, but if I threw a bunch of sunflower seeds in front of Draven, which I'd admittedly done, he'd feel compelled to stop and count them, gathering them. Probably where that puppet version of a vampire had gotten that whole schtick from.

So her drawer was neat. I riffled through the papers with the hand not glowing. They just seemed like handouts from the sisters: schedules, chore charts, information about community activities, etc. I checked out the schedule and chore chart for Sister Mary Katherine on the night of her murder, but sure enough, she would have been killed during "sleep and prayer." Her last chore the day before had been cooking dinner with a few other sisters.

Draven wasn't a fan of the scent of garlic, but it wouldn't harm him, either. Nope, there was nothing here to suggest she had been or hadn't been a vampire.

I checked the second drawer. It was stacked with video game cases.

Roderick perked up at that, his stony head craning over for a look.

So she had been a fan of games. I looked around for sign of a TV. I went to her closet and opened it, as that seemed to be the only place large enough to store one. There wasn't a TV in there. Just clothes, and not a particularly large amount of those.

Roderick pulled a handheld game system that looked a lot like his own out of the drawer. Of course. It'd be easier to hide a game habit with a smaller system, assuming the habit had to be hidden from the other nuns at all. Were games considered some kind of indulgence not allowed? Or perhaps the content of the games was suspect?

I went back to the drawer and flipped through her collection. Nothing rated beyond EVERYONE or TEEN at most.

So she liked video games. I knew two vampires who'd gotten hooked on video games within moments, especially when they were feeling blue.

But there were more normies who liked video games than vampires, that much was true.

Roderick turned on the system and I didn't say anything. If police had been through here looking for any information, they hadn't taken that. And

Roderick's stony fingers wouldn't leave fingerprints anyway.

A sudden memory of what I'd read when flipping through those papers drew my attention.

Opening that drawer again, I took out the schedule. There. Scheduled for this weekend. Dancing and bowling video games in the rec room with some senior members of the community.

The nuns weren't against video games.

But maybe Sister Mary Katherine had been a little *too* addicted to them and felt she'd had to hide her hobby? She *had* gone off for a release day party all alone in the middle of the night.

I put the paper back and shut both drawers. That still didn't help me.

Anything I thought could point to her being a vampire could be explained by her being a normal human.

Humans got addicted to video games.

Humans might not have a single snack or glass of water in their rooms, even if a lot of them did.

It wasn't like I'd found a bottle of blood.

Um, wait a minute. I was forgetting a big one. *The* big one.

I whipped the schedule out of the drawer for the third or fourth time and looked again.

What I noticed about Sister Mary Katherine's name was that every time it came up on the chore chart, her task had happened after five o'clock at night. There was nothing scheduled for her during the day. At any point during the whole month. In fact, every sister's name seemed to be assigned to this or that thing during the day at some point— tending to the rose bushes, shoveling the walkways —but never Sister Mary Katherine.

At night, the schedule had read "sleep and prayer." Who could pray as they slept?

Someone not sleeping at all.

Was it possible Sister Mary Katherine had avoided walking around in the daylight? Had she explained this to her fellow nuns as some sort of allergy or light sensitivity?

There it was again, though. Something that could be explained by her being a normie human. This one with a medical condition.

I wondered why it hadn't come up during any of the articles I'd read about the victim. True, the nun interviewed hadn't known much about her, but that was surely a point of note they could have brought up. News stories lapped up those kinds of details, an existence full of challenges.

Then again, perhaps the nun had predicted that and withheld the information precisely *so* the media didn't make a spectacle out of it.

The light in my palm started flickering and I shook it out, stacking the papers and putting them back in the drawer once more.

My hand went dark, the light from Roderick's game the only thing glowing in this window besides the blue moonlight.

It was all circumstantial. I shook my hand again. I was tired. Too tired to keep up all of these enchantments.

Nothing was so definite as finding Draven's venom in Sister Mary Katherine's neck puncture wounds.

But hadn't I decided it would have been too hard to bite through the woman's habit? Not impossible, I supposed, but there was the lack of blood, too.

I scratched my own neck, thinking back to Draven's and Qarinah's necks. Both had blemishes there, a pair of them, where they'd been bitten themselves. Qarinah's were more noticeable than Draven's since her transformation had happened so much more recently, but they were kind of like freckles. Easily passed over.

Still, they were there.

So I could, at least in theory, say the victim had had those wounds from long ago if she'd turned vampire long before this.

I started pacing the room, doing my best to keep quiet. Roderick played the game on silent, so there was no worry about sound from that carrying out into the hall.

How would *Draven's* venom have gotten into her wound if he'd never been anywhere near her?

I stopped moving.

Lazarus! Hadn't I seen him near her neck? With some sort of dropper?

A *dropper*… Had he been *planting* Draven's venom in the woman's neck wounds? Perhaps he'd poked through the scars to make the wounds seem fresh.

But why? Why would he do that?

And *how*? Draven did *not* give his venom out freely, and he barely fed these days, so it wasn't like you could detain one of his bloodbags and quickly extract what little there was on their wounds. Besides, if his intent wasn't to turn the bloodbags, they wouldn't have much venom in their system.

He'd given *me* some venom a couple of months ago for a potion, but he'd never just hand it off to anyone else. Especially since it had been an unpleasant experience for him just to *collect* it.

My breath caught in my throat.

He'd given *me* some venom. And I hadn't used it all!

I massaged my temples, trying to piece it all together. Lazarus had broken into my house—

No, of course he hadn't. That would have gone noticed, I was sure. Lazarus just strolling down the street went noticed. And besides, Doc Day vouched for him being at First Taste all night, then Ginny had vouched for Lazarus's whereabouts during the day.

So who *had* been seen near my house today?

Who'd *asked* to confirm my house was my house?

Valentin.

And the eye dropper! I gasped. He'd been carrying that expired eye medicine in his pockets, hadn't cared that it was expired to begin with—because he hadn't intended to use it. He'd just wanted… the eye dropper?

No one had told me how Valentin had gotten back downtown from Vogel's. He could have swung by my house before or after he'd gone into the store, as soon as Chione was out of sight. He'd *asked* her to leave, after first asking her to wait for him.

After confirming he was right by my house.

So while I'd been in the park, after seeing Valentin at the funeral parlor, he'd gotten a ride to my house to steal the venom! I searched my memory, trying to remember if the bottle of Draven's venom had been where I'd left it amidst my potions ingredients. But Lien had been moving things around, using almost everything up.

But she hadn't wanted anything to do with the bottle full of venom this morning. I remembered that much.

And maybe it hadn't been there later in the day.

My power boosting potion I'd left on the front table had been gone, too.

And I'd seen a pale-pink bottle in Valentin's pocket this afternoon. Could he have stolen that from me, too?

But why?

Why any of it?

If I was right, that meant Valentin had gone

back to the funeral parlor shortly before sunset when Ginny had been trying to talk to Draven. Walking to there from Vogel's was doable in that amount of time. He'd been the reason Lazarus had been coming back from the front door when Draven was on his way out. At that time, Valentin must have handed over the eye dropper, Draven's venom, and instructions for when Sister Mary Katherine's body returned. Just moments before Draven himself had headed out that same door!

The cheek.

Were Valentin's warnings to Lazarus earlier, about how the nun might resurrect, true because she might have become a vampire or because she'd *already been* one in the first place?

What could kill a vampire? It wasn't exactly a topic I'd ever wanted to address with Draven or Qarinah. Not even Ravana had mentioned such a thing.

Whatever method it had been, it was something Valentin thought might not really work. Despite the state of that woman's decrepit, withered body, he still thought she might come back to life...

The state of her body. Thin skin clinging to bones. White hair.

Where had I seen something similar before?

The escape room! When Ginny had trapped us in there with too much para-paranormal, Draven and Qarinah had weakened. Draven, being older, had withered more rapidly, his skin growing thin and brittle and wrinkled, as if he'd been losing all of his insides and withering away.

That could almost be confused for a vampire draining a human's body of blood entirely.

Broomie's brush head lifted, as if wondering where my thoughts had gone. Whispering, I explained my theory to both her and Roderick. He set down his game on the bed, the glow from the screen brightening his stony face.

"Valentin and Lazarus," I said. "They covered up what happened! They framed Draven. I don't know the motive or if either had a hand in the actual killing—I didn't find shoeprints in the snow that would seem to indicate that, but the whole scene was a mess. I can't say if Lord Aleksandru has a hand in this, either. He must, right? But we have to head back and stop Lord Aleksandru from punishing Draven. We have to—"

Roderick's stony head whipped around, toward the window.

A speck of darkness covered up the moon, growing bigger, moving closer.

Roderick tensed and changed into his human boy form, slamming his stony feet to the ground with a crash that wouldn't go unnoticed.

"What's that?" I asked aloud. I waved a hand in the air, reaching for Broomie.

Stiff, straightened Broomie. She wasn't moving. "Broomie? WOLG!"

Nothing happened. My magic didn't come when summoned.

"Para-paranormal?" I wondered out loud. I took a look at Roderick. He didn't *seem* any weaker. But the stuff seemed to affect every paranormal creature differently. Proximity was enough for me to lose access to my magic. And the greater the amount of the substance, the nearer it was, the worse things got—

The form was getting larger.

Something was barreling straight our way.

A voice shrieked out into the night.

Roderick let out a human-like scream and wrapped his arms around me and Broomie, knocking us to the ground.

Under Roderick's stony grip, I shut my eyes tightly as the small window shattered and a large, blurry figure flew right onto the bed with a feminine shriek and a grunt.

Something clattered to the ground beside us. I peeked open one eye to get a look.

Lying as stiff as a board amidst the tiny pieces of glass flickering in the moonlight was Broomhelen, her fluffy tufts impossible to mistake.

Chapter Twenty-Two

"Lien! What in the world?" I skidded over to her, letting out a wince as my boot heels cracked against broken bits of glass, and gently rolled her on her side on the bed to get a look at her face.

Behind me, Roderick shuffled to pick up Broomhelen in one hand, Broomie in the other.

Both as stiff as an inanimate broomstick would have been.

"Lien," I said, nudging her by the shoulder. Her eyes were closed, thin scratches of red across her tawny complexion, including one far too close to her eyelid for comfort.

"LAEH," I said, waving my hands over her face. She wasn't stirring.

Nothing happened.

"LAEH," I said again, yanking down on my

witch's hat's brim to center the magical energy flowing all around us.

No warmth in my hands. No magical energy I could sense of any kind.

My eyes flicked to the stiff broomsticks in Roderick's hands.

"Para-paranormal," I whispered. It'd been months since I'd dealt with the stuff. A cursed, flowing red substance born from the act of a witch and another paranormal working together—to cause death.

Roderick jumped, tucking both broomsticks behind his back, and growled toward the wide-open window. Remnants of glass still stuck out of the corners of the frame like jagged daggers.

I snatched the broomsticks from Roderick's stony hands to free his up for whatever he sensed and tucked them behind the bed against the wall, their lifeless brushes flipped upright.

I was in such trouble. And I'd led Broomie and Roderick right into it. Lien and Broomhelen, too, because I knew with a kick to my gut that she would have freaked out when she'd sensed me missing from town and headed straight here to find me. She must have sensed my magical energy. At least until it had been ripped from me.

"What is it?" I asked Roderick, standing by his side.

Off in the distance, helicopter blades cracked

out across the night sky. More news coverage for the murder…?

Lien let out a groan.

"Lien!"

Her hand cradled her forehead and she rocked back and forth on the bed. "Don't… go…" Her voice cracked, soft and delirious.

A harsh cackle rang out across the frigid moonlit night. I shivered, and not just because I could no longer use an enchantment to warm myself.

I glanced to Roderick, looking for a sign that nearby para-paranormal was affecting him. His stony brow furrowed, his shoulders tense, but he didn't seem to be in danger of growing immobile or turning back into a boulder.

"Dah… lia…" croaked Lien. "Look… out…"

A dark, shadowy figure appeared through the broken window, far off and overhead. As she grew nearer, her silhouette grew clearer. A witch on a broomstick, holding a flask in one hand. It glowed red and clear, catching the moonlight even before the witch herself came into focus.

"You look positively frozen, dear," said Isadora Poplar, Queen of the Witches and cruel grandmother who wanted me dead. She came nearer, jostling the vial between two fingers.

I tensed, my eyes darting around to look for Sally and Mabel, Isadora's sisters equally as wicked, but they were nowhere in sight.

So it wasn't to be three witches against one? If

I'd had access to my magic, perhaps I might have an iota of a chance.

The helicopter-blade-like sound grew louder and louder as the silhouette drew nearer.

But that was just it. Para-paranormal affected every witch in proximity *except* the one who'd played a role in creating it. Which meant Sally and Mabel would also have been powerless in proximity of the sample of red, oozing goo Isadora dangled in front of us there... but Isadora wouldn't, if she were the one who'd played a part in its creation.

"You killed Sister Mary Katherine," I said loudly.

She was just outside of the window now, as clear as she was going to be in the moonlight and the red, oozing glow of the substance in her hand. Her broomstick had *two* heads, as I'd learned last month during our introduction, and they spun around with a wild, thumping sound, not unlike a helicopter in flight.

Isadora herself looked young enough to be my sister, her bright orange hair in an angled bob as harsh as her sharp cheekbones. Her alabaster skin was particularly frightening tainted in red radiance, her rich, violet witch's hat angled over her head just enough to rim her face in deep shadow.

"Well, I had some help," Isadora said. "Can't take all the credit." She shook the vial again.

So did that mean the wicked substance had been

created when Sister Mary Katherine had died? But did that make the nun a human?

No. My mother and Eithne had set out to create para-paranormal once together, and Mother's death had been the catalyst. A paranormal's death counted as the necessary sacrifice.

That just left whatever other paranormal she'd worked with.

"Your sisters helped?" I offered. There was Valentin's involvement, I wasn't doubtful about that, but he was a human.

Then again, I hadn't exactly given the man a thorough examination upon arrival. *Bananaberries.*

"No. This stuff is old, *dear.* Not created in the past few days. My sisters had a different task." Isadora's eyes flicked to the bed beside me, and I took a look as well. Lien was sitting up, still cradling her head. Those scratches had left red marks all over her skin. "To lead my intrepid niece here on a wild goose chase, to keep her out of the way."

My hands curled into fists at my side. "So the ones who helped you kill the nun were the vampires —and Lazarus," I said, hoping I might get her talking and filling in the blanks.

"Who?" Isadora tittered, still floating up and down as a chilly, night wind gusted in through the open window. "Oh, is that the reaper's name? Yes, I suppose he played a role—though I've never met him." She shivered exaggeratedly. I noticed she didn't deny killing the nun, even if she'd insisted the para-paranormal was nothing new. "Never much cared for his kind, truthfully." Her eyes flicked to Roderick. "No other paranormal compares to the power of a witch."

Roderick growled and I put a hand on his shoulder, forcing myself not to wince at the iciness of his stone skin.

Voices carried down the hall from behind us, and I could just make out the words "crash" and "call the police" before Isadora rolled her eyes and took her hand off her broomstick's shaft. "PEELS OT," she called, and though my connection to magic was severed in the proximity of her para-paranormal, there was a distinct crackle in the air as magic soared overhead and through the door and wall behind me. One after another, what could only be human bodies fell to the floor.

"Can't exactly wipe out the entire convent, can I? Enough attention is being drawn to the death of just one little ol' nun. As if she *really were* a nun."

"I know she was a vampire," I said boldly. Isadora hadn't denied a vampire's connection to the crime. I'd noted that, too.

"Hmm, why, yes, she was. Clever girl. I don't think anyone else in your sorry town has caught on to that fact, have they?"

Not that I knew of. But more importantly, exactly how *Isadora* knew anything about what was going on in Luna Lane…

"You conspired with Lord Aleksandru?" I

ventured. "Or was it just Valentin, all behind Lord Aleksandru's back?"

"The Vampire High Council knows nothing of the matter." She flicked her free hand in the air before clutching her broomstick's shaft again. "I could not jeopardize our relationship with them, as they supply the venom we need for so many of our potions. Though it's easy to manipulate their human servants into working with you quietly if you use enchantments and tug them *just a little bit* past the line of blood madness."

"Valentin is blood mad?" I hadn't caught any of the signs. He was clearly a bloodbag, and he was eccentric to be sure, but I highly doubted Lord Aleksandru, a member of the Vampire High Council, would have been anything but careful when it came to making sure his walking, talking, portable bloodbag stayed on the right side of the line of blood madness.

Then again, there was that stain on the faucet. What could that have been?

"At first, I'd been offering him extra venom myself," Isadora explained. "I had quite the stock for gargoyle creation, you know. So I dangled it in front of him. Just a little here and there—enough to get his mind weak and susceptible to enchantment. Quite a glutton. Swallows the whole stuff up with abandon, as if afraid I'll take it away."

Did that explain the stain he'd washed off in the sink, then? Vampire venom *was* similar in shade to blood. Perhaps he'd just gotten some venom before he'd come into town. His master would have been sleeping by dawn.

"Promise a human bloodbag they'll become a vampire for too long, and they grow impatient," Isadora continued. "Inject just *a little too much* venom into their veins and that impatience can be worked into a desire to please—to do anything for the promise of being turned. I didn't even need to cast enchantments on him the past few days. It grew quite tiresome."

"But you said you offered him venom from your stock. Who but a vampire could inject it straight into his veins?" I bit my lip. Was there some sort of enchantment for that? Unless... "Sister Mary Katherine herself. She was *working with* you."

"Ding dong, clever stone witch again!" Isadora laughed and Lien groaned. "She didn't expect me to *kill her*, of course, but them's the breaks. Nothing but my full plan would work to draw you out of Lien's infernal protective barrier."

I winced. I'd played right into Isadora's hands. But I was still unclear how everything fit.

"Why would the nun—the fake nun—work with you?" She'd looked so much like Draven's mother from that portrait. But Draven's mother had never become a vampire. He'd wanted her to, but she'd refused. Right?

"Not all vampires are happy with the Vampire High Council," Isadora explained. "Maria Catalina never wanted to become a vampire in the first place. Against her religion, you see. But the High Council would rather imprison any out-of-control vampires than execute any. So they'd never have granted her wish to end her eternal torment. I did her a *favor*, really, and she wouldn't have objected to her death —but for the fact that it came a bit earlier than she'd agreed to."

"What would she have wanted in exchange?" My mind scrambled to make sense. "Surely not… to see Draven?"

"Why, yes! Even if she thought his soul was lost, she never stopped loving him. After she turned herself, she couldn't abide the shame of telling him what she'd become, so she staged a fake death and supposedly 'died young.' And how did my clever stone witch piece that together?" Isadora's smile was haunting, almost as if her lips would break open to reveal needle-sharp razor teeth.

"You met Draven last month. You likely heard me call his name—you could have described him to her. And she… She was his mother."

"Yes, that was strange. You see, I wasn't about to let that wretched vampire get away with helping you thwart our plans on the train. So I went snooping around Transylvania to see what I could come up with to fight back. His sire was in prison, so there was no reaching her—shame, she seemed the type of wicked paranormal I could abide." Her voice positively crackled with mirth. "But there was gossip that the vampire Ravana was due to face justice for old crimes as well. A complaint from hundreds of years before, dismissed for lack of evidence, and an unwillingness on the part of the victim in question to pursue justice: A vampire keeping a low profile, who hated drinking blood and didn't want anyone to know her name."

"Maria Catalina," I said, echoing the name Isadora herself had provided.

"Draven's own mother. Ravana had turned her —against her will—as what she thought would be a favor to the vampire they both then had claim to call 'son' in their own way, so Maria explained. When Maria rejected the gift already given, Ravana helped her stage her death and hide away, pleased to have Draven all to herself. When I told Maria I knew where he was and that her hiding away was doing her *no good*, she agreed to try to meet him one last time. And then I would grant her the wish the High Council could not: the sweet release of death."

Something tugged at my skirt and I jumped. Not taking my eyes off Isadora, I shifted slightly. Lien, still cradling her head, grabbed on to my skirt. "Run, Dahlia. Don't—" But she fell back, her cheek clunking against the handheld video game system Roderick had left on the bed.

"Hmm." Isadora studied Lien curiously.

I was probably going to die. Running would just hasten the inevitable.

But at least I wouldn't go to the realm beyond without answers.

"Maria never got to see Draven," I said softly.

"On the contrary. She saw him from afar." Isadora shrugged. "She wanted to go speak to him, but I managed to get my sisters to draw Lien as far away as they had yet and so I could talk some sense into the wretched vampire recluse—see, if she actually got to *talk* to him, I couldn't so easily frame him for her murder." She *tsked*. "And since Valentin had just landed, I figured it was time. What perfect pretense this wedding of the vampire and her human lover created for the High Council's visit. Valentin had been working on a way to encourage his master to travel to Luna Lane, to get past Lien's wretched anti-witch barrier and report to me from the inside. We thought the pretext might be reporting the results of Ravana's trial directly to her vampire children. Perhaps mentioning the plight of Maria Catalina at last, after all these years. And then they get an inquiry about an approval of marriage and a possible new vampire created in your little town—how perfect. Delightful!" She brought the hand holding the flask up to her mouth and let out a little cackle. Then her laughter suddenly cut short and her eyes narrowed on me. "It was as if it were meant to be."

"You wanted Draven arrested for the murder," I said. "As revenge for helping me last month."

"Yes, and see, Valentin would do anything

Maria Catalina and I asked of him when she'd drunk him past the line into blood madness—dreadful business for her, you can imagine, but I kept dangling the prospect of seeing her son again in front of her, so she did as asked. I didn't tell him she was well and truly killed, you see, so he had hope she'd just played dead and would turn him at last—since his master was in no hurry to do so."

He *had* mentioned the possibility of the nun popping back to life on Lazarus's examination table.

"But he was all right with framing Maria Catalina's son?" I asked.

"He didn't know the reasons behind any of it." Isadora lifted her hand from her broomstick's shaft and made circular motions over her ear with one finger. "Blood madness meant the man didn't even *care.* I had to fish out another vial of my own stock of venom just to keep him satiated once he'd arrived outside of your town. Since by then, Maria Catalina was already dead. I thought about killing him then rather than dealing with him further, but he still had a role to play in framing your heroic vampire."

"He stole my sample of Draven's venom from my house."

She laughed. "I told him to find your house and look for a venom sample there. It was only a guess. But I suspected if you had any venom in stock, it would have come from him. The two of you appeared to be quite the bosom companions when you fought together on the train."

Bananaberries. She'd been right.

"His task then was to plant the venom he found in your cupboards in Maria Catalina's wounds. His temptation to drink it himself would have been great, but with the promise of being fully turned should he complete this last task—I was glad to see he followed through."

"It was Lazarus who did the planting, though," I pointed out. "Valentin gave him the venom and a dropper for the job."

"Ah, yes. The reaper would have had to carve those wounds open again, too." Isadora flourished her hand in the air before clutching her broomstick again. "When I kill, I don't *need* to open flesh. Unless I choose to." Her smile curved sinfully across her features again. "It all worked out beyond expectations, if I do say so myself. With your beau in trouble, you fled here."

"He's not… We…" I shook my head. "He's my friend."

Isadora laughed. "That's right. You have that human beau. Humans make for the *best* witch fathers, I have to say. No way would I taint the bloodline with anything as gauche as *stone* like your mother did." She shivered as her gaze flicked between Roderick and me.

I wouldn't let her distract me. I was almost to full understanding. "I surmised para-paranormal made Maria Catalina wither—to death."

Isadora looked at the red, glowing substance in

her hand. "Always good to have on hand. What's a death or two or three or seventy or so in your history?"

It was my turn to shudder. What monsters had I descended from? And I certainly didn't mean my gargoyle father.

"My sisters and I all have some stored in special places. We make them with our broomsticks as the second paranormal, so they're not affected by our own vials, either." Her eyes glistened at that little nugget of information. I hadn't known that was possible. Did that mean the *broomsticks* had participated in the murders that had created the stuff? "Of course, we've vowed not to bring the stuff out much—being able to take a sister's powers away on a whim does little to endear her to work with you, you see—but we all agreed after the disaster of last month, it was time to go home and gather some. For just such an occasion."

She gestured with the bottle at Lien and me. It was just as Lien had warned me. My heart clenched at the sight of stiff, lifeless Broomie. I'd never see her again if Isadora killed us here, with that stuff in her hand.

Not until the world beyond.

There was that to hope for, at least. Reuniting with her—and with my mom—in such a faraway place.

Even if I'd be leaving so many I loved behind.

I gripped Roderick's hand.

"So you killed Maria Catalina when the para-paranormal withered her and aged her, weakening her. You were working with Valentin, but he's still human, and Lazarus never left Luna Lane—"

"I've never met the reaper, but yes, he played a part in framing Draven, as you guessed."

"But then he…" My brows narrowed and Roderick squeezed my hand back, his stony grip weaker than I'd expected it to be. "His connection!" I shouted. Ginny had insisted Lazarus was a good man—er, reaper. That his frightening side had only been because he'd opened himself up to the realm beyond in order to prepare a body for its final rest. "You spoke to him through his open connection to the realm beyond! You controlled him when he was in his reaper trance! He wouldn't have *framed* Draven otherwise. He wouldn't have messed with a body like that!"

"Excellent deduction." Isadora shook her head. "A pity those smarts were tainted by all those rocks in your brain." Her voice grew hushed. "But I'm glad my sisters aren't here to see your little sleuthing skills at work. You're the embarrassment of the family, even more so than Lien, though her betrayal stabbed her mother right through the heart." Isadora snorted. "Though I might thank her for that. Another excuse to kill off a potential heir—my next child will have *so much* magic at her disposal!" She waved the oozing, red vial in my direction. "And with this failure of a branch of the family totally wiped out, I can start with a clean slate."

"I'm sorry, Lien," I said. She'd given up everything to help me. She'd pinned her hopes on me. And all of the training we'd done together had been for nothing if I couldn't even *use* my magic when confronting Isadora. Lien had even floated the idea of using para-paranormal of our own, and I'd refused, pointing out how the stuff was made.

And even when Lien had pointed out the witch royals would have had no qualms creating the substance themselves, the plan to avoid fighting one of them when they still had their magic and we didn't… had been for me to not set foot outside of Lien's barrier.

But I'd walked right into Isadora's trap.

"You knew I'd want to prove Draven's innocence."

"And needing to investigate a murder outside of the barrier around Luna Lane would mean drawing you out from it at last." She whirled the para-paranormal around in the air. "Though I do wonder if you'd left it to the professionals if they would have even come to the right conclusion." She shrugged. "Then again, once you're dead, no one will be able to dissuade them from convicting their current suspect."

"I'm sorry, Draven," I whispered, though it was evident he would never hear my apology.

"Only one thing left." Isadora gestured the flask

at Lien on the bed. "Have a little fun with your deaths." She smiled wickedly. "It's not like we're in any *rush* this time, now are we?"

Roderick growled and stepped in front of me, spreading his stony arms out. His brows drew together again, like he was trying to do something— to transform into his more humanoid form, maybe —but nothing happened.

Perhaps that was the para-paranormal at work on him, after all.

"It's okay, Roderick," I said. "Go," I whispered. "Go back and tell my friends what happened here—"

"Oh, I don't think so." Isadora uncorked the flask in her hand with her thumb. A flash of the stuff sizzling on Ravana's skin made me lean over and cover Roderick, shielding him as best I could and closing my eyes. Roderick fought me, trying to get me off, no doubt wanting our positions to be reversed...

But the sizzling, fiery sensation I'd expected never came.

Instead, over the incessant din of the helicopter broom heads, came what could only be construed as *gulping*.

I opened my eyes and stood straighter, watching as Isadora downed the last of the flask.

She tossed it to the snowy banks beside her, and it landed with a *thud*.

She'd *drunk* the para-paranormal?

And she wasn't dead?

Never in my life would I have thought anyone would *look at that stuff* and *ingest it.*

Isadora laughed, her skin growing a bright, fiery red. "I take it you don't know about para-paranormal's boosting effects for the witch who created it." Her laughter grew hollow now, more echoing and wicked. "For those up to the task of handling it." Her hair shot upward against her wide hat brim, almost as if truly caught on fire.

"EMAG OEDIV EHT OTNI DNES!" She took her hand off of her broomstick and waved them both in the air, her eyes glowing red.

"Did she just say *send into the video game?*" I asked aloud, doing the quick work of disentangling her enchantment.

No one would answer me, though.

No one *could* answer me.

The room illuminated in red, and I felt my whole body ripped apart, atom by atom, the pieces flying upward like square, digital pixels, then dragging down into the bed. Into the handheld video game.

Chapter Twenty-Three

"What. Is. Going. On?"

It was hard to describe the voice echoing out into the strange world around me. It sounded electronic but lyrical, like each syllable had been input into a machine and spurt out as a tinny, musical note.

Blinking, I tried to look around, realizing I could only turn my entire body at once. One way, and then one hundred and eighty degrees the other way. Along a flat, flat axis.

I wasn't even in three dimensions anymore.

"Dahlia?" That voice echoed out again.

I stared at my hands. They were more like peachy blobs, comprised of square pixels and ending in no fingers whatsoever.

"Dahlia," the voice repeated.

I turned my entire body around to find a digital

Lien in front of me. It was hard to see her at first. She looked more like a thin line, but then my eye darted to the side and I realized I could see our reflection on some enormous glass wall as large as the sky.

Digital Lien and Digital Dahlia. Witches made of pixels.

Overhead, a strange sound echoed out over the soft, electronic music. Like pounding in a distinct pattern, the thuds sort of ricocheting out in staticky stereo.

In the reflection, I saw the pixelized gargoyle form of Roderick, flying up and down in a repetitive beat.

"What is this?" Lien asked, holding her blobby, tawny hands out in front of her.

The enchantment Isadora had used rushed back to me. "I think we're… in a video game." My own voice was lyrical, almost like little, tinny beats, too, but we could understand each other.

Roderick nodded vigorously in the reflection, his movement like a video game sprite's simple animation.

"Not a new game, by the looks of it," said Lien. She sounded better, I realized. No longer wounded or sick. Being transformed into a video game sprite must have healed her while the magic had reassembled her in this form. "You're all right!" I waddled over, my footfalls like little electronic squeaks, and tried to reach forward and hug her, but only one arm moved at all and it was just straight forward and back, like a punch.

Lien reached her arm forward for a punch, too, and our fists bumped. "Later," she said. "If we survive this, I will be *supremely* cross with you."

"Right." I winced. Or at least I tried to. "I suppose you won't let me explain myself—"

"On the contrary," said Lien succinctly. "Explain away at a later date. There's *nothing* you can say that will inspire me to forgive you."

"I suppose I deserve that." I waddled toward Lien, but I couldn't push past her. I checked the reflection again. There was no sign of our broomsticks anywhere, but the para-paranormal had rendered them inert even before this.

"I know this game," I said. "Roderick, was this what you were playing on Sister Mary—Maria Catalina's handheld game system?"

Roderick nodded in the reflection.

"But I've seen it even before this," I said, thinking.

"Does it matter?" Lien asked. "How do we get out of here?"

"It's an older game. A platformer I played as a kid," I explained. My digital eyes widened. "Draven was also playing this! On his TV!"

Roderick nodded excitedly.

Lien jumped up and down in place. "Great. That's so helpful to know. Since he's not here, I don't see how that—"

I jumped too. Jumped and kicked, one little digital-booted leg flying outward. Then I jumped and punched. That was the extent of my movement, it seemed.

I flipped around. "We have to go this way. The end of the level has this big platform to climb up, I remember that much."

Lien sighed. "And I don't suppose Isadora is going to just *let* us win if we reach the end?"

"Well, I mean, it's just the *first* level of many, many more in the game."

"Peachy." Lien jumped over me, kicking out her foot as she flew overhead. I supposed that was how one of us passed the other in this game. She punched and punched nothing, and I flicked my eyes to follow the path of her fist upward. There was a number reflected in the glass screen. A number counting down from 364.

"That's a timer, isn't it?" Lien asked.

My eyes widened. We'd wasted so much time just milling about here already. "Go!"

I leaped over Lien's head with a mighty digital witch kick. She had no familiarity with this game. At least I'd played it a long time ago.

Roderick flapped his stony wings and flew overhead, pressing forward. He was so cute in digital pixels. If only this weren't a life-or-death game, I might stop to appreciate it more.

A fireball flew at us from the blackness of off-screen.

"Whoa!" shouted Lien. "ECI!" But of course, she wasn't able to use any magic.

"Punch it!" I shouted, remembering watching Draven do the exact same thing—and finding it weird his little avatar could punch the fire.

Lien hesitated, so I jumped up, sending a punch right into the fireball. It exploded with a scratchy noise and I kept moving. "Don't stop!"

Almost as soon as I'd said that, a dangerous ledge awaited overhead. Roderick flew over it, but the most Lien and I could do was jump. "You have to jump the gap!" I told her.

"That's too dangerous!" she shouted back.

"Trust me! That's how platformers are." Though my body remained stiff, I hobbled forward, and just as I reached the ledge, I jumped.

I flipped around on the other side to watch Lien. To her credit, she moved as fast as she could, her digital body moving from one animation to a second and back again, and then she leaped.

I tried to smile at her, but I wasn't sure our little digital figures even had mouths, despite using them to speak somehow.

"Keep going!" We moved forward, jumping up bricks to pass over dangerous enemies, punching and kicking the fireballs and little rat-like enemies that came our way. Roderick helped too, swooping in to take out the flying bird enemies, punching them with his gray, blobby digital stone fist.

At last, we reached the end of the level, which

was one giant upward climb. A hundred seconds waited on the counter.

"Up!" I said. Roderick was already on his way.

"How?" Lien asked, stopping and tilting her pixelated head just slightly.

"Trust you can do it! Double-A jump!" I didn't have a controller, but I thought really hard about it, as if I were pushing the button. Double A. Jump, jump. Real quick. Up and jump. Punch and kick.

Lien lagged behind me, but she was making steady progress.

I kept imagining Draven playing the game and how I'd been frustrated by his game addiction. Now I couldn't wait to play this for real with him—in Games Club, away from this place.

Safe and home and free of Isadora's torment.

"Watch out!" shouted Lien.

I'd just made a final leap to the top platform. The level's biggest enemy awaited, a giant owl, swooping downward.

"I didn't see all of this part," I admitted. I didn't really remember it from when I'd been a kid, either. I went to jump and kick, but the owl's beak slammed against the top of my witch's hat.

My whole body blinked in and out of existence, and I collapsed on my rear end on the platform.

It *hurt*. My gaze flicked to the reflection of the screen. Where I'd seen three hearts before, there were now only two.

"We only get three hits!" I screamed at Lien as she leaped to the final platform.

"Or what?" she asked, punching her fist into the air as if waiting for the owl to just fly right into her attack.

Roderick swooped in, but the owl's mighty wings slapped him, too, and his face scrunched up as he flew backward. He, too, lost a heart.

"Or we die," I said simply, kicking out into the air.

Lien let out a grimace.

The owl swooped down and Lien went to punch, but she, too, flickered in and out, her eyes closing as she soared back and the owl swooped up again. We all had two hits left.

Roderick flew as close to us as he seemed to be able to, gesturing from one side of the screen to the other.

"Roderick's played this game recently," I reminded Lien. "He's trying to tell us something."

Lien was back on her feet, kicking repeatedly in the vague direction of the owl, doing double-A jumps with each kick. "What? Pray Tell? Should We Do, Kid?" She kicked as the owl swooped down again, but the owl's beak hit her first and she blinked in and out, falling down to the ground.

"Lien! Don't risk it again!" I shouted. I looked at Roderick's eyes in the reflection of the whole screen, the way the owl just paced back and forth on the edge of the screen.

"Roderick," I whispered. "What can we do?"

Roderick's face scrunched up again, his wings beating harder and harder.

And then he zoomed straight up and hit something, a brick block appeared out of thin air, and he… glowed.

When he stopped shining, he turned into a human boy again, albeit a digital one, his skin no longer gray like stone but a medium brown.

He'd lost his wings and he fell to the ground, just as the owl swooped down. He crouched. "Belly," he said, the first word I'd heard him speak.

Lien and I crouched, too.

As the owl neared, we all jump-kicked upward, and the owl blinked once, twice, three times, its face twisted in agony in the reflection.

It crashed against the side of the screen, exploding from the power of our triple hit.

"Roderick," I said softly, reaching a blobby hand toward him.

"Dahlia…" he said softly, as if testing the word on his electronic, tinny tongue. "Mom?"

I reached forward to fist-bump his shoulder. I wished I could hug him.

As the explosions died down, the entire screen went black.

"Hang on," Lien said, touching her own fist to my back.

There was still so much more to this game.

The blackness sort of wavered around us.

"Dah… lia…" said a voice, echoing and familiar. And not at all electronic. "Dahlia, head for the light!"

At the edge of the screen, a single pixel had refused to turn black. "Let's go!" I shouted, jumping over Roderick to lead the way.

They followed and we headed for the single white pixel, like the display itself had broken.

And we burst back through—to real life.

Chapter Twenty-Four

It took me a moment to figure out where we were when we appeared back in three dimensions. It was dark and cold, and there was trampled snow beneath my boots. I shivered as I looked around.

Lien sprung into action before I did, no sign of her wounds. She pulled a long, sharp dagger out of the belt cinching her dress. It was black and it shined in the moonlight. I knew what that was. The onyx dagger.

Roderick was a human boy. A little on the muscular side. He blinked hard, but then seemed as on top of things as Lien. He took point in front of me.

There was a red glow emanating up above.

Isadora still flew overhead. We were in the Holy Home of Mother Mary's courtyard, the broken window leading to Maria Catalina's room just off to the side.

"Take cover, darn it, Lia!" Sheriff Roan's voice snapped me into action.

"Come on," I said, grabbing Roderick by the arm. We bolted for the water fountain in the center of the courtyard, shut off for the icy, winter months, sliding behind its marble, Lien at our feet.

"Take this," she said, shoving the cold hilt of the onyx-pike-turned-dagger into my hands.

I flipped over onto my knees, my flesh digging into the hard, icy snow, peeking around the shiny white marble.

A gunshot ricocheted out into the empty air. Sheriff Roan was there, between two bushes at the edge of the courtyard, firing up toward Isadora overhead.

I'd never seen him shoot his firearm. He usually kept it locked at his station.

"What's he doing here?" Lien asked. "TCE-TORP," she said, then she let out a curse. "There's still no accessing our powers."

Isadora cackled and sent a wave of energy from her hand toward Roan, who dove back into the bushes.

"Roan!" I shouted.

Lien and Roderick both grabbed me by a shoulder, and I realized I'd been about to run out to see if he was okay.

"Our options are limited," Lien said. "As long as

she *emanates* para-paranormal, we're helpless. The dagger can only do so much."

"And I'm not about to teach Isadora the value of love to weaken her in the next five minutes," I said, remembering how Eithne had fallen—albeit willingly—to my dad's pike because she'd loved me like a daughter.

Lien snorted. "You'd need several thousand years for that, and I'm not sure even that much time would do the trick."

"Then how can she be defeated?" I asked. "Even *with* our magic?"

Lien didn't have an answer.

I stopped struggling and looked around the courtyard for signs of anyone else hidden among the bushes.

Over the sound of crackling magic and the occasional shot of Roan's gun, there was something else familiar: tinny, electronic music.

I crawled around to the other side of the fountain, following the sound.

"They're back," said Qarinah. "Enough, Draven. Enough!"

Draven?

At the edge of the fountain, Draven and Qarinah leaned against the marble, both looking tired, their skin starting to sag. In his hands, Draven held the video game system we'd been sucked into, but his fingers were only slowly pushing buttons, the movement on his screen rather limited.

"Dahlia?" he asked as I crawled on my knees in front of him.

"Draven, you're here!" I took hold of his arm. He was cold, but not the kind of usual, unnatural cold his skin possessed. He was shivering.

The game system fell from his weak fingers and onto his lap.

"I'm glad we found you," he said. "Hello to you, too." His gray eyes—the red lines around the irises so much fainter than usual—roved over my head and toward Lien.

"Hello," said Lien stiffly. Her whole body went rigid, and her cheeks darkened.

Her cheeks… darkened?

"But I don't understand. Why are you here? What happened to you being arrested?" I asked.

"Lazarus's connection to the dark entirely snapped when he stepped away from the body for a time," Qarinah explained. "He realized he'd been manipulated almost all day because he'd opened that connection as he'd been preparing himself to handle a body. Ginny was the one who noticed something was still a bit off about Lazarus and encouraged him to take a walk around town with her for some air. Then he realized…" She went quiet.

"My mother," said Draven simply, his voice cracking, and tears glistening across his pale eyes. "The victim was my mother. All this time… And when I see her at last, it's too late."

I grabbed his hand and squeezed—but not too hard. His skin felt like brittle paper. "She saw you before she died," I said. "I only just learned… But she was here. To see you. And she saw you last night when you went to the game store."

Draven let out a groan. I couldn't tell if it was pain from him aging in the presence of para-para-normal or something more. Deeper, emotional.

Shivering, I squeezed my arms together across my chest.

"Mayor Abdel arrested Valentin," Qarinah said. Her hair was growing gray, her breaths a bit labored. "With Lord Aleksandru's permission. The Frenchman told us everything he knew, cursing the fact that now *no one* would turn him into a vampire, and Lord Aleksandru freed Draven." She smiled. "We even got an apology out of the old bat."

Draven laughed weakly. Old bats, indeed.

"So it would have all come to light even if I *hadn't* ventured outside of the safety of Lien's protective barrier." A sense of vertigo overtook me. "I'm sorry," I said to my cousin.

Lien sighed, her gaze flicking up to the glowing red light that was Isadora. "I'm not sure my barrier could have held up to that kind of power. And me constantly leaving the barrier myself, well… They could have used para-paranormal on me at any time. The barrier could have crashed." She bit her thumb. "I thought I could keep you safe. I thought I had enough power. But I was wrong—"

"Don't blame yourself." Draven tried to smile, but his lips were so thin, it was like the mere movement cut his flesh. "This one never listens."

"I was trying to clear *your* name!" I said.

He chuckled. "And she also has to do everything herself."

"That's not…" I bit my lip. "Who else came?"

"Lord Aleksandru wouldn't risk losing his vampire self," said Qarinah softly. "He's clearly upset he didn't recognize Maria Catalina as soon as he laid eyes on her body—because he knew about her, another thing that upset Draven to learn." Draven muttered something indistinguishable. "But she'd been drained so much, her appearance changed." Qarinah held up a spotted hand as if to illustrate. "Nonetheless, killing a vampire is a serious crime in the eyes of the High Council. More serious than almost anything else. He gave us permission to apprehend the witch—through any means necessary."

"Good luck with that." Lien scoffed.

"Roan is here and Faine wanted to come—"

"We told them we would handle it ourselves," Draven said. "Turns out we had good foresight to convince them all to stay. What good would they be against a witch using para-paranormal?"

"What use is *anybody*?" Lien asked.

Qarinah sighed and leaned over into the empty fountain, pulling out first one long stick and then another, handing our stiff broomsticks to

Lien and me in turn. "We found them in the room, too."

"Broomie," I whispered, running a hand over her shaft.

"How did you find us here?" Lien asked, clutching Broomhelen to her chest, the broomstick's shaft towering over her head.

"Followed the red, glowing light." Draven shrugged one shoulder to the witch high up above and behind us.

There was a *click, click* sound and Roan let out a curse. He chucked the handgun up at Isadora and she guffawed, shifting her dual-headed broomstick just right so that its blade-like flying action smacked the handgun back down into the snow.

"He's defenseless." Qarinah's breath caught in her throat.

I got to my feet, holding my inanimate broomstick companion to the side like a walking stick. "There has to be something we can do. Her sisters aren't able to come near her, either. Having her alone… It has to count for *something*."

In my other hand, I gripped the onyx dagger, determined to squeeze some kind of chance out of it.

Roderick stood beside me, just a boy. A human boy.

"Roderick?" Qarinah asked quizzically. She stood, too, and took his hand.

He nodded at her, still too shy, perhaps, to speak.

"Stay back," I said. "Both of you—I'm not sure what you can do like this."

Qarinah shook her head. Ahead of us, Isadora was shooting waves of energy toward the bushes in which Roan was hiding. They rustled as he crawled quickly, narrowly evading each blow.

"That's my love," she said. "We won't go down without a fight." She looked for all the world like an elderly woman, beautiful and full of wisdom, fighting the gravity determined to sink her body downward to stand up straight.

Beside me, Lien brought Draven to his feet, wrapping an arm around him and keeping him snug against her side. He was unnaturally old now, so weak.

"That witch killed my mother," he said.

If I was going to fight, they would fight, too.

And I knew that Isadora wouldn't be satisfied with just my end. There'd be no sacrificing myself to allow them to get away.

A bush nearby rustled and out popped Roan, taking his place at Qarinah's side and heaving deep breaths. He took her face in his hands a moment. "Human again? You're beautiful," he whispered, then the two exchanged a quick kiss before grabbing hands and joining the line in the courtyard facing off with Isadora.

"Oh, that was *fun*," she said. "The video game did get rather *boring*. I did wonder what Maria Catalina saw in such a thing on our trip here, as she hardly stopped playing the thing, but I'm glad the vampire managed to call you out from that enchantment. Shooting at a little rat crawling through the bushes was so much more entertaining."

I held the dagger high above my head. "Leave, Isadora," I said, for all the world projecting more confidence than I felt. "Leave or feel the wrath of this blade."

Isadora casually kicked both legs out into the air, her flame-like hair flittering around her head. "You're *joking*, are you not? I *am* para-paranormal. You are nothing without your powers. And you're far too soft to make any of your own and turn the tables on me. It's over, filthy-blooded child." She huffed her nose in the air. "You've all lined up for your execution. Makes things convenient for me."

She spoke, the enchantment on her tongue lost to my ears, waving first one and then the other hand above her head, keeping her grip on her broomstick with her thighs alone.

"What now?" Lien asked darkly.

"Now we say our farewells," said Draven. "I am sorry we didn't get to know each other better, you and I, fair Lien. Perhaps things could have been… different."

Her cheeks darkened again. "I'm sorry, too," she said softly.

What was going on here? I'd thought Lien didn't trust anyone in Luna Lane.

"I love you, Qarinah," said Roan. "Lia… Little

Roderick? You look great. Even you, Draven. Wish we'd gotten to know you better, too, Lien," he added.

Qarinah nodded, and I wondered if I'd misinterpreted Draven's words to Lien—my whole town didn't know Lien well. It was only natural to wish we'd had more time together.

"My love for you all is great," said Qarinah. "And if I'm to die today, I know I at least won't be left to mourn anyone." She brought Roan's hand to her mouth and kissed his knuckles.

"Mom," said Roderick, and Roan and Qarinah both let out little yelps of surprise. "Mom… I'll protect you."

"Roderick, no—"

But he dropped Qarinah's hand and darted in front of me, yanking the dagger from my grip.

He couldn't fly, but he brought it high above his head, chucking it as far as it could go.

Isadora smiled even as her lips moved, boundless energy in her hands. The dagger was going to crash to the ground, nowhere near her.

It started downward—and then flew back up.

It flew back up, on its own, lightning-fast, and went straight for Isadora's leg.

She screamed and lost her grip on her broomstick, tumbling down, the dagger still embedded in her thigh. The energy she'd been harnessing in her hands flew upward instead of at us—exploding into a giant firework of red energy.

Isadora fell, no longer glowing, her back smacking against the hard snow just as the explosion rung out into the air.

Where she'd been, there materialized a ghost. Ginny put her spectral hands on her hips and glared down at us. "Did you forget y'all can't see me when para-parnormal's around? I wasn't about to let these three head off alone to save my best friend, whatever they might have insisted." She gestured toward the vampires and Roan—the vampires, who were already regaining some of their undead beauty.

"Ginny!" I shouted. "Thank you!"

She looked taken aback, kind of stumbling in the air. "Yes, well, of course you'd need me. Not like para-paranormal can take a *ghost*'s abilities away. We just sort of… stop existing." She shrugged. "At least as far as everyone around us thinks." She sniffed, her nose in the air.

"Come here, you!" I shouted, just as Broomie's brush head flickered to life. "All of you!" I said, grabbing Roderick in front of me, hugging chirping Broomie, grabbing Ginny as she approached—or more accurately, just putting my hands through her cold, mist-like being. She solidified just a bit at the top of her back so I could give it a pat, rubbing my cheek against Broomie's bristles.

"It's not over!" Lien bounded across the snow, *tearing* open the pouch on her belt and taking out a pale-pink power-boost potion. She tossed some of it down her throat then threw it my way.

"*Watch it*," said Ginny as the vial soared through her. She bristled as Broomie caught it for me.

Lien hovered over Isadora, using Broomhelen—her brush head wagging like a puppy with its tongue out—to slam down against Isadora's chest on the ground.

"Watch out!" I screamed before chugging back the potion myself.

A couple of things happened in just a matter of seconds.

Roderick turned gray—then he grew stony wings, even on his boy-like form.

Draven popped into a bat and took to the sky alongside him.

Isadora's helicopter-like broomstick spun its heads faster and faster, diving straight down for Lien's exposed back.

And I channeled all of my strength, calling on the magic around me, feeling my skin turn to stone from head to toe.

And I, too, grew stone wings.

Broomie and I flew off into the air side by side, aiming straight for the helicopter broomstick.

Draven popped back into vampire form just in time to grab hold of Lien and roll her and Broomhelen away, his impact full-force and the three of them tumbling off into bushes nearby.

Roderick slammed a stone hand against the front of Isadora's broomstick's shaft.

And I spun around, my wobbly wings making

me flutter up and down, and kicked my leg between its dual heads.

Sparks flew as Broomie whapped the shaft and Roderick punched into the top of the shaft, splintering the wood.

The dual brush heads tried and tried to keep moving through my arm, but I added another video game double-A punch from below.

A brush head went flying off into the snow.

The other hung on by a thread.

And the shaft fell, lifeless, to the ground below.

"*No!*" Isadora shrieked. She got up now, crawling, the dagger still in her thigh. "Broomhansel! Broomhorace! You… You… monsters!" she screamed.

My gaze flicked to the broomstick in pieces below, my gut weighing heavily. It wasn't the first time Broomie and I had killed a broomstick—a cat's soul on its very last incarnation. Able to die before its witch did. Perhaps hers had even housed two cats.

She'd never have a companion broomstick again.

"EID!" shrieked Isadora. "EID!"

There was no mistaking that enchantment. She was trying to kill us—any of us—in one blow.

Light soared out of her hands as she waved them around wildly, limping forward, her thigh oozing blood that dripped on the snow.

"I don't think so!" Ginny flew in a flash between

Isadora and Roderick, Broomie, and me, taking a hit from one of Isadora's blasts.

Ginny laughed and sneered, her hands on her hips. "I'm already dead, witch."

Isadora's face was as red as a tomato and she shifted her hands to the side. "EID!" she shrieked—straight at Qarinah and Roan.

Qarinah and Roan… who were standing strangely, Qarinah coming up from kissing Roan's neck. She wiped her arm across her lips, which were bright red with blood.

She'd been feeding. For strength?

No.

To turn him. To turn Roan!

I didn't quite recognize him at first, but there from my memories danced the man with a full head of chestnut hair and a trimmer physique. The one I'd known as a child. He ran forward, his skin ghostly white, his eyes rimmed in red, and took the blast straight on.

He kept moving.

Ginny looked over her shoulder to us. "Vampires are dead, too, you know. She'd have to word her enchantment differently if she wants to inflict a final death on a vampire like she did before."

But Isadora, her violet hat slipping off her head, was clearly not in a thinking mood.

She screamed as Roan charged her, tackling her to the ground. In the scuffle, the dagger slipped out of her flesh.

"My turn," I said, flapping my wings and feeling a bit nauseous. I took hold of Broomie and slid on her shaft, wings and all, needing to feel one with my broomstick to move forward fast.

"ETATIVEL, ARODASI."

A voice echoed out in the chilly night above.

Roan's vampire fangs snapped together as he snatched at Isadora's neck, and she only just managed to roll out of reach, kicking her boots at this chest. Before she could slam back into him, she started flying, wobbling into the air without finesse.

"I have them!" she shouted. "Leave me! Leave me!"

Sally laughed. The svelte, dark-skinned witch rode her stiff broomstick with its pine-needle brush side-saddle. She waved a hand lazily and directed her elder sister up toward her.

"It doesn't appear so, *Your Majesty*." She spoke the title with clear disdain.

"Fight them!" Isadora shrieked, even as she flailed in the air. "Kill them! Get Mabel! Do it!"

It was now or never. They were getting away.

I directed Broomie toward the dark dagger in the snow, and we snatched it up.

"Wait!" said Lien. She stumbled to her feet. "Just... Just let them go."

I hovered in the air, my gray skin turning peachy once more. "Wait? But we—"

Lien shook her head and pointed to the top of a tall pine tree. Another figure rested there, a broomstick at her side. "My mother's here, too. I'm not ready to take on all three. You dealt a blow. That will have to do." Her gaze flicked to the shattered pieces of the two-broomsticks-in-one.

Draven's hand came down on my shoulder and Broomie lowered us to the ground. "Please, Dahlia. Let us go home." He smiled at me, a quick quirk of his lips, then at Lien as well. She looked to the ground as Sally's and Mabel's cackling echoed out into the air.

"See you again, child!" said Mabel, mounting her broom.

Isadora shrieked and then Sally took hold of her on her broomstick. Off they flew in the direction of the swollen moon.

Sighing, I held Broomie out beside me. "I hope you know what you're doing. That might have been our best chance."

"It was until Sally and Mabel realized they could approach." Lien nodded at me and let out a deep breath. "Good work, though. She won't be in a good position as Queen without a broomstick, you know."

"Perhaps you bought yourselves some time," Ginny said, floating nearby alongside Roderick. He'd transformed into his small, gargoyle form again. Perhaps he felt most comfortable that way. "Maybe all the in-fighting will keep you off their radar for a spell."

"You really think Isadora might be deposed?" I asked.

"You know families," Draven said. "Too often fighting." He brushed past and held a hand out to vampire Roan. "Welcome to mine… brother."

Roan grinned broadly, showing off two brand-new fangs, and gripped his hand back. "Hadn't decided at first that I was going to join *this* way." He smiled broader as Qarinah stepped up and slipped an arm around him. "But I have no regrets." He winked at me.

All three vampires hugged.

"Maybe we should all move in together?" Roan asked as he pulled back. "The three of us—"

"No, no, no." Draven held his hands up in surrender. "I learned my lesson. I was selfish and wrong, and I will give my sister her space. I think having you two lovebirds under the same roof as I might be *too* close-knit a family for my tastes."

Roan and Qarinah slapped their thighs as they laughed, and it was time to spread the hugs all around. Even Lien got in on it, albeit as just the recipient of a few embraces and never the one handing them out.

At least not until she held her arms out toward Draven, her mouth moving softly.

They embraced.

Whatever she'd said had lit up Draven's once too-sorrowful expression.

Chapter Twenty-Five

"And you're going to keep your phone with you at all times," Cable said from the tablet propped up on the chair beside me.

First Taste had been transformed, all of the tables shifted to the side to make room for several rows of chairs. After the disaster of the past week, Qarinah and Roan had opted for a small ceremony, but it was packed to the brim, Chione, Erik, and Ryan running around to make sure everything was settled. Mayor Abdel stood by to perform the wedding, Lord Aleksandru beside him to offer the Vampire High Council's blessing.

True, Qarinah had transformed her fiancé into a vampire outside of his presence, and a member of the Vampire High Council being present was required for a transformation, apparently, by their laws. But he *had* said that she and Draven could do whatever was necessary to take out the witch who'd killed a vampire, and they'd convinced him it had been an integral part, so he'd given his blessing.

Thank goodness. I wasn't about to lose them to another Vampire High Council crime. I wondered if the vampire lord was eager to please them to sweep his own assistant's role in the whole mess under the rug.

"Dahlia? Are you listening?"

"Huh? Oh, yes, of course, Cable." I bounced Falcon on my knee. The tablet with Cable's face was seated in Falcon's seat, technically, but the little boy had insisted on climbing on my lap and had promptly fallen asleep. It was rather late for him, but vampires had to get married at night, naturally.

In Cable's apartment in Scotland, sunlight streamed through the window. He'd dressed up despite not being here, complete with tuxedo. He'd even swapped his glasses for contacts. He looked rather dashing.

"Dahlia, if you can't stay safe, I can't concentrate on my work. I have to come back—"

"One semester," I reminded him. "We agreed on you finishing out the semester as you promised your colleagues you would and then we would talk about it more."

Flora and Fauna were playing with Roderick—completely human boy at the moment, in a little tuxedo of his own—near the entrance leading to Hungry Like a Pup next door. Giggling and shrieking, they all ran around, holding Faine's and my phones out in front of them as they caught imaginary monsters they could only see through the phones' cameras, apparently.

Cable let out a sigh. "I worry about you."

"I appreciate that. But a phone isn't going to save me. I wasn't going to call for backup. I wouldn't have called the police."

"But I—you could have called me!"

"I didn't want to worry you. There was nothing you could do."

"Then I shouldn't be here," he said softly.

I *tsked.* "I won't be responsible for you not doing what you love."

Cable didn't comment on that. "So where's your phone now?"

"Roderick has it." I shifted one arm out from behind Falcon and grabbed the tablet, showcasing the kids playing around. Faine and Grady stepped through, both of their hands piled high with trays of food. Grady snapped at them to be careful, but they disappeared into the café, shrieking about the monster moving.

"He looks so… human," Cable said. It wasn't the first time he'd chatted via video with a human Roderick. Roderick hadn't said much, but he'd said Cable's name.

"He's getting stronger," I said. "And so am I. I'm not alone," I pointed out.

I put Cable on the tablet back on the chair and looked over my shoulder. At the bar, Draven, complete with punk-rock tuxedo and a leather black jacket, was mixing drinks for human guests. Lien, in a sparkly, orange, off-the-shoulder dress, was beside him, squeezing blood from literal bloodbags donated from Dr. Corbin's hospital into a few wineglasses for the vampires.

She and Draven were talking. Laughing, even.

I'd never seen Lien's dark eyes sparkle with quite the brightness they were now. She kept grabbing a mug she kept nearby and sipping from it, perhaps drinking coffee, as I knew she was wont to do, then putting the mug down and picking up a new bloodbag to pour it into a wineglass, trying to stay busy, glancing at Draven out of the corner of her eye even as she worked to fix the vampires' drinks.

"Something's brewing there." Ingrid nudged my shoulder from behind as she took a seat in the empty row, pointing toward Draven and Lien behind the counter.

"Beer?" I asked.

Ingrid chuckled. Milton shuffled alongside her, a stack of cards in his hands that he kept shuffling. She was dressed in a pale-green business suit with a floral blouse, Milton in a powder-blue corduroy suit that looked a few decades out of date. His wife's reading glasses were still around his neck.

"Hi, Ingrid," I said. "Cable, your mom's here." I lifted the tablet up to face Cable's mom and uncle.

"Hi, darling." Ingrid made kissy noises at the screen. "Lovely day there, apparently, huh?"

"It is." Cable waved. "Hi, Uncle Milton."

Milton mumbled. "Don't like that TV show."

"I'm not a TV show," Cable said. "It's your nephew, Cable."

Milton muttered and kept shuffling. Ingrid waved a hand. "Oh, he's in a bit of a mood tonight. He wanted to go to Spooky Games Club and I told him there's a wedding instead today."

"We're still going to play some games afterward," I told Milton. "Qarinah and Roan both wanted to play, too."

"No video games," said Cable, chuckling. He'd heard all about vampires' addictions.

Milton started humming, satisfied that he was on his way to Games Club, apparently.

"And don't *you* look beautiful," Ingrid said. "Oh, Cable. I wish I could get a pic of the two of you together."

"Go ahead," I said, holding the tablet beside my face.

Chuckling, Ingrid brought her phone out of the purse over her shoulder. She snapped the picture and then spun the screen around so we could see.

There I was with a tablet held up to my cheek and a little sleeping werewolf on my lap. Even though I was seated, she'd gotten a good shot of my black, sequin mermaid dress. Spindra had *insisted* on making something special for everyone in the wedding party. For me, apparently, that meant a dress that was poured on me to hug my curves and then flared out at about the knee to poofy, black, sparkling tulle. It was beautiful—and I was grateful for my warmth enchantment since it was sleeveless as well—but I could barely move in it.

Instead of leaving my witch's hat at home, I'd given it to Broomie to borrow. Along with a sparkly, black bow tie made from the same black tulle as my dress that Spindra had crafted for her, which was tied neatly below her brush head.

"Well, look at you, Broomhilde," Ingrid said. "May I get a picture?"

Broomie chirruped and flew up from her seat, posing in the air sort of as if a model lounging on chaise chair. Ingrid laughed and got her pic, too. I scratched under Broomie's bristles before she took a seat.

"Cable, are you eating enough?" Ingrid asked.

"Yes, Mother," Cable answered.

"You look thin."

"I'm *fine*, Mother."

I spun the tablet around to look at him. He looked tired for sure, but he looked all right.

"He's not getting enough fresh air," I guessed.

Cable rolled his eyes. "Is this some sort of team-up now?"

"Gentlefolk and paranormals." Mayor Abdel's voice carried across the pub from where he stood on top of a small dais the town hall team had dragged into the bar. "If you would take your seats, we're about to get started."

"Oo, oo," said Ingrid, sitting down.

Everyone else milling about took their seats, and Faine slipped in two chairs down, grabbing Falcon from me to put on her lap and mouthing, "Thank you."

Grady appeared half a minute later with his daughters and Roderick in tow, directing them to their seats in our row and confiscating the phones.

"But we almost had him!" Flora whined. Roderick nodded glumly.

"Well, then, you'll just have to be fine with letting him go," Grady said sternly, slipping the phones into his suitcoat pockets. I wouldn't have room to store mine anywhere in this dress.

The whole Vadas family had on matching red-and-black dresses or suits. Faine's dress was the most red, but her eclectic fashion sense was making her little girls look adorable, too, with their poofy red-and-black skirts and red headbands through their hair.

Spindra slinked by in a silver dress, moving as slowly as if on a runaway, and Ginny floated nearby, the two whispering to one another and giggling. Even Ginny had changed her usual outfit to a more formal dress, a faded pale lilac baby doll dress with a short skirt. Lazarus hadn't come. He would never be comfortable around such crowds. But we'd spoken since, and he'd apologized for scaring me.

I'd apologized for sneaking around his place and

smashing his window—which I'd fixed, of course, Roan wagging a finger at me all the while.

"Hello, Dahlia," said Doc Day as she took her seat in front of us. She'd left her lab coat behind and looked quite elegant in a dress in a floral design. "Doctor Corbin wanted to thank you for your help the other day."

Without the barrier around Luna Lane, I'd gone —escorted by Lien, mind you—to Doctor Corbin's hospital once and did some magic on a few patients. Nothing too mind-blowing, mind you. Just nudging some injuries along, soothing some pains whenever patients were sleeping. Nothing that might draw more attention to weird goings-on in Creekdale.

The murder of the nun there was still "unsolved," at least in the public eye. And unsolved it would always be.

"Of course," I said. I'd try to get there as often as I could, but there was still a real danger out there, royal infighting or not. And we had no confirmation they weren't still a united front.

Jamie, First Taste employee and Doc Day's boarder, sat down beside her in a brown suit. He nodded at us.

"How do you like having a new boarder?" I asked him. I knew Doc Day was fine with it.

Jamie gulped and took hold of his neck. "He asked me if I'd be willing to donate some blood—"

"He was fine with you saying *no*," Doc Day said, chuckling. "Just be glad that Valentin fellow has been locked up in the sheriff's jail cell all week before Lord Aleksandru's replacement assistant can be summoned to take him home for trial with the High Council. Now *that* was a rude fellow."

The lights overhead dimmed and I tapped on Cable's tablet screen to reduce his light a bit, too, before Broomie floated by and wrapped her shaft around him, acting as a floating tablet stand.

"Excuse me," I said to Faine and the kids and Grady, shuffling out past them to the side of the aisles.

"Bridesmaid!" whispered Fauna.

Flora nudged her. "Groomsmaid."

Fauna looked puzzled. I just smiled.

Scooching around the rest of the seats, I made my way to the door leading to the pub's storeroom.

In stepped Roan, looking like a model for long-tailed tuxedo suits. "Ready, kiddo?" he asked.

I gave him a quick hug. "Congrats... Dad."

I didn't mean any disrespect to my mom's choice to stay single after my dad or to insult my biological dad out there somewhere by it. But Roan had always been the closest thing I'd had to a father, and I wanted him to know that this evening.

His glowing, red eyes watered up a bit. That glow would still take some getting used to. As would having Luna Lane's sole law enforcement officer being only available at night. "Thank you, Lia," he said.

We'd planned this a little different than most

marches down the aisle since Qarinah had no parent present to give her away. I looped my arm through Roan's, flinching just a second at the coldness of his skin, and escorted him down the aisle, waving at all the faces looking our way. It was a good thing we went slow, as it was a bit hard to shimmy in the tight mermaid-style dress. Goldie and Arjun clapped excitedly from the front row as we approached, both wearing layered Indian formalwear in bright pinks and golds, a golden chain clipped from Goldie's nose to her ear.

Once Roan and I got to the platform where Mayor Abdel and Lord Aleksandru stood, I nodded at them and took my place off to Roan's side, cupping my hands together in front of me.

The soft, rumbling thunder that usually echoed out of First Taste's speakers was replaced with Wagner's "Bridal Chorus," only this rendition was spooky, played on an organ but with liberties taken with the tune, mixing in a bit of Wagner's "Ride of the Valkyries," which made it seem perfect for Halloween.

Or a vampire bride.

Draven had moved out from behind the bartop and he stood now beside his vampire-sister, their arms linked.

She was beautiful, a sight to see in a pale white dress made almost entirely from lace over a solid white base, buttons all the way down her back and up to her throat.

Spindra had outdone herself.

Draven and Qarinah walked down the aisle, fangs on joyful display. Qarinah held a bouquet of black orchids in one hand, and she sniffed it, perhaps to hide the broad smile of her lips, as they neared where Roan, Abdel, Lord Aleksandru, and I awaited.

Draven's head turned noticeably to Lien, who waited behind the pub counter. She blinked rapidly and looked down, adjusting the glasses on the bartop, though they hadn't seemed out of place. In her other hand, she reached for a mug that she sipped at as Broomhelen's tail-like shaft whipped back and forth from her spot on a stool in front of the bar. No one else was looking at Lien by then, but I winced for her sake when I noticed her face grow pale, her nose scrunching as she spit the contents of her mug back into the ceramic.

Her lips were bright red. Could she have added some blood to her coffee without realizing? Her eyes blinked rapidly and she stared downward, as if trying to sink into the floor.

Trying not to laugh, I focused again on the bride as she reached her groom. She squeezed Draven's hand and he stepped aside, opposite me.

Everyone's heads turned as a strange, loud noise echoed out from the darkness.

Broomie shook her brush head to bend around and stare at the tablet she held curled up on her shaft.

"Sorry." Cable's voice echoed across the quiet room. He grabbed a handkerchief and blew into it —that had been the sound we'd all heard. Like an elephant's trumpet. "I can't stop crying at weddings. Gah. Contacts." He started fumbling at his eyes.

"I can mute him," Ingrid said, standing up.

"Don't!" I shouted. I looked to Roan and Qarinah for confirmation. They both beamed at me and nodded.

"We want it as if he were here for our big day," Roan confirmed.

Laughter broke out across the room, but Cable's next honking blow still carried out over the raucousness.

Broomie actually jumped in place.

"Let me at least turn his volume down." Ingrid reached over Broomie to hit the tablet's buttons.

Draven nodded my way. "I can already tell he's going to blubber a lot when the two of you get married." He winked at me, not a trace of sorrow to be found on his expression.

Now it was *my* turn to flutter my eyes and stare at my feet.

Join the Spooky Games Club in Werewolves and Wargames

Dahlia Poplar, Luna Lane's homegrown witch, has had enough of mystery and murder. Luckily, the royal witches after her may be preoccupied after the blow Dahlia and her friends dealt them the last time they tried to attack. Ready to spend a snowy February warm and cozy at home, the only thing that could have made her first Valentine's Day with her boyfriend better would be if they didn't have to confine their celebration to a video chat.

Thankfully, her best friend has quite the plan for holiday: Faine's parents and in-laws are visiting Luna Lane to spend time with their grandkids, and the kids aren't into mush or romance. Instead, the family wants to stage an elaborate paintball wargame, which is something the kids enjoy in the werewolf village in Canada. Of course, the Spooky Games Club was practically made to participate.

Unfortunately, the pretend wargames result in an actual murder—and someone near and dear to Faine is thought to have killed for real. It's up to Dahlia to gear up for the fight and sleuth out the truth. Otherwise, her loving, supportive, and optimistic Galentine will never be the same.

Witchy Expo Services Mysteries:
Magic, Conventions, and Murder

Witchy Expo Services. We host your convention, expo, or trade show—with a dash of magic!

Set up in a matter of days, our expos can host even the largest of crowds in our witch-run village of Cauldron Cove. We can offer what no other expo planners can: breathtaking illusions, instant teleportation from one end of the center to the other, floating item storage, and all the exceptional, magical touches that will make your event one-of-a-kind. Inquire about Cauldron Cove hosting your next event today by contacting Bernadette Toothaker, award-winning Head Witch General Manager of Witchy Expo Services for eleven decades.

Nimue Toothaker is ecstatic that her world-famous grandmother is about to retire and has chosen her as her successor in the family business. She's only been working on the expos for a few years, but she's confident she has what it takes to lead her fellow witches and warlocks in the business that defines their entire village. Unfortunately, her grandmother's sole condition for Nimue taking the job is that she share the position with her arch rival, an irritating warlock possessed of two minds—quite literally.

First up is Bookshop Con, where indie booksellers from across the nation host authors and sell books to passionate readers. Nimue's grand plans clash with her co-manager's persnickety demands, but their arguments cease to matter when a celebrated author drops dead in the convention center lobby. Nimue suspects murder, but she knows that if she ends the convention prematurely, the magic at work will destroy her beloved hometown. It's a race to catch the killer before they strike again—all while trying to prove she can handle the job she's so desperately always wanted.

About the Author

Amy McNulty is an editor and author of books that run the gamut from YA speculative fiction to contemporary romance. A lifelong fiction fanatic, she fangirls over books, anime, manga, comics, movies, games, and TV shows from her home state of Wisconsin. When not editing her clients' novels, she's busy fulfilling her dream by crafting fantastical worlds of her own.

Sign up for Amy's newsletter to receive news and exclusive information about her current and upcoming projects. Get a free YA romantic sci-fi novelette when you do!

Find her at amymcnulty.com and follow her on social media:

amazon.com/author/amymcnulty

bookbub.com/authors/amy-mcnulty

facebook.com/AmyMcNultyAuthor

twitter.com/mcnultyamy

instagram.com/mcnulty.amy

pinterest.com/authoramymc

Killer Runway

DARIA WHITE

In this case, fashion is death…

Bianca's determined to live a normal life in Edenville with her family, and she has no intention of getting involved in another case. While attending a fashion show, a model, also a childhood friend of her sister, collapses off the runway. Dead. Not the show Bianca planned on attending.

Detective Sims shows up to solve the case, but Bianca can't keep silent. Too many clues are surfacing, and with a month-long fashion event in town, the suspects remain in Edenville. There's no harm in Bianca investigating one more time, though Detective Sims wants her to stay away.

Can she discover the motive behind this unexpected death? Bianca's life at risk with another killer isn't wise. Not to mention the lives of her loved ones.

Old Flames

ELISA KEYSTON

Laney isn't looking for love. She's perfectly happy with the life she's built for herself in the little town of Foreston, Washington. She's a successful businesswoman, the owner of an alterations shop with a clientele across the northwest. She's the chair of the local Victorian house museum's annual fashion show. And she has a reputation for a magic touch: the rumor around town is that anyone who wears one of the period costumes she designs in her spare time will be blessed with good luck.

That's what they say, anyway. Laney knows the truth is a bit more complicated—anything she wills while sewing has a tendency of coming to pass. It's a supernatural gift from the fae who are said to inhabit the woods surrounding the Paine Estate, and it's taught her to keep a guard on her notorious redheaded temper. But keeping her temper becomes difficult when journalist Paul Nelson comes to town to do a feature about the museum. With his stunning good looks and swoon-worthy English accent, Paul is charming, irresistible… and just so happens to be Laney's ex.

Laney wants nothing more than to keep Paul at arm's length, but when she stumbles across a series of break-ins at the museum, she may have no choice but to trust the dashing reporter who once broke her heart to help her catch the culprit. And when a nearby forest fire threatens the safety of the town—and of the woods—will Laney be able to put her old feelings aside in order to protect the magic of Foreston? Or will that same magic lead to an unexpected happy ending?